ALSO BY KATE O'SHAUGHNESSY

The Lonely Heart of Maybelle Lane

Lasagna Means I Love You

the WRONG WAY HOME

Kate O'Shaughnessy

Alfred A. Knopf
NEW YORK

Text copyright © 2024 by Kate O'Shaughnessy
Jacket art copyright © 2024 by Shelley Couvillion
Watercolor stains art by BoszyArtis / stock.adobe.com
Leaves and branches art by moleskostudio / stock.adobe.com

Visit us on the Web! rhcbooks.com

Educators and librarians, for a variety of teaching tools, visit us at RHTeachersLibrarians.com

Library of Congress Cataloging-in-Publication Data
Names: O'Shaughnessy, Kate, author.
Title: The wrong way home / Kate O'Shaughnessy.
Description: First edition. | New York : Alfred A. Knopf, 2024. |
Audience: Ages 10 and up. | Audience: Grades 4–6. |
Summary: When twelve-year-old Fern and her mother abruptly leave their isolated, off-the-grid community, Fern wants nothing more than to return, but things get murky as she slowly adjusts to her new life and discovers unsettling truths about her old one.
Identifiers: LCCN 2023007368 (print) | LCCN 2023007369 (ebook) |
ISBN 978-0-593-65073-8 (hardcover) | ISBN 978-0-593-65074-5 (library binding) |
ISBN 978-0-593-65076-9 (trade paperback) | ISBN 978-0-593-65075-2 (ebook)
Subjects: CYAC: Mothers and daughters—Fiction. | Adjustment—Fiction. |
Friendship—Fiction. | Cults—Fiction.
Classification: LCC PZ7.1.O8435 Wr 2024 (print) | LCC PZ7.1.O8435 (ebook) |
DDC [Fic]—dc23

The text of this book is set in 12-point Dante MT Pro.
Interior design by Michelle Crowe

Printed in the United States of America
10 9 8 7 6 5 4 3 2 1
First Edition

Random House Children's Books supports the First Amendment and celebrates the right to read.

For Mom and Langdon

1

Before we came to live at the Ranch, Mom and I were like tumbleweeds. We never stayed anywhere for more than a year, maybe two.

Or at least that's how I remember it. Then again, with every passing year my memories of what life was like before are becoming less and less solid. It's like I'm looking at the past using pieces of a broken mirror.

What I do remember: Our freezing cold house in Boston, with the cracked board on the front porch. Our studio apartment in Brooklyn, with the half fridge and its "Mean People Suck" sticker that was ripped all around the edges, because Mom tried—and failed—to peel it off. My friend Mallory, who smelled like strawberries and loved the color pink. I knew her in Buffalo, but I can't remember if we met at our apartment complex or at school. I was six when Mom and I came to live here, and I'm twelve now. The memories have only grown foggier.

A cough from across the room brings me back to myself.

When I look down, I realize I've dropped a stitch halfway through the row on the sweater I'm making. A beginner's mistake. Stupid. Now I'll have to go back and fix it.

My mind wanders like this sometimes when I'm knitting. I think it's the rhythmic click of the needles, the push and pull of the yarn. Dr. Ben says I need to focus on the work, so that's what I try to do.

But then the coughing starts up again, and it sounds even worse than before. It's Iris, one of the adults. She's coughing so hard one of her knitting needles slides from her lap and clatters to the floor. She's only a little bit older than Mom, but since she's been sick, it's like she's aged thirty years. She's gotten so thin you can see the outline of bones in her hands, and her skin has this yellowish white tint to it, like when you stay in cold water for too long. One of the other women goes over and puts her hand on Iris's shoulder, murmurs something to her, and then helps her stand and walks her out of the room.

I watch them go, pressing a hand to my chest in sympathy. That cough must hurt. I say a silent prayer that the herbal teas and salves Dr. Ben has her on will start working their magic soon.

I put my needles down and take a breath, trying to re-center myself in the present. This is something Dr. Ben does all the time, even if he's in the middle of a conversation. He stops talking, closes his eyes, and breathes in, loud and slow, through his nose. And then he'll open his eyes and continue right where he left off.

I try to do the same thing, but my nose is still too stuffed up from a cold to get much air through. I look around to see if anyone else is struggling to focus right now. The great room is filled with the gentle sounds of needles clicking, along with the occasional *snap* or *pop* from the fireplace.

Next to me, Meadowlark is bent almost in half, her nose inches from her work. Her bangs are in her eyes, and the tip of her tongue is stuck between her teeth in concentration. She's only knitting a simple hat, but even from here I can see her stitches are uneven.

Our seats are by the double windows overlooking the field. It snowed yesterday, and the trees are frosted with ice. It's pretty, but as the sun continues to sink, I know Meadowlark will struggle in the fading light. Her up-close vision isn't good, even under the best of circumstances, and it doesn't help that the cold presses through the glass, making our fingers numb and clumsy.

Meadowlark reminds me of a cloud. Maybe it's her fine, wispy white-blond hair or her pale, almost translucent skin. She's lived here two years longer than I have, and she's a few months older, but for some reason I feel protective of her. I think it's that not-quite-there quality of hers, like she could blow away with a strong gust of wind. I tap her gently on the shoulder, meaning to point out her mistakes so she can fix them. But at the last second, when she looks up at me, I stick out my tongue and cross my eyes instead.

She smothers a smile. Then she clears her throat and

closes her eyes, composing herself. When she opens her eyes, she bulges them out and curls her lips, so it looks like she's toothless.

I stifle a laugh. "You look like a possessed turtle."

"Hold on, hold on. I can do better." The next face she makes is so hideously ugly, so *strange*, I feel like I'm about to split apart at the seams. Soon we're both shaking with silent laughter.

One of the adults shushes us, which only makes us laugh harder.

I'm making another face at Meadowlark when the doors to the great room creak.

They're wide and wooden, twice the size of normal doors, so they're loud. The clicking of needles stops—everyone looks up as the doors swing open.

It's Dr. Ben.

Both Meadowlark and I stop laughing. I grab my needles and start unraveling my last row, the one with the dropped stitch. Meadowlark bends over her hat.

First, he goes over to the fire, where Meadowlark's mom, Dahlia, sits. If Meadowlark is a cloud, her mom is an oak tree. Strong and solid. She's got long blond hair that goes all the way down to her sturdy, thick waist, and a very pretty face that's been weathered by the sun. She nods at whatever Dr. Ben is saying to her, and then he puts his hand on her cheek for a moment before he continues. They aren't married or anything like that, but they might as well be. She's special to him. And that makes her special to the rest of us, too.

He moves among our group quietly, stopping every now and then to inspect hats, mittens, sweaters. He drops in like this occasionally. It's never on a schedule—sometimes he'll surprise us twice in three days; other times he won't come around for months. I keep glancing up to watch him. Even from a distance he'd be easy to recognize, because he always wears the same thing: a pair of jeans with a worn brown belt and leather hiking boots. In the winter, he wears a sweater one of us has knit, and in the summer, a loose undyed linen shirt.

I'm not the only one who's nervous. I see the flash of eyes all around me, the tucking of hair behind ears and shifting of bodies.

Dr. Ben is the leader of our community. If something is broken, he fixes it. If there's a threat to our family, he stands up to it. He's the person who finds compromises and solutions. Everything we have—everything the Ranch provides us—is because of him. Even the animals seem to respect him the same way the rest of us do. Somehow they just *know*.

And as long as you live up to his ideals, life is beautiful. It all makes sense.

Soon he comes to a stop next to me and Meadowlark. He turns to her first. "May I?" he asks, gesturing at her hat.

After she hands it to him, she immediately starts chewing on her thumb cuticle. As he turns the hat over, inspecting it, my heart is in my throat. I wish I'd pointed out her mistakes earlier, instead of making stupid faces at her. I wish I'd helped her when she still had a chance to fix her mistakes.

But he only nods once and gives it back to her.

Then he picks up a corner of the sweater I'm working on and rubs it lightly between his fingers.

"It'll do," he finally says. "But there's room for improvement here, don't you think?"

I swallow hard. Truth is, I don't like to knit. I'd rather be outside with the men, rounding up the goats and cooping the chickens for the night, feeling hot inside my coat from the effort as my breath fogs out in the cold. Still, his comment stings. I'm glad Meadowlark didn't get in trouble, but I also know my work is much stronger than hers. I can do vertical mosaic patterns. I can make all kinds of things, whereas she hasn't graduated from hats yet. So why did he point out my shortcomings and ignore hers?

For a second I think about the way Dr. Ben pressed his hand against Meadowlark's mom's cheek. But no, that's not fair.

So all I say is, "Yes, Dr. Ben."

Because, at the end of the day, he's right. There *is* room for improvement. I have to stop daydreaming and goofing around. I have to focus harder on the work, on *my* work, because the work is what sustains us.

"Well, I *did* come in here with a purpose, not just to distract you all," he adds, in a voice loud enough so everyone can hear. "Would you mind joining me in my office for a quick chat, Fern? I have a couple of things I'd like to talk over with you."

I point at myself, because maybe I misheard him. "Me?"

"Yes, you. It shouldn't take too long."

After a second, Meadowlark nudges me and widens her eyes. She mouths, *"Go!"*

I accidentally knock my needles to the floor as I stand. I feel everyone's eyes on me as I bend down to gather them up, and as I trail along behind Dr. Ben.

From across the room Mom tilts her head and knits her eyebrows together, like she's asking me what's going on. I shrug my shoulders a tiny bit—I have no idea. She frowns, and her eyebrows come together even more.

Have I done something wrong? I try to figure out what it could be. Did I break something or leave a gate open to the grazing pastures without realizing it?

Or is it something worse?

As Dr. Ben and I leave the great room, the doors boom shut behind us.

I guess I'm about to find out.

2

I try to keep my footsteps light on the hallway's stone floor, to make as little noise as possible. In front of me, Dr. Ben walks slowly, his hands clasped behind his back. Everything about him is peaceful, whereas everything inside of me is a storm.

As we go, a drip of ice-cold water falls on me from above. I glance up to see a spot on the ceiling that looks spongy and damp. Another leak, probably. There have been a lot of them this winter. The rumor I've heard is that the Ranch was an abandoned convent before Dr. Ben bought it. That makes sense to me, because there's something special about it. Something holy. But there are also always repairs that need to be made.

We get to his office. I've only been inside once before, when Mom and I first arrived years ago, so I try to take in as many details as I can. It isn't big or fancy. Like Dr. Ben himself, it's humble. There's a fireplace with a small fire crackling, and a few lamps—powered by our solar panels—

throwing off a warm glow. His desk is simple, made of well-sanded and -oiled pine. It was built here, on the Ranch, same as most of the furniture.

Behind his desk, a bookshelf displays artifacts and gifts people have given him during his travels around the world.

"Please." He motions at a wooden stool in front of his desk. "Sit."

I do as he says.

"Fern." He laughs a little as he shakes his head. "Sit up. Straighten your shoulders. Take up space."

I hadn't realized it, but the second I sat down, I hunched my shoulders and wrapped my arms around my stomach. I immediately straighten my back and let my hands fall to my lap. "Sorry."

He considers me for a long moment. "Do you remember anything about when you first got here?"

"A little."

"You were always *clinging*. Onto your mother, onto whichever adult was caring for the littles that season. Dahlia and I joked that your chosen name should be Ivy, because of how tightly you clung."

I don't smile along with him—the memory is too embarrassing. I hate that that's how he thinks of me as a little kid.

He leans back in his chair. "I was the same as you, you know. At your age, I could've been an 'Ivy,' too."

"Really?" It's hard to imagine him as anything but what he is now. Thoughtful. A leader. No—a visionary. Someone who sees the truth of the future. The idea that I could ever be someone like him feels impossible.

"Yes, really. Anyway, I'm sure you're wondering why I asked you here this evening."

I nod, trying not to let my anxiety show.

"Don't worry. It's nothing bad. Or at least I hope not. I wanted to talk to you about your rite."

I lean back in surprise. He's talking about my rite of passage, something all kids living on the Ranch go through. It's an honor, really. After your rite, you're considered an adult, and you're entrusted with a lot more responsibility. Most of the time it happens around the spring equinox of the year you turn fifteen. But I don't even turn thirteen for another six months. So why would he bring it up now?

"What about it?" I finally ask.

He fixes me again with his even stare. His eyes are so blue they're almost hard to look at. "I think you're ready."

I'm so surprised—shocked, really—that I grab on to my stool with one hand, like the earth itself is shifting beneath me.

It's an unspoken rule that you don't talk about what happens during your rite. Dr. Ben says it's between you and nature. But even so, whispers get out. And there seems to be one thing that unites everyone's rites: they can be dangerous. A couple kids have gotten hurt. Last spring one of the boys came back with a broken arm and a nasty-looking cut above his eye that's since turned into a ropy scar.

My thoughts flash to Rain. Because sometimes whatever

happens during the rite is so dangerous you don't come back at all.

"Me?" I manage to say. "Now?"

"You have so much potential, Fern. Do you know that? It's deep inside, but it's there. You walk through the world so small, shoulders rounded, eyes down. That's why I was hard on you before. With your sweater. Because you're like me. I can see it. Inside you're strong. Destined for greatness. You have a quiet strength, a quiet power. We just need to break the shell. And while, yes, it's early, I think you're ready for it."

"But won't it be—" I swallow. "Isn't it dangerous?"

"Yes," Dr. Ben says simply. "But you need to understand something. I am responsible for crafting the next generation. A generation who will understand how to live in harmony with the land. How to be ready to survive the fallout of war, of climate change, of disaster. I do not take this responsibility lightly. Because it's coming, sooner than society thinks. And to survive, you need to be tough. You need to go through the gauntlet of hardship and come out the other side stronger."

"Do you think— Can I talk to my mom about it?" Mom and I don't always see eye to eye on everything, but a part of me feels like I should check in with her when it comes to something this big.

There's a flicker of a reaction on Dr. Ben's face. Disapproval, maybe. Even I've noticed Mom's been acting . . . a little weird lately. She's been asking more questions than usual, for one. Not just *how* questions but *why* questions. Like she doesn't trust Dr. Ben's judgment all the way. She's been showing up late to meals and chore hours. Dr. Ben has her on a water fast right now, to get her mind sharp again. To get her back to understanding why the rules are what they are and why he's the one who makes them.

"You can talk to her about it, if you'd like, but our community is all family in the same way, Fern. Blood doesn't run deeper here. You should know that by now."

"You're right," I say quickly. "I shouldn't have asked. I'm sorry."

"No, no," he says. "Ask for her counsel, if you respect it. If you respect *her*. It's just . . . there's a weakness in your mother I don't see in you. An indecisiveness. And I worry she might end up holding you back from the growth I know you're capable of."

I'm embarrassed for Mom—for both of us—that this is how he sees her. I don't want to be weak or indecisive. I want to be the person he says he sees in me. "Never mind. Really. I don't need to talk to her. I—I want to do it early. I'm ready."

"Good, Fern. Very good." He leans back, and his eyes are cast into shadow. "I have one piece of advice for you, then, as spring draws nearer. Prepare for the unexpected."

3

With every breath I take of the cold midmorning air, I feel more alive than ever. The sky is a brilliant and sharp winter blue as Meadowlark and I finish cleaning out and replacing the bedding in the last chicken coop. The roof of the coop and the trees all around us are dusted with a layer of powdery snow from last night, and the sunshine is making everything sparkle.

"Can you help me with the feed bag?" Meadowlark calls to me. "It's heavy."

A couple of the Rhode Island Reds are clucking and cooing around her feet. They're my favorite breed of chicken we raise. They're the most sweet and sociable, and some of them will even let you pick them up and stroke their feathers.

"Sure," I say, going to help her. The bag *is* heavy, and by the time we've refilled their feeder and changed out the coop's dirty bedding for fresh, we're both sweating. I don't mind, though. In fact, I love it. Chores change seasonally, and the two of us are on chicken duty through the end of winter.

It's the only chore the two of us have alone together, and I like the chickens and their gentle energy. The eggs they lay have rich, bright orange yolks. Every time we eat them, I like knowing I was a small part of their production.

Meadowlark and I are just sitting down on a stack of logs next to the coop to catch our breath when we notice a tall figure crunching toward us across the field.

"Hello, girls," the man calls. It's Ash, and he has a steaming mug in each hand. "We made cider with some of the leftover Idareds, and I saw you from the caf and thought you might appreciate a hot drink."

"Yes, please," I say, holding out my mittened hands. Meadowlark does as well.

Ash gives Meadowlark her mug first, and then hands the other one to me. As he does, he nods approvingly. "Fern. Nice work out here."

Ash is the closest thing we have to a teacher on the Ranch. Once a week for an hour or two, all the kids gather in the great room and Ash takes us through lessons. Mostly he teaches us things we need to learn to take care of the Ranch and the land. Basic math, lots about seasonal planting, some carpentry skills, things like that. He's not necessarily *strict,* but he doesn't tolerate "wasted time," as he puts it. Basically, he's not the kind of person who'd walk two mugs of cider across a snowy field without good reason.

Which makes me feel proud. Word spread quickly after my conversation with Dr. Ben last week, and people are paying attention to me in a way they didn't before. I have a hunch that even this mug of cider is because of it. Before, I was just a kid in everyone's way, someone to be told where to run off to and what to do. But now it's like I'm taking up a new kind of space. I'll be the youngest person on the Ranch to go through the rite of passage, and it's like people are starting to actually *see* me now.

Once Ash leaves, and we've both blown enough heat from our cider so we can drink it without burning our tongues, Meadowlark asks, "Has your mom said anything else to you yet?"

"No. Nothing yet."

Meadowlark winces. "I'm sorry."

Mom is the only adult who doesn't seem proud or happy for me. When I told her about my conversation with Dr. Ben, she just frowned and said, *"Now?* He thinks you should do it now? Why?"

Dr. Ben's words about her came back to me then. *Weak. Indecisive.*

"Yes," I told her. "Now. Because he thinks I'm ready for it. And I *am* ready for it."

Ever since we had that conversation, we haven't talked much. Of course, we don't always talk every day anyway. We're often on a different schedule, and at meals adults tend to sit with adults and kids with kids. It's also kind of a hassle to go back and forth to the adult women's dorm, because it's on the other side of the Ranch's sprawling main house. But still. There's been a new tension between us.

Meadowlark and I sit together in easy silence for a few

more moments, sipping our cider, before she asks me another question. This one she barely whispers, her voice so quiet I can't hear her.

"Sorry, what'd you say?"

"I just— Are you going to tell me about it?"

"About what?"

"Your rite," she says. "Will you tell me what I should expect? For when it's my turn?"

"I mean . . ." I shift uncomfortably. "The whole point is to get through whatever he throws at you without preparation. If I told you what happens, it wouldn't be fair. You'd only be cheating yourself."

"I would tell you," she says. "If I was the one doing it early."

Suddenly, I feel unsure. Maybe she would. And maybe I'd want her to. But Meadowlark can afford to knit bad hats and break rules. Her mom is special to Dr. Ben. Mine isn't. "Then I guess it's good you're not."

She stiffens, almost like I've hit her. "I thought you were my best friend."

"I am. Of course I am."

She stands and pours out what remains of her cider. "Okay, fine. You're right. I never should have asked. Let's finish up out here."

"Meadow—"

But she's already moving away. I stay put for a few more seconds, squeezing my eyes shut, before I dump the rest of my cider, too. I haven't even gone through my rite, and already things are getting more complicated. Is this what happens when you grow up?

Tonight's dinner is one of my favorite meals, tomato-lentil stew with flaky cheddar biscuits. This'll probably be one of the last times we'll have it for months—we've almost run out of the tomatoes we canned from last summer. But I still feel all weird from my conversation with Meadowlark earlier, and I'm struggling to enjoy it.

She's sitting next to me, like normal, and we aren't ignoring each other or anything as obvious as that. I don't know if she's upset with me or if I'm upset with her. Whatever it is, there's definitely something off between us. And I don't like it.

I crane my neck to see if Mom has come into the caf without me noticing, but every time I check, she isn't here. Even though she's on the water fast, she's still supposed to join the rest of us for meals. The only other person missing from dinner tonight is Iris, but that's because she's been too sick the past few nights to get out of bed. Maybe Mom is with her.

". . . Fern? I said, what do you think?"

Oak is staring at me from across the table. I didn't hear his question. He turned fifteen last month, so his rite will be happening this spring, too. A week ago, he wouldn't have ever sat with me for dinner, but now it's like I'm the only person he wants to talk to. Next to me, Meadowlark tears her biscuit into two pieces and doesn't say anything.

I'm about to ask Oak to repeat his question when there's a loud clattering noise. Across the caf, Dr. Ben is standing in front of Yarrow, one of the men, talking angrily to him. There's a mess of food on the floor, and Yarrow is backing away. Dr. Ben must have knocked his plate out of his hands. Yarrow's been helping himself to extras at mealtime every day for months, and I guess Dr. Ben finally noticed.

I sit on my hands, curling into myself. Dr. Ben certainly isn't perfect—we all know he has a nasty temper. He doesn't lose it often, but when he does, watch out. Part of me wishes he had just pulled Yarrow aside and asked him privately to take only his fair share.

Dr. Ben closes his eyes and breathes in, recentering himself. When he opens his eyes, he doesn't seem mad anymore. He puts a hand on Yarrow's shoulder and talks in a very calm manner. And maybe this *was* the right way to handle it, because from the look on Yarrow's face, I can tell he'll never help himself to more than his fair share again.

Soon conversation starts up like nothing happened. Dr. Ben goes to sit at his usual spot by the fire, next to Meadowlark's mom, and opens his journal. I watch as she reaches out and squeezes his hand before going back to her meal. Across the room, Yarrow cleans up the mess on the floor, red-faced, as everyone else pretends not to notice.

A few minutes later, the door to the caf swings open.

And—it's Mom. *Finally.*

Her cheeks and nose are flushed, like she's been outside. Her eyes find mine, but only for a second. She starts looking around, stopping only when she sees Dr. Ben. She hurries over to him.

He doesn't look up at her or stop writing in his journal. "What is it, Magnolia?"

Oak is trying to say something else to me, but I shush him. I strain to listen.

"Weather's not looking good." Mom twists her hands together, something she does when she's nervous. "If you're heading north, you might want to get on the road sooner than planned."

Dr. Ben's face is expressionless as he listens. Every couple of months, he leaves for a few days. I'm pretty sure it's to give talks and lectures, to spread the word of what's to come—that sort of thing. Sometimes he brings back new people. That's rare, though, and it only happens if he thinks they've got what it takes.

He tips his journal shut and stands. It's funny—I don't think of Mom as that tall, but she's taller than Dr. Ben by at least a couple of inches. But Dr. Ben doesn't seem short to me. Not at all. He always seems like the tallest person in the room.

"Fine. I'll leave tonight," he says. "Please get someone to pack up my things."

"Of course," Mom says. "Right away."

He turns and strides out of the room. Mom glances at me one more time before she follows him out. Her eyes are saying something, but I can't tell what it is.

Later, I head to the women's dorm to find Mom. Inside, it's softly lit and smells like a combination of the lavender essential oil mixture we use on the bedding and something pungent and medicinal. Most of the women are here, getting ready for bed. Two of the older women are sitting on Iris's bed, chatting softly as they tend to her. One is braiding her hair, and the other is massaging a tincture onto her arms and hands, which must be the source of the smell. Iris's eyes are closed, and she has a small smile on her lips. Iris is—*was*, I guess—Rain's mom. She got sick soon after Rain's accident. It doesn't feel fair that she should have so much to deal with at once. Not that life or nature is fair. Which is why it's so important to be strong, to be prepared. But still. I'm glad to see her feeling okay and getting taken care of tonight.

A few rows down, I spot Mom sitting on her bed, rifling through the drawer of her pine nightstand. I go over and touch her on the shoulder to get her attention. She gasps in surprise and spins around, like I've scared the daylights out of her. A few of the other women glance over to see what's going on.

Is this all it takes to scare her these days? A light touch on the shoulder?

"It's just me." I draw my hand back. "Relax."

20

Mom lets out a long breath. She smiles, but it comes out more like a grimace. "Sorry. You startled me."

I wait to see if she's going to say anything else. I know it's stupid, and it shouldn't matter to me, but I came here because I want her to acknowledge me. To say she's proud of me, that she believes I can do it.

But then I see a half-eaten biscuit tucked in between the folds of her blanket. Mom shifts her body, hiding it from view.

She's supposed to be on a water fast. Why can't she try just a little bit harder?

"So, what's up, honey?" she asks. "Is there something you wanted to talk about?"

"Nothing. Forget it. I should probably go to bed."

"Yeah. Me too." She reaches out to squeeze my hand and says, "Love you."

I don't say anything in return.

When I get back to the dorm, Meadowlark is already in bed. There are ten fifteen-and-unders in total on the Ranch; the six of us girls share this room, and the four boys have a room closer to where the adult dorms are.

Usually, Meadowlark and I use our before-bed time to talk, brush our teeth together, or play cat's cradle or card games she invents. Though "game" isn't quite a good enough word. She creates these long backstories for the cards, so that playing a game with her is like stepping into a different universe, where the Queen of Hearts is desperately in love with the Ace of Spades, but they need to escape deep into the hills so the King of Diamonds, who wants to eat her heart for the power it will give him, won't find them. I was hoping to talk to her tonight, try to make things feel normal again. But I guess that'll have to wait until morning.

After hanging my day clothes in my cubby and brushing my teeth with our homemade mint scrub, I crawl into bed.

Most nights, I fall right asleep.

But tonight, despite how tired I am, all I can do is toss and turn and stare at the dark ceiling.

4

It feels like I've only been asleep for a few minutes when someone starts shaking me.

Or maybe I'm dreaming it—I snuggle deeper under my blankets. In my mind it's summer, and I'm in one of the row-boats on the pond, rocking back and forth. I can almost feel the tickle of wind and the sunshine on my face and the lapping water—

"Frankie," a voice whispers urgently. "Wake up."

Mom is the only one who calls me Frankie instead of Fern, and only occasionally, by accident. Because that was my name, before. I open my eyes.

"Mom?" My voice creaks as I sit up on my elbows. She's kneeling next to my bed. The dorm is dark and heavy with sleep, but I can see she's already dressed for the day in her thick wool sweater and waxed work pants. "What are you doing here?"

We get up at sunrise. No earlier and no later. Dr. Ben says consistency within our schedules and across our community is important. It took me a while to get used to it, but I've grown to love it. Now it's like my body knows to wake up my mind without an alarm of any kind.

So why is she here when it's still dark?

"What time is it?" I ask. "Is something wrong?"

In the bed across from mine, Meadowlark stirs. She's got the covers pulled up so far that all I can see is a puff of her white-blond hair.

"Shh," Mom says, glancing at her. "Nothing's wrong. But I need you to get dressed. Warmly."

"Why?"

"Because the two of us are going on an off-site for Dr. Ben."

I sit up a bit more, trying to make sense of her words. An off-site is an errand or a job where you actually leave the Ranch. Only people Dr. Ben really trusts go on off-sites. I don't think Mom's been out on more than three or four of them in the six years we've lived here. There's no way he'd schedule her for one right now, not when she's been acting so . . . different. And kids rarely get to go, either. Something about this doesn't feel right.

"What are we going to do?" I ask.

She presses her finger to her lips. No one else is awake. Meadowlark flips over and mutters something I can't make out and hugs a pillow to her chest, but she doesn't open her eyes. "I can't say anything other than this is what Dr. Ben wants. Get dressed and meet me by the fireplace when you're ready. And be quiet."

Suddenly, I remember the last words Dr. Ben said to me during our meeting. *Prepare for the unexpected.*

A surge of energy courses through me. Because maybe this is it. The beginning of my rite. It isn't anywhere close to the spring equinox yet, when rites usually happen, but maybe that's what Dr. Ben meant by "unexpected."

So I nod, not making a sound.

When Mom leaves, I pad silently from my bed into the changing room, shaky with nerves. I'm extra quiet as I slide the door shut behind me. From my cubby I pull out my sweater, the thick fuzzy brown one I made last month. I put on my long underwear, two pairs of wool socks, and then my work pants as my last layer. Except for the secret blue fish I stitched on the inside pocket, they're exactly like Mom's, exactly like everyone else's. Well, everyone else's except for Meadowlark's, which have a red fish to match my blue one. We aren't supposed to focus too much on our lives before the Ranch, but one thing I do know about Meadowlark is that before she lived here she lived with her parents in Florida, by the ocean. Her dad came to the Ranch with her and her mom originally, but he left before Mom and I got here. I don't know the details. And I don't know when or how it happened, or if it was connected to her dad or to Florida, but drawing little fishes somehow became *our* thing. And that's what matters.

I want to wake her up, to tell her there's a chance my rite is about to happen. Maybe she'd give me one of her fierce hugs and wish me luck. I know I could use it. And I almost do—I even creep back into the dorm, to her bed.

But I don't. I just press my hand lightly on her shoulder and tiptoe out of the room.

Mom's waiting for me by the fireplace in the great room, like she said she'd be. The fire is down to embers now. Someone will be back to build it up as soon as the sun crests the trees.

She's pacing back and forth, twisting her hands. The only light is from the dying fire, but I can see she's got a woven tote bag slung over her shoulder, so full of stuff that it's lumpy and bulging.

She doesn't notice me right away, so I go and touch her elbow. "Mom? I'm ready."

She startles and spins around, just as jumpy as last night. Her shoulders relax when she sees it's me. But only a little.

She nods toward the doors. "Come on. We don't want to be late."

I follow her into the foyer, where we keep all our coats, hats, and winter boots. The stone floor is so freezing cold I can feel it through both pairs of my socks. Mom and I put on our last layers in silence.

When we go outside, the cold air is shocking, but it feels kind of nice.

Mom closes the main door gently, so gently, behind us.

Maybe she's going to drop me somewhere, and it'll be up

to me to get back to the Ranch on my own: no supplies, no food, only my wits and my inner strength.

A new wave of anxiety comes over me. Even though I'm dressed warmly, it's cold out here. Really cold.

You're ready, I tell myself.

The snow crunches beneath our feet as we walk down the long driveway toward the double garage where the van and Dr. Ben's private car are kept.

I assume we're headed to the van. We all share it. Whether it's going out to sell at farmers markets or picking up supplies, it's always the van that's used. Well, we *kind of* share it. Dr. Ben has the only set of keys, but he lends them out for off-sites or . . . for other things, I guess. Like what's happening right now.

The garage's automatic lights click on as we approach, and as soon as they do, Mom starts walking twice as fast, almost like she's running.

She walks right past the garage door.

And then right by the garage, period.

She's going so fast we're almost to the metal gate at the end of the Ranch's driveway before I can catch up to her.

"Mom." My breath fogs out in giant puffs in front of me. "Mom, what are you doing? The van's back there."

She doesn't respond. She pulls the metal gate open just wide enough for me to slip through.

Out on the road, I can see a car is waiting, its exhaust rising like steam. I look more closely. It's a taxi.

She motions me forward. "Go."

I don't move. I haven't been past the Ranch's gate in a long time. Not since we started living here, six years ago. "Shouldn't we be using the van?"

"No," Mom says. "Not today."

That's enough to get me moving, but something still feels wrong.

Because doesn't Dr. Ben trust us enough to lend us the van keys?

As soon as I'm through, Mom follows. She tries to close the gate quietly, but metal still snaps against metal, which makes her wince.

We're outside, I think again and again, trying to find that special feeling I always imagined I'd feel when I stepped out beyond these gates.

But it doesn't come.

I try to make sense of why we would be taking a taxi. Maybe there was something wrong with Dr. Ben's car and he needed to take the van. Like maybe the van drives better in the snow and he wanted to be safe, given the snowstorm Mom warned him about. Not that any snow is falling yet, but still.

Prepare for the unexpected, I remind myself as I slide into the taxi's back seat.

We drive for a while. I try to stay awake, but the taxi is so warm and it's still so dark I can't see anything through the windows, so I fall asleep. Part of me knows I should probably get all the rest I can before I'm dropped off.

When I wake up, the world is softly lit by the sunrise,

and the snow glows almost pink. Meadowlark and the others should be getting up right about now. I sit up taller and stretch my arms above my head. From now on I'll stay awake so I can report every little detail back to Meadowlark. Because I've decided: If she wants to know, I'm going to tell her everything about what happens. She's my best friend, and sometimes it's worth it to break a rule or two for the people you love the most.

But the farther we go, the less certain I am about what's actually happening.

We drive until the snow-covered woods and long winding roads are far behind us. We drive until all I can see is gray asphalt and dingy buildings. We pass gas stations and diners and strip malls. It makes me feel dirty and uncomfortable.

Finally, after what seems like forever, the taxi pulls into a wide parking lot. It's a sea of old cars with big dollar signs and numbers written on their windshields in hot-pink marker.

The number on the meter is high. We used to take taxis sometimes when we lived in Brooklyn, but I don't remember them being this expensive.

How long was I asleep for?

Mom reaches into her tote and pulls out some cash. I stare at it. How on earth does she have that? Did Dr. Ben give it to her? I haven't seen money in . . . I can't remember the last time I saw money. I've never been to the farmers market, or out on an errand, so I guess the last time would have been when I was six.

I don't have time to ask, because after she pays, it feels like she gets out of the taxi before it even stops moving.

There's a man in a big parka leaning against one of the cars. He straightens up when he sees us walking toward him.

"You're late. I didn't think you were coming," he says to Mom as soon as we get close. "Paul said you were going to be here over an hour ago."

I glance at Mom. *Paul?* I think. *Who's Paul?*

"Yeah, well, here we are." She turns to the car. "Is this the one?"

"Yep." The man slaps the roof. It's the color of dry dirt, and bits of paint are missing here and there, with rusted metal showing through. One of the doors isn't the same color as the others. "I rotated the tires and checked the oil yesterday. Should be good enough for your needs."

Mom peeks in one of the windows. "And you got everything else?"

"Everything that was on the list."

"Fine. Good." Mom takes an envelope out of her stuffed-full tote bag. "And if anyone asks—"

"I never saw you. Or your kid," he says, winking. "I know."

I step closer to Mom.

She gives him the envelope, and he hands her the keys.

He taps the envelope to his forehead. "Pleasure doing business with you. Drive safe and have a good life."

"Thanks," Mom says. "You too."

After he's walked a far enough distance away, I turn to

Mom. "Who's Paul? And 'have a good life'? What's that sup-posed to mean?"

"It's just something people say. Come on. Let's get warm."

The car door sticks from the cold, so I have to pull with my whole body to get it open. It's as cold inside as it is outside.

As soon as we're both in the car with the doors shut, I face her. "What's going on?"

She turns the engine on and starts fiddling with some of the knobs.

"Damn," she says. "I think the heater's broken."

"I *said*," I repeat, "what's going on?"

"Nothing's going on. We're doing exactly what we're sup-posed to be doing." She reaches behind her into the back seat. There are two red duffel bags. They look brand-new—and completely synthetic. She unzips one of them and pulls out a bright yellow blanket that still has its tags on it. She rips them off and tries to hand it to me. "Put this on your lap."

I press my back against the car door. I don't want that thing anywhere near me. "What's it made of? It looks like it has dyes and chemicals in it."

"I'm not asking, Frankie," she says, pushing the blanket closer.

"Fern," I say loudly. I still haven't taken the blanket from her. "My name is Fern!"

"No." Mom reaches over and forces it onto my lap, tuck-ing it in roughly around my legs. "Your name is Frankie."

I can tell by the look on her face I'd better not argue if I want to get anything else out of her, better not take the blanket off. I press my teeth together. I'm probably imagining it, but I can almost feel the dyes and chemicals seeping through my pants, into my skin.

She pulls into the road, her blinker clicking. Then she turns left.

West. Away from the rising sun.

"This isn't the way home." I point behind us. "The Ranch is back there."

Mom doesn't look at me. "I know, baby."

"Does this have anything to do with my rite? Because this isn't an off-site, is it?" I swallow, the question I'm about to ask so horrible I can barely get the words out. "Does Dr. Ben even know where we are?"

"Of course he does." Only then do I notice her hands are clutching the wheel so tightly I can see the white outline of her knuckles.

We drive all day long. We eat canned cranberry beans and pickled vegetables Mom brought from the Ranch, and only stop to use the bathroom. I keep asking where we're going and when we're going to turn around and go back. She only gives me vague half answers that don't actually tell me anything.

"It'll all be clear soon." And "Don't worry. Try to rest." And "I'm trying to focus on the road. I promise I'll explain more later."

I get angry. I raise my voice. I beg. But she still doesn't give me a good answer.

We drive until the sun arcs through the sky and sinks down in front of us, making it hard to see.

She hasn't dropped me anywhere. We haven't picked anything up. No fuzzy chicks, no bags of seeds for the greenhouse, no new knitting needles or garden trowels or other tools. Nothing.

Finally, we pull into a motel parking lot right off the highway. Mom grabs both duffel bags and gets out. I don't move.

She opens my door for me and stands there. "Come on."

"No. I'm not moving until you tell me what's going on. You promised." To make my point, I slip my hand through the grab handle and grip it as hard as I can. "When are we going back to the Ranch?"

Mom sighs. A deep whooshing sort of sigh, like some important part of her is slipping out of her mouth and into the cold night air.

"Honey," she says. "We're going to try something new for a little while."

My heart starts beating so hard I can almost feel it in my throat. I stare at her. "What? What does that mean?"

"It means . . ." She swallows. "It means we aren't going back."

And just like that, my world cracks open.

5

We stay in the parking lot for more than an hour.

I beg her to get back into the car, to take us home. I say please. I cry. She tries to physically pull me out of the front seat, but I cling to the handle so hard she can't get me out.

Exhausted from the effort, Mom slumps down onto the pavement, panting. "Please. Please get out of the car."

"No!" Through my tears, I say, "Why do you always give up so easily? On everything? You've always been this way!"

She looks so tired. And . . . hurt. But I don't care. I want her to feel bad, and hurt. I want her to feel as terrible as I do.

"I didn't give up," Mom says. "I *woke* up. Ever since Rain died, things have changed for me. Dr. Ben acted like it was just the natural way of things, but it wasn't. It never should have happened. He was only fifteen years old. And I know Ben could see me losing faith in him." She motions at me. "He wants to punish me. Don't you get it? To remind me who's in charge. And he planned to do that by putting you in a dangerous situation. Where you could have gotten hurt." She swallows. "Or worse."

"My rite has nothing to do with you! Dr. Ben sees things in me. He's proud of me. And unlike you, I'm not afraid of hard things." My voice shakes. "I'm not scared. And you shouldn't be, either."

"Rain died during his rite, honey," Mom says. "I can't let that happen to you."

"Rain died because he was weak," I tell her. "I'm not weak."

Mom stares at me. "You don't mean that, do you?"

The news of his death was a shock to everyone. Well, almost everyone—it doesn't seem like Dr. Ben gets surprised by anything. I'll never forget the wail Iris let out when she heard what had happened. Dr. Ben gathered us all together in the caf and talked about death and how it's a natural part of life. How, throughout history, death has been nature's tool to create stronger communities of animals and people. Iris cried silently and nodded the whole time. Dr. Ben hugged her tightly, his arm never leaving her shoulders.

For a second, I let myself remember Rain. I remember the way he smiled with his whole face. The way he gave extra food to Meadowlark every time he was on caf duty, because she's always been so small. The time he stitched up one of the hens and carried it around in his coat for a week after it had been attacked by a fox. The memories make me ache. But then again, maybe kindness is weakness.

I slump back in my seat. "I don't want to talk to you anymore."

"I'm sorry," Mom says. "I'm sorry you're hurting. I'm sorry if you feel confused. But I'm doing this to protect you. It'll make sense to you. One day."

I start to cry again. "I won't ever forgive you. Now or 'one day.'"

Mom nods, looking like she's trying to hold back tears of her own. "That's a risk I'm willing to take."

At some point I'm too tired, too spent to fight her anymore. I let her take me into the motel. Once we're in the room, she locks the door, turns the dead bolt, and pulls the blinds.

We don't talk for the rest of the night.

Well, *I* don't talk to *her*. Because how could I? She's obviously lost her mind. She keeps talking about how change is a positive force in life, how I should be open to new experiences. I ignore every single word she says. Eventually, she stops trying.

After she falls asleep, I lie on top of the stiff motel bedspread in my clothes and stare at the ceiling tiles. I know I won't be able to sleep, so after a while, I go and peek through the blinds. I can see the flash of headlights from the highway, hear the thrum of tires against the road.

In my head I try to count the places we lived before the Ranch. I remember Brooklyn, Buffalo, Boston. And Cleveland, I think. There were more places, but I was too little to remember them. There was never a set time for when we ate, for when we woke up, for what chores we did. I remember more than once getting back from school to see the car packed up, Mom ready to take me somewhere new, without any warning.

Honestly, before we moved to the Ranch, the rocking feeling of being in the car, with all our bags and belongings shoved in the trunk, was what felt like home most of all.

And I don't want to go back to that.

I can't.

In the morning, she doesn't turn the car around. She doesn't say, *Sorry, Fern, I don't know what I was thinking. We'll go home now, and I'll make it right.*

She just keeps driving.

Over the next few hours I try to talk sense into her. Because we have to get back, and soon. The longer we stay away, the worse it will be. I tell her that we can still smooth it all over, that she obviously lost her temper about something, but it isn't too late to turn around.

"Please," I say. "He'll forgive us. He'll know we didn't mean to leave. We'll—"

She veers off the highway so quickly the tires shriek. The car behind us swerves and honks its horn in a long, angry blast as it whizzes by.

"Enough." Mom lets out a shaky breath. "That's enough. I already told you. I got scared. I didn't . . . I stopped recognizing myself." She motions between us. "I stopped recognizing *us*. It was time to go."

Part of me feels like laughing. I can't believe she doesn't see it. Because it's the same as it's always been. *We're* the same as we've always been. The two of us in a car, leaving, off to somewhere new. The problem isn't the Ranch. The problem is her.

After that, I stop talking. For hours. Days.

Every night we stay in the same dreary kind of motel off the highway, with a TV bolted to the wall and multiple locks on the door. Some of the rooms stink; it's a bitter, almost smoky smell. It's so unlike home that it makes me want to cry. Which I do. Mom brought food from the Ranch, and she buys fruit and nuts when we stop for gas, but I barely touch any of it.

Everything is gray and unreal. I feel like someone died. Like *I* died, as if my own edges are fading away. It's like the Ranch is the only thing that makes me solid. The only thing that makes me *me*.

Signs fly past: Ohio, Indiana, Oklahoma, and still I don't say a single word to Mom. She tries to talk to me. She tells me we're driving the southern route, to avoid the snow. She tells me little things she knows about each state we drive through. She points out places on the road signs where she's either visited or stayed for a while. Her words wash over me like water.

After our third day in the car, the snow starts to melt, and we don't have to wear all our layers anymore.

Soon the rocks turn red, the sky blue.

And we still haven't tried to contact the Ranch, not once.

Tears leak from the corners of my eyes every time I think about what the look on Dr. Ben's face must have been when he realized we were gone. About Meadowlark sitting at the foot of my empty bed. Her fingernails, chewed down all the way and bleeding. I can only imagine the hurt she feels that I left without saying goodbye. That I disappeared in a moment when things were unsettled between us.

And if it hasn't turned to anger already, I'm sure it will soon.

I didn't know, I think fiercely. *I didn't know. I never would have left if I had known.*

Somewhere in Arizona our ugly brown car starts sputtering. When we stop for gas, it doesn't turn back on.

"It's a sign. Please, Mom." My voice is all croaky because it's the first thing I've said out loud in days. "Even the car wants us to stop driving and go home."

"No," Mom says. "We just need to jump it."

I don't know what "jump it" means, but I don't ask. Mom goes over to talk to a man in a pickup truck, and a few minutes later there are black cables snaking from his truck to our car.

She turns the key. The engine coughs and makes a *ruh-ruh-ruh* sound. Then it dies.

Mom tips her forehead on the steering wheel and closes her eyes. "Please. Just a little bit farther."

It must work, because the next time she tries the key, the car stops coughing, and its engine rumbles to life.

After that, we keep on driving.

At some point the next day, once we've passed into the state of California, I fall asleep. And when I wake up, the mood in the car feels different. So does the air coming in through our cracked-open windows. Heavy. Salty, even.

I sit up and yawn.

Mom smiles at me. It's the first time she's smiled since she got us into this mess. "Hey, sleepyhead. Guess what? We're here."

I don't smile back. But I do look out my window to see where "here" is.

We're turning left at a big faded sign. It says:

WELCOME TO THE LIGHTHOUSE MOTEL
in beautiful Driftaway Beach, CA
CABLE TV! OCEAN VIEWS!

I can't help it: I gasp as we pull into the parking lot, because it's right at the edge of the world. Even from the car, I can see the huge waves smashing against rocks, the spray dusting down on all the parked cars like tiny raindrops.

The ocean.

I'm so amazed at how close we are to it I forget to be mad. As soon as Mom parks, I jump out of the car and run to the low wooden fence that separates the parking lot from the water.

It seems to go on and on, forever. Dr. Ben says the ocean is the cradle of all life. That it's infinite and full of power.

And it is. It's that and more.

Mom comes to stand next to me. The salty wind whips at her hair. "It's beautiful, isn't it? I've always loved the Pacific Ocean. There's something majestic about it. Wild."

Another wave crashes, which is enough to wake me up.

Because we've reached the Pacific Ocean. We're as far away from the Ranch as land allows us to go.

An ache starts in my chest. I think about my soft bed and its low wooden frame, exactly the same as those around it. Our fields overflowing with vegetables that feed us through the year, the gentle clucking of the hens. The dinging of pots and pans in the caf, the chatter over meals. I think about the dense woods cocooning the property, with the meandering, secret paths we made ourselves with wheelbarrows full of mulch.

Here, I can barely see a single tree. From where I'm standing, all I can see is ocean and pavement and wide-open gray sky.

Mom reaches out to take my hand and I don't have the energy to stop her. I feel numb as she pulls me along.

The office we go into is tiny, with all sorts of posters taped to the walls, their edges curling up from the damp sea air. I notice one in particular, probably because it's the biggest. It's a picture of a woman in a white dress on top of a cliff, facing out toward the sea. But you can kind of see through her, like she's not actually there.

In faded white print, it says, "The Spirit of the Sea."

And below that, in smaller print: "Want to learn more about our local legend? Grab a brochure today!"

"Hi there," comes a voice. "Checking in?"

It belongs to the man sitting behind the desk. He's younger than Mom but older than a teenager—I think. It's hard to tell with adults. He's got messy black hair and he's wearing a faded T-shirt that says, "The Kooks."

And he's reading a *book*. A faded paperback with a scaly creature on the front. I stretch my neck, but I can't see what the title is. One glance is enough to tell me it's not the kind of book you'd find in the Ranch's library.

"No," Mom says. "Not exactly."

He closes his book and puts it onto the desk, facedown, waiting for her to go on.

Mom takes a small step forward and rubs her palms nervously down the sides of her hips. "I'm Mag—I mean, Jamie. . . . Jamie Silvana?"

It's weird hearing Mom use her born name. Everyone at the Ranch calls her Mags, which is short for Magnolia. Actually, hearing "Jamie" isn't weird—it's terrible. It's like she's introducing someone who no longer exists.

He still doesn't say anything. He tilts his head to the side, like he doesn't understand.

Mom's cheeks are turning red. "My friend Paul was corresponding with your dad on my behalf about the housekeeping position? And our . . . special circumstances?"

There's that name again. Paul. We don't know a Paul—or at least I don't.

"Oh!" He hurries out from behind the desk, reaching to shake Mom's hand. "Hey! Of course. It's so nice to meet you. I'm Alex. Alex Reyes. Sorry, took me a sec. My dad's in the Philippines for the next few weeks, visiting family. He'll be so happy to know you arrived safely."

He turns to me and smiles. "Hey. You must be . . . it's Frankie, right? I'm Alex."

"Fern." I flick my eyes back to Mom and lift my chin defiantly. "I actually go by Fern."

"Oh! Sorry. I thought the letter said . . ." He trails off. "Well, never mind. Welcome to the Lighthouse Motel, Fern."

Lighthouse. The word is familiar, but I can't quite remember why or what it is.

"What's a lighthouse?" I ask. "Is it something to grow plants?"

Alex laughs like I made a joke.

"No," Mom says quietly. "It's a building that helps guide ships away from the shore by flashing lights toward the sea."

Alex has stopped laughing and has a funny look on his face. "Oh. Uh, yeah. There used to be a lighthouse here until it burned down in the early nineteen hundreds. And now it's a motel. Go figure." He claps his hands together. "Okay, well . . . right. Follow me, and I'll show you to your new digs."

Mom and I trail after him, out of the office and down a

cement walkway, which is separated from the big parking lot by a low wall. We pass door after door with dull silver numbers on them. When we're almost at the end, we stop at number 15.

"Here we go." Alex fumbles to get the key in the lock. Once he does, he pushes the door open, and we step inside.

There are two beds with dark green quilts, a worn wooden desk, and a television on the wall above a dresser. Everything is old and a little shabby, and the air is as damp and salty in here as it is outside.

"It's not much, but it's clean," he says, like he's reading my mind. "We also put in a mini-fridge and a hot plate for you to use."

I want to know what a hot plate is, but I don't want him to give me another weird look, so I stay quiet.

"It's perfect," Mom says. "I can't thank you enough for all of this. For what you and your dad are doing for us."

Alex waves a hand at her. "Nah. It's our pleasure." He gives us both another warm, crinkly smile and runs his hand through his hair. "We figured you'd need a couple of days to get settled before getting to work. So take your time."

"I'd actually like to start tomorrow, if that's okay," Mom replies.

I have no idea what they're talking about. "Start what?"

"My job," Mom says to me, as if that explains everything.

"Tomorrow?" he asks. "So soon?"

Mom nods. I stare at her.

"Well, if you're sure. . . . Then okay. Whatever you want.

You can meet me in the office at seven, and I'll introduce you to Dina. She's the head of housekeeping, and she's been threatening retirement for years. I'm sure she'll be excited you're here. She'll get you all set up."

Mom keeps thanking him as he leaves, right up until he shuts the door behind him.

Job? I think. Everything is jumbled. I don't understand anything. I sit down on the edge of one of the beds and start to cry.

"I don't want to be here," I say. "What's even happening? Who's Paul?"

Mom sits down next to me and tries to put her arm around my shoulder, but I push her away. "Stop. Don't do that."

She moves over, giving me space. She clasps her hands in her lap. "Do you remember Forest or Kestrel? From the Ranch?"

"Of course I do."

Forest was short and stocky, with a big bushy beard. Kestrel was his daughter, five or six years older than me. They disappeared from the Ranch about three years ago, after leaving for an afternoon hike around the perimeter. Dr. Ben put together a search team to comb the property, just in case they'd been injured somewhere and needed help. But they were never found.

"Forest's real name is Paul," Mom went on. "And they didn't disappear. They left. By choice. And they helped us leave, too."

That makes me cry even more. Because I don't understand

any of it. Why they would want to leave, and why they'd want to drag us out with them.

Eventually, I stop crying and start to hiccup. When I'm breathing normally, Mom goes on. "We've been living at the Ranch since you were six. It was becoming all you knew. I thought it was time . . . I think it would be good for you—for *us*—to try something new. Which is why I want us to try living in the world."

"We were *already* 'living in the world,'" I tell her. "At the Ranch. And it's not safe out here. There are chemicals in the food, and heavy metals in the water, and—"

"Give me a couple of months," Mom says, brushing a tear off my cheek. "I want to try living away from the Ranch for a couple of months. And if at the end we aren't happy, if *you* aren't happy, we'll reevaluate. I promise. The Ranch will still be there in a couple of months. It'll still be there in a year. What do you think? Can you do that?"

No.

The word rings through me so strongly it's like my bones are vibrating.

Because *no.* I'm not willing to risk it. I won't risk losing the only place that's ever felt like home and being told there isn't a place for us there anymore. The one place where we'll be safe if the future becomes scary. Which it will. I won't risk losing Dr. Ben's respect and faith in me. I want to be the person he sees in me.

But Mom can't know this, and I can tell her mind's made up already.

She needs to think I'm giving in. That I'm okay with her plan. But on the inside, I'm going to fight. I'm going to claw our way back home. Back to safety. Back to the place where things make sense. I'll do whatever it takes.

So I take a deep breath, and I lie. I lie with everything I have.

"Okay," I tell her. "I can do it."

The next day Mom and I wake at dawn, like always.

I'm grateful for this tiny bit of normalcy.

We're almost out of the food Mom brought from the Ranch. She uses the last of the oats to make oatmeal on the hot plate, which, she explains, is kind of like a portable stove.

I couldn't sleep much, so instead I thought about my plan all night. I have to get in touch with Dr. Ben. He's the one who'll be able to talk sense into Mom. He could talk sense into a rock. And then, once they've talked, he'll find a way to bring us home. I know he will.

Which means I have to figure out *how* to get in touch with him. The Ranch has no phones and no computers, because living without all that stuff around is a lot better for your nervous system. I guess the way Dr. Ben organizes his trips away from the Ranch is by paper mail. It has to be, right? Which means the only way I can contact him is by sending him a real physical letter, which is something I've never done before.

Mom starts rifling through the dresser beneath the TV.

She unpacked both our duffels last night, because I couldn't bear to help her. "Want to wear some of your new clothes?" She pulls out shirts, pants, underwear. "Look at all this blue, Fernie. Your favorite. So nice, right?"

I stand a little so I can see, mostly because she called me Fernie instead of Frankie. There are lots of blue clothes. But they're not the soft blues of robins' eggs or the deep navy of natural indigo. They're bright and sharp and unnatural. I chew on my lip. "But the dyes—"

"No. A few months isn't long enough for the dyes or the chemicals to hurt you, okay? Try not to think about it."

Even so, I don't touch any of them.

It's been strange spending so much time with Mom. We see each other in passing on the Ranch, and some entire days go by where I don't see her beyond mealtimes in the caf. It's been years since we've been around each other this much, and it feels awkward, like we're trying on clothes that stopped fitting a long time ago.

After she showers, Mom puts on an outfit I've never seen before. It's brown and white and synthetic-looking. She scrapes her long hair back into a tight ponytail and clips a piece of plastic to her chest that says, "Jamie."

"What's that for?"

Mom touches it. "So people know my name, and that I work here. As a housekeeper."

"What does a housekeeper do?"

"Mostly cleaning and tidying rooms, making the beds— that sort of thing."

We do that at the Ranch, too, but no one calls it "house-keeping." And it's never only one person. We all share the load. Sometimes you're on laundry, other seasons you're assigned to dish duty in the kitchen or compost shoveling. We take care of each other, together. I don't see why this should be any different. I will live by the Ranch's principles, whether I'm there or not.

So I stand up. "I'll come with you. And help."

Mom opens her mouth like she's going to tell me not to, but then she closes it. "Okay."

An older white woman with dyed yellowy blond hair meets us outside the office. She introduces herself as Dina. She takes Mom to a big closet and gives her a cart she'll have to push from room to room. Then she gives us a checklist of what to do: strip and make the beds, vacuum, clean the bathroom, throw away the garbage. Things like that.

"I'll check the first room after you've finished." Dina's eyes flick to me, but she doesn't say anything about me being there.

"Okay," Mom replies. "Thank you."

After Dina leaves, we start on the first room. Since the narrow cement walkway between rooms is open to the parking lot, I can see and hear the ocean as we go. Across the lot, two people are sitting on the hood of a car facing the water, drinking from steel mugs and eating pastries from greasy paper bags. A few seagulls are perched on the fence nearby, watching them with beady eyes, no doubt hoping for some crumbs. I can't stop looking at the ocean. Being so close to it makes me feel better, even though it's cold and foggy this morning. It's something about the rhythmic pounding of the surf. I shiver a little, grateful for my thick sweater.

It makes me wonder what's going to happen to the sweater I was making the day before we left. Will Dr. Ben have someone unravel it? Will Meadowlark have to do it?

Mom knocks on the first door. "Housekeeping!"

When no one answers, she uses the key Dina gave her to open it.

I trail behind her as she pushes the cart inside. It bumps and rattles over the doorsill. The room is empty, and very messy. Especially the bed. The sheets are twisted, like the person got up two minutes ago. There's also an empty plastic water bottle and torn food wrappers on the bedside table.

I stare. "I can't believe they left it like this."

"This? It isn't that bad. When people stay at hotels or motels, they know there will be cleaning services."

"That seems really rude," I say, and Mom laughs. I frown. "What? Why is that funny?"

She touches my cheek. "It's not. I'm sorry for laughing."

We start by stripping the bed and remaking it with fresh sheets. I help her tuck the corners in, just so. She cleans up the wrappers and water bottle, and then we start on the bathroom.

As we work, I can't help but notice that it isn't only the food wrappers. There's plastic everywhere. Plastic wrapped around a tiny piece of soap. Tiny plastic bottles in the shower. In one single room there's more garbage than we make in a week on the Ranch.

I imagine each little piece drifting on top of the ocean, fish and turtles choking on it, dying with plastic scraps in their stomach. I imagine the cleaning chemicals we're using— which are *nothing* like the homemade supplies we use at the Ranch—soaking through the rags and into our skin. Poisoning us.

I crouch down on the bathroom floor and hold my head in my hands.

Mom comes over and kneels next to me. "This is a lot. I know." She rubs my back. "Why don't you go back to our room and lie down?"

"But I should help you," I say, head still in my hands. "No one should work alone."

"No. This is my new job. They're paying me to do this, which means it's my responsibility, not yours. If anything, you should be starting school, not working." She sighs and gives my shoulder a squeeze. "But for the meantime, I got you a surprise. Now seems like as good a time as ever to give it to you."

At that, I look up. "What is it?"

"You'll have to go see for yourself. It's in my tote bag, wrapped in paper."

"Okay." I stand up shakily. On my way out of the room, I turn around. "Mom?"

She stops scrubbing and pokes her head out of the bathroom. "Yeah?"

"We should tell Alex the motel needs new cleaning supplies. He might not know how toxic all this stuff is."

"Okay, honey," Mom says. "I'll make sure to mention it."

When I'm back in our room, I go directly to Mom's tote bag. And there it is—a rectangular package wrapped in brown paper and twine.

I unravel the twine and unfold the paper, careful not to tear it so we can use it again for something else.

It's a book. One I've never seen before. There's a picture of a girl on the cover, with a long brown braid down her back. There's a horse, too, and something flying in the sky. An airplane. I trace my finger over the words at the top. *Finding where you belong is always worth the fight.*

I read part of the back cover, and immediately I can tell it isn't the kind of book Dr. Ben would allow in our library. The Ranch doesn't have books like this, or the kind I remember from when I went to school, with their bright colors and pages full of illustrations and cartoon-like pictures. Not that those books are *banned* at the Ranch—he'd never put down a rule like that. It's more that the Ranch's library is practical, filled with books about permaculture, carpentry, animal husbandry, and some about making your own essential oils, natural cleaning supplies, and body products, and other stuff like that. There are also books written by Dr. Ben himself, which were hand-bound at the Ranch. My favorite is the one he wrote about the six months he spent traveling in the Amazon by riverboat.

Dr. Ben says most books have mainstream society's misguided ideas about how a life should be lived written right into the fabric of their stories. Even if the stories are fiction. Even if they're about wizards and witches or other magical stuff. And because of that, he says it's better to avoid them altogether. Otherwise, you risk forgetting the true danger we're all *really* in. Which is why we don't have these kinds of books back home.

I don't want to get any of society's misguided ideas in my head. I want to stay focused. So instead of reading it, I grab a pen and open to the book's blank inside back cover.

Dr. Ben probably had my rite planned for the spring. Near the spring equinox, to be exact. I know it isn't a perfect plan, but I feel like if I can figure out a way to get us back before then . . . maybe I could save this. Maybe I could still save *us*.

Spring Equinox, I write at the top. *March 20th.*

Today is January 7. I draw three boxes, and divide those into smaller boxes, until I have a makeshift three-month calendar. I number the days and count them up. Seventy-two. I have exactly seventy-two days until the spring equinox. Seventy-two days to get us back home.

Again, I know this isn't the most ideal plan ever. It might fail spectacularly. And yet something deep in my gut tells me if I can figure out a way to get us home by then, to be back in time for what Dr. Ben had planned for me, everything will be okay.

After slipping the book beneath the mattress, I lie down on the bed and try to remember everything I can about sending letters. I know where it's going, obviously. There can't be too many sustainable futurist communities in New York State called the Ranch, so I feel like that part should be easy.

But the actual sending . . . I'm not sure. Sometimes I help package things to be sent by mail—homemade mint tooth scrub in little glass jars, knit hats, and things like that. But an adult takes them away to get shipped. I don't know where or how.

I close my eyes. Alex at the front desk would probably know. Or even Dina. Or maybe I should stop a stranger on the street, so the fact that I'm asking how to send a letter won't get back to Mom. The idea of talking to a random stranger makes me nervous, but it does seem like the safest option.

Anyway, it's way easier to focus on the how instead of thinking about what I'll actually write in the letter to Dr. Ben.

Because how can I possibly explain Mom's decision to leave when *I* don't understand it?

I must fall asleep at some point, because I wake to the sound of the door opening and Mom coming in. The light is a little different outside, too. It's darker and heavier.

"Sorry. I didn't mean to wake you," she says. "Feeling any better?"

I sit up on my elbows. "What time is it?"

"Almost four." Mom unties the white apron from around

her brown dress and tosses it on her bed, and then takes her hair out of its ponytail. "Are you hungry? I can make us something."

I shake my head.

"Then how about a walk? I'm done for the day, and we haven't really explored yet."

"Okay," I say, sitting all the way up. Despite everything, I *am* curious to see more of the place she was willing to give up the Ranch for.

The weather's grown moodier since I fell asleep. Even so, California winter is different from winter back home. The air is chilly and heavy with gray fog, but it's not so cold that I need to wear my hat.

We leave the car parked where it is and set off through the parking lot on foot. We pass a couple who keep turning to stare at the ocean as they unload black suitcases from the trunk of their car.

"Driftaway Beach isn't big," Mom explains. "You can walk the whole thing. It's only about ten blocks long."

"How do you know?" I ask. "Have you been here before?"

"A very long time ago."

"Oh. Have *I* been here before?"

"No. It was before you were born." Mom nods to the left. "Come on. I'm pretty sure the main streets are this way."

And she's right: Driftaway Beach is tiny. You can walk from one end to the other in about twenty minutes. There are so few trees here. All around us is pavement, ocean, and in both the near and far distance, a coastline of sandy-colored cliffs. It's nothing like the Ranch, where the untouched land and dense woods stretch for miles. To get to the farthest edge of the property is an hour's hike.

We walk by store after store. There's a restaurant called the Seafarer, advertising its "famous" crab sandwich. Little iron tables are crowded together outside, damp from the wet weather. There's a clothing shop that, according to its colorful sign, sells "knickknacks and accessories." A tiny grocery store has produce displayed outside, with faded notes marking the prices. As we pass, an older lady in a clear plastic raincoat picks through the display of wilted lettuce.

There's trash on the streets and sidewalks, too. Lots of it. Smushed paper cups in the gutter, long strands of clear plastic, bits of food wrappers. I flinch every time I see a piece. We barely made any garbage at the Ranch. We composted most of our waste and used it as fertilizer.

As we walk, one shop in particular catches my eye because it's so . . . pink. The building itself is painted bright pink, and it has a pink sign in the shape of a teapot that says BIRDIE'S TEA SHOPPE on it in white cursive. A few women are leaving the shop, laughing and chatting with one another.

I start moving closer to the windows so I can see in. I'm curious if the inside is as pink as the outside. But Mom grabs my arm to stop me.

"Let's keep walking." Her eyes dart between me and the tea shop. "I don't want to stop here."

I pull my arm away from her. "Why not?"

Mom's eyes don't leave the shop's wide front windows.

"Because I want to show you something. There's a pretty path back to the motel that goes all along the ocean."

"Okay," I say, relenting. Because walking right next to the water does sound nice. So far, listening to the pounding of the waves has been the only thing that's helped my brain stop spinning.

The walking path Mom takes me to is a couple streets away from the pink tea shop. It's pebbly and gravelly under our feet, a mix of beach and pavement. Like the motel's parking lot, there's a low wooden fence lining the far side of the road—I guess to keep people and cars from falling into the water, which is fifteen or so feet below us. The water comes directly up to the land. That's how close the town of Driftaway Beach sits next to the ocean.

I wonder if this feels at all like Florida. I wonder what Meadowlark would think of it. My heart gives a squeeze.

Walking to the left would lead us straight back to the motel. Not too far to the right, the street ends at the base of a huge cliff. It's so tall that when I crane my head all the way back, I can't see to the top of it. And it just *rises* straight up—there are no paths up or anything. There's only the sheer rock wall of the cliff.

Mom wanders over to a metal stand with words engraved on its top. All around the base of the stand are flowers and candles. I follow her.

"Gosh. I'd forgotten about this," Mom says, her eyes scanning the words on the plaque. "The Spirit of the Sea. It's a big deal around here."

"What is it?"

"A local myth. Or mystery, I should say." She clears her throat. " 'This bluff is the haunting ground of the Spirit of the Sea,' " she reads. " 'If you're—' "

"What's a haunting ground?" I ask.

Mom thinks for a moment. "It's where ghosts live. Spirits. If you believe in that sort of thing."

I'm not sure if I do believe in them—or what Dr. Ben would say about them—but this seems like the kind of place that might have one. With its misty fog and low-hanging clouds and cold ocean spray that clings to your clothes and hair in tiny droplets.

"Keep going," I say, pointing at the plaque.

Mom clears her throat. " 'If you're lucky, you might see her in her white dress, with a flickering lantern held aloft, on the very top of the bluff. Some say it's the ghost of Amelia Lester, the lighthouse keeper, who died in the fire that burned down the lighthouse in 1903. Locals say she was so devoted to her job that she continued it in the afterlife. The story goes that her spirit moved to higher ground to better cast her light, which is said to beckon the souls of drowned sailors back to land, so they can finally make their way home, and find peace.' "

She reads more of the plaque silently. "It says that locals claim she appears on particularly dark, foggy nights on top of the bluff, which is inaccessible by foot. If I'm remembering correctly, lots of people have tried to prove that someone is faking it, but no one's ever been able to figure out how they'd get up there. We should keep our eyes peeled for her."

"Huh," I say, because I wasn't really listening to that last part. Something else has grabbed my attention.

I'm staring at a little building across the street. It has two blue mailboxes out front. The building's sign reads UNITED STATES POST OFFICE: DRIFTAWAY BEACH, CALIFORNIA.

Of course.

The blue mailboxes! The memory comes back fast: Mom dragging me to the post office when we lived in Brooklyn. I remember because sometimes there were dogs on the sidewalk I always wanted to pet, but Mom never let me. But the most important part of the memory: we went there to send packages . . . and *letters.*

That's it, I think. That's where I have to go.

7

<<<<<

Our lives pretty much follow the same pattern over the next week.

Mom and I get up before sunrise so we can eat breakfast together, because her shift starts so early. At first, I wasn't sleeping well, partly because Mom talks in her sleep. It woke me up the first night or two, and I thought she was trying to tell me something. But then she mumbled about dandelions and rolled over. It's strange; I'd totally forgotten she did that. Only on the second night did I remember she used to talk in her sleep all the time when I was little, too.

After breakfast, I help her clean the motel rooms, even though she keeps telling me I don't have to. I make the beds while she does the bathrooms, because I can't bear to touch the cleaning chemicals. If Mom's talked to Alex or Dina about making our own safer supplies, I haven't heard about it.

We don't talk a lot while we work. Mostly I let my mind go blank and focus on the task. That or I think about what I'm going to say in my letter to Dr. Ben.

We go back to our room for lunch. On our second full day here, we ran out of food from the Ranch entirely, so we started walking to the little grocery store every day after Mom's shift. Our mini-fridge isn't big enough to hold a lot of produce, so we get only what we need for the next day or two. It's strange to see how much out-of-season produce they have there, like underripe cantaloupes and sickly-looking pale red tomatoes. It doesn't seem right to be able to eat fresh tomatoes in January. We don't buy any of that stuff, though. We stick mainly to the basics, things we'd be eating at home right now, like oats, winter greens, squash, and eggs.

After lunch, Mom encourages me to hang out in our room. To rest, watch TV (absolutely not), read my new book, do whatever I want. But I always choose to go with her.

"I don't want you working all day," Mom says. "This is my job, not yours."

More than that, I can tell she feels weird about the way the guests look at us—at me—when Mom knocks and says "Housekeeping!" in an upbeat voice and they're in their room. They tend to give me a funny look, like, *Why is there a kid here?* I'm always relieved when she knocks and the room is empty, and I can tell she is, too.

But then on our fifth day, she *makes* me stay in the room after lunch.

"Can I at least go for a walk by myself?" I ask. "I could get us groceries."

From the walks we've taken together, I've already memorized the route through town to the post office, so I could get there with my eyes closed. Take Gusty Way two blocks from the motel parking lot, left on Main Street. Right on Moonraker. Then one more left to get to Ocean Road, and the post office is right there. I memorized the street names and even made a map in the back of my book, right next to the calendar.

"No. Not yet. Just—stay in the room, okay?"

"But—"

She puts her hands up. "My answer for today is no. But I'll think about it."

Her answer for the next few days is no, too. At least she picks me up some yarn and knitting needles, which I requested the first day she made me stay back. I don't like knitting—it makes my mind feel itchy—but it's good, important work. It connects me to what I would be doing at home. I'm working on the same style of sweater that I was making when we left. I'm trying to re-create it as closely as I can, but I'm messing up more than usual. I'm distracted, so I take lots of breaks to open the curtains and look out the window. Yesterday a big crew of men on motorcycles arrived in the parking lot and parked their bikes by the water. They all wore black leather jackets. They spent a few hours laughing and talking before roaring off on their bikes, like a swarm of loud mosquitoes. Lots of guests come and go. Most people seem to stay here for only one night, maybe two.

I like to watch the seagulls wheel and cry. There are some other types of birds I've noticed, but I don't know their names. I listen to the pounding of the waves and try to imagine what kinds of sea animals might be out there, lurking under the surface.

But mostly I feel . . . empty. Back home, every day is filled with such purpose. And sure, on some bitter cold mornings, especially in the late winter, when there was freezing rain instead of snow, I would dream about climbing into my bed and spending hours there. But now that I *can* spend as much time as I want lying in bed, it seems . . . pointless.

On our tenth day in Driftaway Beach, a day after I finish the sweater and have moved on to a new one, Mom surprises me with something.

"Here," she says over breakfast, handing me a small object. "I got myself one, too."

I don't realize what it is until I flip it open and see the buttons on the inside. "A phone?" I snap it closed and immediately toss it on the bed. "I don't want it."

"I got you an old kind," Mom explains. "It doesn't have the internet or anything like that."

"I don't care. I still don't want it."

Mom takes a sip of her coffee. The adults don't drink coffee at the Ranch, only tea. Mom started drinking coffee again on the drive here. I don't like how fast she switched *or* its bitter smell. "You know, Dr. Ben has one."

"A phone? Yeah, sure." I don't believe her. No way. Dr. Ben

has a lot to say about technology, and most of all, phones. He says they disconnect us from the world around us, from other people. *Hyper-connection means lack of connection* is what he likes to say. And at their worst, they emit radiation that can make us sick. "They're too unhealthy."

"That's not why he didn't want us using them."

"What's that supposed to mean?" I ask.

"It was more about . . . control. A couple other people had them, too. How do you think I got in contact with Paul?"

It makes no sense. In all the years we lived there, I never once saw Dr. Ben touch a piece of technology. I never once saw *anyone* touch a piece of technology. There's just no way she's telling me the truth about this. If multiple people had phones, I would have noticed. Right? Part of me wishes it might be true, because calling Dr. Ben would probably be easier than sending him a letter. But I know she's lying. "You're only saying that to make me use it."

"No. I want you to use it so you can go out on your own in a way that feels safe to me."

Now *that* catches my attention. "Wait—what?"

"If you take it with you," Mom says, "you can walk around Driftaway Beach while I'm working, so you don't have to stay cooped up in here. I've programmed my own number in there for you." She reaches over and grabs my phone, opens it, and taps a few buttons. "See? I'm okay with you going out as long as you send me a text every fifteen minutes or so."

Honestly? It's worth every bit of radiation if it means I can go out alone. It's the only way I'll get to the post office without her knowing. "I can? Will you show me how to use it?"

She laughs. "Of course."

She shows me how to send a text message. It makes a little sound as I send a text that says "hi mom." Across the room, her phone pings.

"I also want you to memorize my number," she says. "In case you ever lose your phone, or the battery dies, I want you to always be able to get in touch with me."

I wiggle my phone at her. "The battery is full."

"Right now it is, sure," she says. "But that might not always be the case." She writes her number on a piece of paper and presents it to me for a few seconds. Then she puts it behind her back. "Okay, so what's my number?"

We do this a couple more times until I can repeat the whole thing easily, without having to pause to try to remember it.

And just like that, I'm free.

"I want you to text me every fifteen minutes," she reminds me as she gets dressed in her brown housekeeper's uniform. "This should go without saying, but don't go anywhere near the highway. Okay?"

"Okay, yes, got it." I hesitate. "I think I'm actually going to rest this morning, and then maybe go for a walk after lunch. Is that okay?"

"More than okay, honey." She turns around. "Will you zip me up?"

Finally—*finally!*—she leaves. The door clicks shut behind her.

Instead of resting, I spend the morning working on my letter, on Lighthouse Motel stationery I found tucked in the drawer of the nightstand.

I've been thinking about it for days. Trying to put actual words onto paper is something else entirely.

But finally, after about ten drafts, I think I finally have it. I sit back and reread it, to make sure.

Dear Dr. Ben,

Hi. It's Fern. Let me start by saying that I'm so, so, SO sorry. I hope you aren't too worried about us, though I bet you are. Mom's confused about what's best for us, and I think she needs your help. Well, we need your help.

Can you please come get us and bring us home? We're staying at a place called the Lighthouse Motel in Driftaway Beach, California. We're in room number 15.

Please don't be disappointed in us. I know we're off the path. But I'm sure if you talk to Mom, you can get through to her. And if you're willing, please tell Meadowlark I miss her, but that I'm okay.

I really want to come home, and I know deep down, my mom does too. Again, I'm so sorry. I'm still ready for my rite of passage. I'm not scared. I want to be the person you say I am. We will do whatever it takes to make this up to you.

Yours, with gratitude,

Fern

To be safe, I shred the drafts and flush them down the toilet. I tuck the final letter in the back of the book and slip it under the mattress. I'll go for my walk and send it during Mom's afternoon shift.

I'm not sure how long it will take for a letter to travel across the country, but it can't be that long. If I can figure out how to do this, we could be back *way* before March. We could be back next week!

Lunch drags on and on. Mom uses the hot plate to reheat soup in a used metal pot Alex lent us. "You seem happy. Did you have a good morning?"

"Fine. Yeah. Good."

"Have you started reading the book I got you?"

"A little," I lie, and Mom smiles.

"Want to read some now, together?" she asks. "Where is it?"

"No!" I almost shout. I force myself to calm down, to be casual. "No. I want to read by myself."

"Okay. That's fine. I just thought it would be nice to read together." Mom stirs her soup with a spoon. I can tell she's a little hurt by the way she dips her head.

Good, I think. Because I'm hurting, too.

After what feels like a lifetime of minutes dragging by, she gets up to go finish cleaning the rest of the rooms. Before she leaves, she stops at the door and points at me. "What's my phone number?"

I repeat it easily.

"Good," she says. "Have a nice walk, hon. I love you."

As soon as she's gone, I jump up, take out my letter, and slip it carefully into the pocket of my work pants.

Next I have to find something of value to bring with me. For the hundredth time, I wish I'd known what Mom's plans had been so I could have grabbed more stuff. Or refused to go with her altogether.

But all I have is the sweater I just finished, and my hat. I lay them out on the bed and study them critically. You can *see* that my mind wasn't totally there when I made the sweater. One of the arms is slightly longer, and the neck hole is a little looser than I wanted. Whereas my hat . . . It's made of soft white wool, with a ribbed pattern, and a big yarn pom-pom at the top. I made it last winter, and I loved it so much I asked if I could keep it for myself instead of adding it to the farmers-market inventory.

I press the soft pom-pom against my cheek.

It's worth it, I remind myself.

I almost leave the room without it, but then I remember: the cell phone. I quickly text Mom that I'm going for a walk before turning it off and shoving it to the bottom of my pocket. I'll turn it on to text her again when I get to the post office, but for now I want to keep it as far away from my brain as possible.

On my way out of the room, I bump into Alex. Today he's wearing a black-and-red shirt beneath a blue button-down.

"Hey, Fern," he says. "Haven't seen you much. How are you and your mom settling in?"

"Fine." I shift anxiously. I want to get going.

"Your mom's doing a killer job, by the way. Rooms

haven't gotten cleaned this deeply in years." He grins. "Don't tell Dina."

"I won't." And I hadn't noticed until now, but he's holding that same thick paperback book I saw him with the first day we got here. The one with the scaly creature on its front. I point at it, curiosity getting the better of me. "What is that?"

He lifts the book. "This? Oh, man. It's called *Firestride*, and it's the best fantasy novel published this century. It's about this incredible community of—"

"No. Sorry. *That*." I point again at the cover. "What kind of animal is that?"

"Oh." He seems a little embarrassed. "Sorry. It's a dragon."

Dragon. It's like the word opens an old dusty door in my brain. I remember dragons; they're made-up creatures that breathe fire. There was a book Mom used to read to me when I was little—one about dragons who love to eat tacos, but only if they're not spicy. I haven't thought about that book in a long time.

"Thank you," I say quietly, before we say our goodbyes and I head off.

There's a line at the post office. I take my spot at the end. In front of me, there's a woman with a cat poking its head out from inside her coat. The cat has big, almost snakelike eyes, and it's staring right at me.

"You wanna pet him?" the woman asks when she notices me staring. I shake my head and look away.

After a short wait, it's my turn. A woman with her hair slicked back into a tight bun calls out, "Next!"

I step up to the counter on my tiptoes. I slide my letter across the counter. "Hello. I'd like to send this letter, please."

She picks it up. "Okay. You'll need to buy an envelope and postage. And I'll need the address, too."

"I was hoping you could help me with that," I say. "I need to send it to a man called Dr. Ben. He runs a sustainable futurist community in New York State called the Ranch."

"A what now?" the woman says.

I repeat myself, enunciating each word as clearly as possible. Because I don't know the Ranch's exact address. I only know it's in the northern part of the state, where the trees are tall and green in the summer and the snow falls heavily in the winter. I don't know much about the way the internet works, but having the name must be enough for her to pull up the address in their system. Right?

But the woman only stares at me. "Do you even have any money? How old are you?"

"I'm twelve. And I don't have any money, but I have this." I take my beautiful white hat out of my pocket and slide that across the counter, too. "I was hoping we could trade."

The woman's stare has turned from confusion to disbelief. "Honey, this is the United States Postal Service. We don't *barter*."

The way she's staring reminds me of the way Alex looked at me when I asked what a lighthouse was. Like neither of them believed I could possibly be serious.

71

"But—"

"No. I'm sorry, but I don't make the rules."

I glance behind me; at least three people in line are staring at me now, too. My face prickles as I turn back to the woman. "Please help me," I whisper. "I've never done this before. And it's really important I send this letter."

Her face softens a little. "You need a specific address, with a street number and a zip code, to send a letter. And money for an envelope and a stamp. Real money, not a hat." She pushes it back toward me, along with my letter.

My cheeks burn as I pick them up off the counter. I'm not sure I've ever felt this stupid in my entire life. "Is there an easy way to find that?"

"Money?" She raises an eyebrow. "You think if I knew that, I'd be working six days a week?"

"No. Sorry." My face burns worse. "I meant the address."

She lets out a heavy sigh, like she's tired of talking to me. "I don't know, hon. Ask an adult. Look it up on the internet. Hire a private investigator, for all I know. I don't care how you get it, but you can't send a letter without a specific address. That's step one. Okay?" She doesn't give me time to respond before she loudly calls, "Next!"

And with that, I know my time for asking questions has ended.

Outside, it's started to rain. Not a thick, heavy rain—more like a mist. The little droplets cling to my wool sweater.

I slip my letter to Dr. Ben back into my pocket, where it won't get wet.

There are lots of things I know. For example, I know you can't plant garlic and beans close together, because they need the same nutrients from the soil.

I know how to knit complex cable patterns.

I know how to coo and cluck at a laying hen so she won't peck at your hands when you go to take her still-warm eggs away.

But there are obviously so many things I *don't* know. There are so many things I don't know that I don't know that I don't know them. Like, what a zip code or a hot plate is. Or how the post office works.

I want to smack myself on the forehead with the palm of my hand, which is something I used to do when I got frustrated as a little girl. But instead, I force myself to take three deep, centering breaths.

As I breathe, a favorite saying of Dr. Ben's echoes in my mind: *You only fail if you stop trying.*

So I might not know some things, but I won't stop trying. I'll figure out how to find the address myself, no matter what I have to do.

The post office woman said I could try to look for the address on the internet. There's a computer in the motel lobby, on the desk where Alex sits. That's got to have the internet, right? Maybe there's a way to use it without him noticing.

As I stand there, trying to figure out how and when I'll do that exactly, two girls around my age walk by. One has a green backpack; the other's is blue. They're dressed like it's below zero and blizzarding out here, with hats and mittens and thick puffy coats, even though it's only raining. They're walking arm in arm, and their heads are close together. One of them shrieks with laughter—the blond one. A strand escapes from beneath her hat. It's wispy and pale and looks so, so familiar.

My chest constricts as a wave of homesickness overwhelms me. *Meadowlark,* I think.

I can't bear to go back to our damp little motel room alone.

So I follow them.

8

The two girls are so focused on talking and laughing with each other that they barely notice the rain or that I'm following them. They don't turn around, not once.

Soon we're at the pink building, the one with the teapot sign I noticed when I was out walking with Mom the other day. A bell tinkles as they go inside.

For a minute I stand there on the sidewalk, unsure of what to do. But the rain makes my decision for me—it's coming down harder now, more rain than mist, and I'm getting uncomfortably wet. I don't want it to seep into my pants, into my pocket, and ruin my letter to Dr. Ben. So I hurry toward the pink building and stand beneath the little fabric cover extending from above the door and windows.

The shop—Birdie's Tea Shoppe—even has a pink glass doorknob on its pink door. Now that I'm here and Mom's not, I press my hands and face against the glass so I can finally get a better look inside.

At the center of the shop is the tallest woman I've ever

seen, talking to the two girls I followed here. She's heavyset, with weather-beaten white skin and enormous boobs. Her gray hair is cut short, almost in the same style Dr. Ben wears his. I watch as she motions for the two girls to go sit at a round table tucked into the far corner.

After getting them settled, she turns around, so she's facing the windows—and me. And then our eyes meet.

I turn away, embarrassed to have been caught staring. I should get going anyway.

But before I can talk myself into heading back into the rain, the bell tinkles again.

It's her—the tall woman. She smiles, and like the rest of her, it's big. The smile takes up her whole face. I see it in the corners of her eyes, in the wrinkles on her cheeks. "You wanna come inside, sweetheart?"

I stand there, frozen, not sure what to do or say.

Her smile widens, if that's even possible. "I don't bite. You're staring through the window like a hungry stray. Come on in, and I'll get you all set up."

"But I . . . I don't have any money."

She wipes her hands on her delicate lace apron. It's as dainty as the tablecloths inside, and it doesn't quite match up with the rest of her. "It'll be on me. Come in out of the rain."

"Okay," I find myself saying. "Thank you."

Only when the warmth of the store envelops me do I realize how cold it is outside. My fingers and nose sting.

"This way, sweets." She leads me to a table next to the

two girls I followed. They both go quiet and watch me as I sit down, but then go back to their conversation.

"Do you like tea?" the woman asks. "I can get you our signature tea, so you don't have to bother with a menu. It's chestnut-chocolate. Great with some cream and sugar. Even better with a hot cross bun on the side. How's that sound?"

We don't eat sugar on the Ranch. Ever. According to Dr. Ben, you might as well eat poison. We only use honey from our hives. But I don't want to ask for honey when she's already giving me tea for free, so I nod. I don't need to add any sugar. And I'm pretty sure Dr. Ben would say a sip or two of chestnut-chocolate tea would be okay. We mostly drink chamomile tea at the Ranch, because we grow and dry the flowers ourselves. I don't know about the hot cross bun, though. I don't know what that is.

"Okay," I say again. "Thank you."

She claps her hands together with a loud *smack*. "Good, great! Then we'll start with that. And a name. I like to know everyone's name who comes into my shop. Unless . . ." She tilts her head at me like she's trying to figure something out. "Have you been in here before?"

"No, I'm just . . ." I search for the right word. "Visiting. I don't live here. And my name's Fern."

"Well, then, Fern, welcome to Driftaway Beach. And to Birdie's Tea Shoppe. I'm Babs, and I'm happy to have you here."

She winks at me before moving off to talk to someone at another table. With her gone, everything feels quieter. She's the kind of person whose absence you feel immediately. Kind of like Dr. Ben, but in a different way.

My fingers find the edge of the letter in my pocket. Thankfully, it's still completely dry. I think again about my plan. Mom used to have a computer I'd watch TV on, back before we knew how bad it is for you. I shut my eyes, trying to remember everything. The computer had a screen, buttons with letters on them, and the finger pad that let me move the arrow thing. *What else?* An image comes back to me. The bright red YouTube play button. YouTube was on the internet. If I can find my way to YouTube on the motel's computer, then that means I'm on the internet. And I can go from there.

The motel's office doesn't open until seven a.m.—it says so on the sign out front. If I can get in early, before anyone's there, maybe I can learn enough about how the internet works to figure out what I need.

Then it hits me. Mom's housekeeping key. It opens all the motel room doors, and I saw Dina use hers on the office door. That means Mom's key should work, too, right? My feet don't quite touch the floor, so I start swinging them back and forth in excitement. Every morning, Mom showers after breakfast, spending about twenty minutes in the bathroom. With her key, I bet I can get in and out of the office and onto the internet without anyone noticing. This might actually work.

This new idea, plus the warmth of the tea shop, is enough to lift my spirits. I sit back in my chair to get a better look around. It smells good in here—like baking bread and the sweet, earthy tang of tea. The walls are lined with shelves and shelves of teapots that are all different shapes and sizes. One in particular catches my eye—it's round and white and is decorated in a pattern of little red fishes. Like the one stitched on the inside of Meadowlark's work pants.

She would love that teapot. She loves tea, period. One time, we harvested a bunch of mugwort, a weed that grows around the edges of the garden plots, and dried it so we could make it into tea. Meadowlark said the tea would give us dreams that told our future. The tea tasted awful, like pond sludge, and I didn't dream anything at all. But when I woke up, Meadowlark told me she'd dreamt we were old, with gray hair and wrinkles, which meant we'd survived everything that was going to happen to the earth.

"And better yet, we were still best friends," she'd said, threading her arm through mine.

I'm still thinking about her when the front door to the shop bangs open. It's so loud and sudden that the shop quiets down and everyone turns to see who it is.

It's Mom.

My phone, I realize with a rush of dread. It's still off and deep in my pocket. I completely forgot to text her.

She's in her housekeeping uniform, and it's soaked from the rain. Her eyes have a wild look to them, and when they land on me, they go even wilder.

"Frankie!"

She rushes over to my table and grabs me by the shoulders. "I texted and called. I looked everywhere. You were supposed to text me every fifteen minutes! Never do that to me again! What were you thinking? I thought someone had taken you!"

"You're hurting me," I say, trying to pull away. Mom's acting so frantic and angry I can't help but start to cry.

She immediately lets go. "I'm sorry. I'm sorry." She kneels down and tucks my hair behind my ears. "But don't do that again. Please don't disappear on me ever again."

It's completely silent in the tea shop by now, and everyone is looking at us. I wish I could sink into the floor and disappear.

"What's going on? Is everything okay?"

It's Babs, rounding the corner, holding a tray with a teapot and a single cup, plus a little round roll on a matching plate. That must be for me. She looks concerned, but when she sees Mom, her face changes.

Almost like she's seen a ghost.

The tray of tea in her hands rattles and then falls, and when the teapot hits the ground, it splits in half. Hot tea sprays everywhere, and a few stinging drops land on my ankles. One or two of the guests gasp, and the girls I followed here are staring at us with wide eyes. A man in a white apron hurries over to help Babs clean up the mess.

But Babs doesn't move.

She just stands there, staring at Mom. Finally, she says, "Jamie? Is that really you?"

Mom smiles, but in a way that only makes her look more exhausted. "Hi, Babs. It's been a while."

Mom and Babs go outside for a couple of minutes to talk in private. The shop slowly returns to normal and the mess gets cleaned up, but I can still feel people glancing over their shoulders to look at me.

When Mom and Babs finally come back inside, Mom motions to me. "Come on, hon. We're going."

I glance at Babs. She's looking at me in an entirely different way now, with a new kind of warmth in her eyes. She looks back to Mom. "I'll be over tonight, after I close down. So we can talk some more."

Mom nods tightly. "I know. You said."

"Bye," I say helplessly to Babs as Mom drags me out of the tea shop.

"You *know* each other?" I ask on our walk back. Most of my anger and embarrassment from earlier have ebbed away and made room instead for curiosity. The rain has stopped for now, but the air is thick with moisture and salt, as though the rain stirred up the ocean. "From where? When? Who is she? Did *I* know her?"

I feel guilty for even asking, because I know I should be focused on the future, not the past. But I can't help myself.

"No. I know Babs from a long time ago. From before you were born."

I wait, hoping she'll go on, and she does.

"Babs was my mother's best friend from when they grew

up together in Sacramento. She and her wife, Birdie, were my godparents." Mom pauses for a moment. "Well, *are* my godparents. At least Babs still is. Birdie passed away a while ago."

"Oh," I say. I try to take in all this new information. "What's a godparent?"

"I guess, technically, a godparent is supposed to be a religious thing," Mom explains. "But for us it always felt like it was a way of declaring that Babs and Birdie were like family, even though we weren't related by blood."

Like everyone at the Ranch. I don't say it, though. "When was the last time you saw her? Babs, I mean."

"My dad's funeral. So . . ." Mom thinks. "About eighteen years ago now."

"Wow," I say.

Because what else *can* I say? I've never heard the names Babs or Birdie until now. For the most part, I don't know that much about Mom's life before me. Honestly, sometimes I don't feel like I know that much about Mom, period. I was only six when we got to the Ranch. Plus, no one at the Ranch talks about their pasts. Dr. Ben says it can distract us from the future we're building together, that it doesn't matter. Still, little pieces would come out in conversation, sometimes by accident. But it's weird to think Mom had this whole . . . *existence* before me. I mean, I know a couple of things. I know her parents—my grandparents—died when she was a teenager. Her mom from a disease called ovarian cancer, when Mom was sixteen, and her dad in a car accident two years later. Not even because she told me directly. I overheard her telling one of the other adults.

I don't know what happened to her after that. Which always made me think of young Mom as alone in the world. Like a lone boat, bobbing on a wide, dark sea. At least until I showed up, completely by accident, all because she spent one night with a man whose name she didn't even know.

Despite everything, despite how mad I am at her for taking us away from the Ranch, I slip my hand into hers, and keep it there for the rest of the walk back to our motel room.

Mom goes back to cleaning right away. Apparently, she left her cart in the middle of the walkway when I wasn't picking up my phone, so she's in a rush to make sure everything's still there.

I go to the motel office as soon as she's gone.

Alex is talking to a woman with bright red hair when I push open the office's glass door. I wave when he notices me, then walk over to look at the stand of colorful brochures.

They talk for a few minutes before Alex says, "Let me know if you need help getting anything else set up beyond the ghost tour." The woman thanks him and then heads out of the office. "Take as many as you want," Alex says to me, nodding at the brochure stand. "We get those for free."

"Thanks." I take one of the brochures without even

glancing at it, because that's not what I came in here for. I angle my body so I can see the computer a little better.

It isn't anything like the one I remember, the one Mom used to have. This one is big and clunky, with a screen that's more like a box instead of thin and flat. Still, for the next few minutes, I try to take in every little detail.

"Is there something else you need?" Alex asks me.

"Sorry." I didn't realize it was so obvious I was staring. "I was just looking at your computer."

Alex laughs. "This old thing? Yeah. It's basically an antique at this point."

I walk over, using this as an opportunity to get a closer look. "It's a lot different from the one my mom and I used to have. We had one you closed like a book."

"Oh, a laptop. Yeah. Well, we need something to handle all the software for our reservation system. It's easier with a desktop."

"What's that for?" I point at the thing he's holding in his hand. It's connected to the computer by a thin wire.

"This? This is the mouse." He explains how moving it around and clicking on it controls the little arrow on the screen, doing the same thing the flat pad of our old laptop did. If my lack of familiarity with computers is strange to him, he doesn't show it.

I don't want to be too obvious. So after one or two more questions, I force myself to leave the office, a couple brochures tucked into my pocket.

Tomorrow morning. I'll use Mom's key and sneak in to try to use the internet tomorrow morning.

Later, around eight o'clock, there's a knock on our door. "It's me! Babs!"

Mom peeks through a slender gap in our curtains—to be sure it's her, I guess. Then she undoes the main lock, plus the extra chain she keeps on the door whenever we're in here together. It makes me feel like I'm trapped. There aren't any locks at the Ranch. At least not in any of the rooms I've used.

As soon as Babs walks in, it's like the whole mood of the room changes. Brightens, as though the lamps are glowing a little stronger. She shakes her head in a friendly way when she sees me. "I still can't believe you have a daughter, Jamie. Wow. That's why I thought I'd seen you before," she says to me. "You look so much like your mom did when she was your age. You have the same nose, the same eyes. I'm so glad to meet you."

I give her a shy wave.

She turns to Mom. "I'm so glad *both* of you are here. I can't believe how long it's been."

"A long time," Mom agrees.

Babs pulls a glass bottle with amber-colored liquid from one of her coat's deep pockets, wiggling it at Mom. "I figured we could use something stronger than tea."

"Let's talk outside. I'll grab my coat." She turns to me. "Frankie. Bath or shower for you, please."

"Fern," I grumble, but she pretends not to hear me.

When the door shuts behind them, I race to the bathroom and turn the water on. Before it's even warm, I get in and take the fastest bath of my life. The goat's milk soap we brought from the Ranch is down to a sliver now, so I scrub carefully to use as little as possible. Then, once I've toweled off and put my nightshirt on, I creep over to press my ear against the door.

". . . and Fern? Or Frankie? Which is it?" Babs is saying. "Why haven't you enrolled her yet?"

Enrolled me in what? If only I'd been faster, I'd know what they were talking about.

Mom sighs. "Because I'm worried. She got some basic lessons back at the Ranch, but she's got huge gaps in knowledge. What if she sticks out? What if she sticks out so much they want to take her away from me?"

I stiffen. What she said in the tea shop comes back to me: she was afraid someone had *taken* me. And now here she is, saying it again.

I wait for an explanation, or for Babs to tell her no one's going to take me away. But she doesn't say that. Instead, she says, "You could come stay with me. I have a guest room. I use it as an office, so it would be a tight squeeze, but we could handle this together."

"No," Mom says immediately. "Thank you, but no. I need to do this myself. I need to know I can do this myself."

86

"Do you have a plan?" Babs asks.

"First, I need Frankie to reacclimate. And I need to get back on my feet." She sighs. "I've got nothing, Babs. It's not like we had much before, but I did have that account Mom left me. I was saving it. I thought once Frankie was old enough, I could use it to go back to school. . . . But that's gone now, too. Thanks to him."

"If you want to go back to school, I'm sure there's a way to make it happen. All I know is I'll do whatever I can to support you."

They're both quiet for a while, and then Mom says, "I'm sorry about Birdie. I should have said that to you a long time ago."

Babs says something back, but it's too low for me to hear.

"And I'm sorry I didn't warn you. That we were coming. Or about our . . . situation." Mom laughs, but it sounds more like she's crying. "God, I've really messed things up, haven't I?"

"Don't say that." There's a long pause, and then Babs adds, "I'm glad you're here. Both of you."

Eventually, they move on to other topics. They talk about people I don't know and places I've never been to.

And you know what? I don't care. I pull myself away from the door and crawl into bed. I don't care, because none of it matters. At the end of the day, it doesn't matter who Mom *was*. And unless Babs plans on coming back to the Ranch with us, it doesn't matter who she is, either.

Later that night I wake to the sound of Mom crying. At first, I think she's talking in her sleep again, but no—she's definitely crying.

I glance at the little digital alarm clock set on the nightstand between our beds; it's two in the morning. I don't know why she's crying, but part of me thinks . . . *good*. Because that means I'm not the only one who's been struggling.

I stare at the ceiling, trying to hold on to the anger. But another part of me aches for her. By the way her shoulders are silently shaking, I know she's trying to not wake me up. She's always been like this—private about her hurt feelings. Before I can stop myself, I get out of my bed and go over to hers. I slip under the covers and snuggle in close to her back. I used to sneak into her bed all the time when I was little, before the Ranch. It's been years since I've done this. Years since we've slept near enough to each other that I *can* do this. After a few seconds, she lets out a shaky breath and snuggles me back.

9

After we have a quick breakfast of boiled kasha the next morning, I feel like I'm sitting on nails waiting for Mom to go take her shower.

She washes our dishes in the little bathroom sink, and then finally asks, "Do you need to pee before I shower?"

"No." I kind of do, but the clock says it's six-thirty-three, which means I only have twenty-seven minutes until the office opens. I'll let myself have ten minutes. Ten minutes to look around, figure out how it works. I can do ten minutes every morning until I understand how to use the internet. It might take a few days, but that's okay. I just need today to go well. "You go ahead."

The bathroom door closes behind her with a click. Soon I hear the hiss of the shower and the sound of Mom singing loudly to herself, which is something she's started doing again the past couple of days. Another little quirk of hers I'd forgotten about. She's a terrible singer, but I admire how she puts her whole heart into it. I jump to my feet and go directly to the pockets of her housekeeping apron, which she keeps folded next to the TV. I let out a breath of relief when my fingers brush the key.

The parking lot is quiet, and the edges of the dark sky are just starting to soak up the new light of day. I'm only wearing socks, so my feet don't make any noise against the concrete as I hurry to the office.

Through the glass door I can see the office is dark and empty. There's a handwritten sign that says IF OFFICE IS CLOSED, RING FOR SERVICE ☺ with an arrow pointing to a little button. I insert the key into the lock, praying it will fit.

And it does—it slides right in, and as I twist, I hear the satisfying *clunk* of the lock turning. I ease the door open, and then shut it behind me.

I don't have much time, so I go straight around the back of the desk. There are papers all over the place, covering the letter board that's attached to the computer screen. I glance at them. They almost look like pages of a book, with hand-written notes in the margins. Lots of the printed sentences are slashed through with red. I read one that hasn't been crossed out. *She took her sword and thrust it into the loamy earth.* I'm curious, but I've got no time to waste, so I shove the stack of papers aside. The computer's screen is dark. I tap a button, but nothing happens. I wiggle the little controller thing—the *mouse*—but nothing happens then, either. There's got to be an easy way to turn this thing on.

As I search for a switch, I hear something. I freeze, trying to figure out what it is—when one of the office's interior doors swings open.

It's Alex. He's wearing a pair of jeans and an inside-out T-shirt, like he got dressed in a hurry. He stops short when he sees me.

"Oh, God, Fern, it's just you. The silent alarm went off, and I— What are you doing in here?"

My heart is beating so fast I'm worried I might faint or throw up or both. "I—"

He looks between me and the computer, like he suddenly understands. "If you wanted to use the computer, you could have just asked."

"No, that's not what I came in for," I lie. I can't tell him the truth. If he tells Mom I was trying to use the computer, she'll guess I was up to something. She'd know I would never touch it just for fun. "I . . . was looking for your book."

He goes deep red and glances at the marked-up pages on the desk. "How'd you know I was writing a book?"

"No—I meant the one with the dragon on the front. I'm sorry. I wanted to read it." I hold up Mom's housekeeping key. "And I thought you might have left it on your desk."

"Oh. Okay. Well, like I said. You could have, you know . . . asked."

"I know. I'm sorry. I'll go."

He puts a hand out. "Hold on. Wait right there, okay?"

Before I can say anything else, he disappears the way he came. He's back in less than two minutes, carrying the thick paperback with him.

"Here," he says, handing it to me.

I take it from him. Now that I've told this lie, I guess I have to read it. The cover is creased and worn, and the edges of the pages feel soft against my fingertips, like wilted flower petals. This book has been handled a lot. "Thank you."

"Can't wait to hear what you think. I'm pretty sure I read it for the first time when I was around your age."

My heart's still beating extremely fast. "I should probably—" I motion to the door. "I'm really sorry."

"Yeah. Next time, don't break into the office, okay? Come to me if you want to borrow anything."

"I promise I won't do it again. Are you . . . are you going to tell my mom?"

"Nah. I used to do ridiculous things for books, too. So I get it. Once I pretended I had food poisoning so I could stay up all night in the bathroom with the lights on. Only I wasn't sick. I wanted to finish the book I was reading. I made groaning sounds and flushed the toilet every fifteen minutes to keep up the ruse." He grins. "See you later?"

I nod and hug the book to my chest.

Once I'm back in our room and have returned the key to Mom's apron, I climb into my bed and cover my face with a pillow. I can't go back there, now that I know there's an alarm. But would it have mattered? I couldn't even figure out how to turn the stupid computer *on*.

So what am I going to do?

I don't have much time to think about it, because there's a knock on our door.

I pull the pillow off my face and sit up. Did Alex change his mind and decide to come tell Mom after all?

Mom's just getting out of the bathroom by then, and she hurries to the door.

"Wait—" I say, but she doesn't.

But it's not Alex—it's Babs. I sink back in relief.

When she comes inside, our little motel room fills with smells—yeast and butter, and the distinct scent of coffee. She hands Mom a paper cup. "Coffee for you." Then she grins and wiggles a paper bag at me. "And since you didn't get to try anything at the shop yesterday, I brought you a little something. Fresh croissant. Still warm from the oven."

"No, thank you," I say politely, even though the smell is making my mouth water. Tendrils of steam escape the paper bag, which has little dots of grease all over it. "We already ate."

"It's okay," Mom says. "As long as I've known her, Babs has only used the best ingredients."

"It's true," Babs agrees. "Organic ingredients and butter from pasture-raised cows." She winks. "Only the best for my customers."

"Does it have sugar?"

"Nope. Only flour and butter, babes. Any sugar was for the yeast, and they've done their work and eaten it all up."

"Well . . . okay," I say. She hands it to me. The bag is still warm. I pull out the croissant, which is something I've never had before. It looks kind of like a flaky roll, in the shape of a crescent moon.

And it's one of the best things I've ever tasted. "Wow," I say, with my mouth full. "*So* good."

Babs smiles. "I'm glad you like it. You're welcome to come into the shop and have a bite whenever you want. I've got more than croissants. Much more. All of it on me, of course."

"That's nice of you, Babs, but we can pay," Mom says. "I'll give her some money whenever she wants to come see you. You don't have to give us anything for free."

Babs presses her lips together, like she's trying to keep herself from saying something.

I finish the croissant in three giant bites and look up hopefully. "Do you have another one?"

Babs laughs. Despite the promise I made to myself to not care about Babs, I immediately like her laugh—it's booming and confident. She reaches into her huge red-and-green-plaid purse and pulls out another paper bag. "Sure do. I figured you'd need energy for your big day."

"Big day?" I look between Mom and Babs. "What's that mean?"

Only then do I realize Mom isn't in her brown uniform. She's wearing a white button-down shirt and a pair of blue jeans, and her long hair is down around her shoulders. "I have today off, remember? So I figured we'd go and enroll you. At the local school."

So *that's* what they were talking about last night. Enrolling me in school.

I remember school. Of course I do. I was in first grade when Mom and I moved to the Ranch. Thinking about school makes me think about Mallory, my friend who smelled like strawberries. Suddenly, I remember that I knew her because of school, not because of our apartment complex. Our teacher's name was Ms. Cardillo. It's strange; somehow being back in the outside world is jostling my memories. It's like all these little details are floating up from the bottom of a murky pond.

What I know: school is the sort of thing that's permanent. Deeply rooted. I think about how difficult it is to get dandelions out of the garden—their roots go so deep, sometimes you have to dig a foot down to get the whole thing out.

I don't want to be like a dandelion. I don't want us to grow any roots here at all. I want to be as easy to pull out as a single piece of chickweed.

I put the croissant back down on its paper bag, my appetite gone. "No. I don't want to go to school. Can't you do lessons with me? The way Ash taught us back home?"

"Me? You really want a high school dropout to be your teacher?" I can tell she means it as a joke, but it comes out all strange, like it's painful for her to say. "I don't think so."

"Well, I know I don't want to go to school."

"Fern," Mom says. "You promised me. You said you'd try."

I cross my arms. "Well, I don't want to try *this*."

10

An hour later, Mom pulls our ugly brown car into a parking spot with a VISITORS ONLY sign in front of it. The school is a long brick building in the middle of a sea of gray pavement.

"I know the principal," Babs says, turning around to face me from the front seat. "Adriana Diaz. She's an exceptional woman. Big fan of my cranberry-and-white-chocolate-chip scones." She reaches into her giant purse and takes out yet another crinkly brown paper bag. "A little bribe to help it go smoothly. But she'll be excited to meet you. Don't worry."

I'm not worried about whether she's excited to meet me. I'd rather she *not* be excited to meet me. I'd rather be told there's no place for me at all, so Mom can abandon this plan altogether.

We're almost to the main double doors of the school when Mom says, "Babs, can you sign us in? I need to have a quick word with Fern."

"Sure," Babs says. "See you in there."

When the doors close behind Babs, Mom turns to me. "Okay, honey, I need you to listen. When we talk with the principal, I might have to say a couple of things that aren't true."

"What does that mean?"

"Your education at the Ranch wasn't exactly . . . normal. We didn't keep records or do anything by the book, so to speak. Or at least the way the state government wanted things to be run. The laws in New York are strict about how a child should be educated at home. So if we told the truth, not only could I get in trouble, but every adult at the Ranch could, too."

This, at least, I can agree with her on. We did things our own way at the Ranch. It makes sense that Dr. Ben wouldn't want the government sniffing around. According to Dr. Ben, the government is even worse than mainstream society.

Plus, it must be a good sign that Mom still wants to protect the rest of the adults at the Ranch. A glimmer of hope; it means she hasn't totally lost her way.

"We could just *keep* doing things that way. Instead of"—I motion at the school—"all this."

"Sorry. But this is nonnegotiable."

I stare at her. She stares back at me.

"Fine," I say, relenting. "I won't say anything."

Mom sags in relief. "Thank you."

Once we're inside, Babs hands us our visitor passes. Then we're buzzed into the main hallway.

It is *filled* with kids.

Back at the Ranch, there are only ten fifteen-and-unders, including me. Here it feels like there are hundreds of kids. Running, slamming lockers, shouting, laughing. I'd forgotten how this felt—arriving at a new school. Being the new kid.

It's so loud I want to put my hands over my ears and close my eyes to tune it all out.

"The office is this way," Babs says.

She starts striding right into the crowd, and amazingly, the kids move aside for her. Some of them recognize her, and soon they're shouting hello and holding up their hands for her to slap.

"Hi, Babs!"

"It's Babs! What's up?"

"Are you here to do another baking demo?"

Babs says hello back, slaps some hands, and laughs. "No demo today, I'm afraid. Maybe next month."

Mom and I follow in her wake.

Thankfully, we leave the noisy hallway and go into a small waiting area that's quiet. There are a couple of chairs. And it has plants. Lots of green plants, everywhere. The green and the quiet refresh me.

Mom and I sink into two seats, side by side, as Babs goes to talk to the woman sitting behind the desk. When I glance at Mom, she looks rattled and pale. Maybe that means she won't make me follow through with this.

A few minutes later, the woman tells us to go in.

Mom and I follow Babs into a small office. There are more plants in here, and an older woman sits behind a desk stacked with books and loose papers. She's got tan skin, short black hair threaded with silver, and bright pink lipstick. Her shirt is dark green, almost the color of evergreen needles.

"Babs!" she exclaims, looking up from her computer. She takes her glasses off and smooths her hair as she stands. "I knew I had a new-student appointment, but not that you'd be involved. What a nice surprise."

"Well, you know me—always popping up in unexpected places." Babs lets out a strange, too-loud laugh, then takes the brown paper bag from her purse and holds it out. "Also figured you could probably use a little breakfast."

"You're so thoughtful," she says, taking it from Babs, whose face has gone very red. Then the woman's eyes go to me and Mom, and she smiles.

Mom takes that as her cue and rushes forward. "Hi! I'm Jamie. And this is my daughter—"

"Fern," I say.

Mom forces a smile. "Her name is Frankie, but her nickname is Fern."

"Well," the woman says. "It's great to meet you, Jamie, and . . . Fern, too. I'm Ms. Diaz, and I'm thrilled to hear you're interested in joining us at Driftaway Middle. Now, please sit!" She motions at the chairs in front of her desk.

"So," Ms. Diaz continues, once we've all settled. "Joining midyear isn't ideal, but it's totally possible. Fern was home-schooled before this, is that correct?"

Mom's sitting ramrod straight in her chair, twisting her hands in her lap. "Yes. That's right."

"Good, that's no problem—we've had a number of home-schoolers transfer in since I joined the school ten years ago, and they tend to be some of our most unique thinkers." She smiles at me. "Now, did you bring her records with you?"

"No, I'm sorry. The records were . . . lost," Mom says.

"Again, not an issue," Ms. Diaz says. "We've had more student transfers with insufficient records than you could imagine. We're here to help you. And make sure that Fern succeeds in every possible way."

"Will she need to take any kind of placement test?" Mom asks.

"Nope," Ms. Diaz says. "Grade placement in this district is based solely on age. There will be some enrollment forms you'll have to fill out, but all we'll need is a copy of her birth certificate, her immunization records, and proof of residency. If you're dealing with any issues regarding housing insecurity, we can help you with that, too."

"There won't be any assessment?" Mom says again, like she doesn't believe it. "None at all?"

"No, but if it's something you're worried about, it might be helpful for your own peace of mind to have her take an assessment online. There are a bunch of free websites I could direct you to. If Fern struggles at any point, we can also revisit the need to do an assessment. The success and comfort of our students is our number one priority."

"Sounds great," Babs says. "Easy-peasy, just like I told you it would be. I can fill out the enrollment forms for you, Jamie.

We can do it back at the shop. Maybe this afternoon? I can get us set up at one of the quieter tables."

"I know how to fill out forms," Mom says to Babs. "I can do that much myself."

Ms. Diaz laughs. "Let's not get ahead of ourselves. It'll take a day or two to get the packet together for Fern. As for now, do you have time to do a tour? I'd like to show you our facilities."

"That would be great." Mom turns to Babs. "You can go. I can handle it from here."

"Oh, I'm happy to stay. See how Fern likes it."

For some reason, Mom looks annoyed. "Fine."

We start our tour back in the hallway, which is thankfully empty now.

Classrooms line the hallway, and most of them have colorful papers stuck on their doors. There's the "gymnasium"—a giant room with shiny floors and bright white lights that make my eyes hurt. We see the lunchroom and the library. I'd like to stay in the library, to see what kinds of books they have here, but the librarian is talking to a class right now, and Ms. Diaz says she doesn't want to disturb them.

Before we go into the next room, Mom motions for me to go with Ms. Diaz, and then turns to Babs. "Babs, can we have a word out here?"

Babs glances at me and then frowns. "Okay, sure."

I want to know what they're going to talk about, but I

can't stay out here while Ms. Diaz is waiting for me, so I follow her into the room.

And I'm so glad I did.

Because it's an entire room dedicated to computers. There are dozens of them on glass desks. A couple of kids are working quietly around the room.

"This is the computer lab," Ms. Diaz starts. "We offer coding classes, and—"

"Can anyone use these?" I interrupt.

"Of course," Ms. Diaz says. "As long as you're a student here."

I glance over my shoulder, checking to make sure Mom is still in the hallway with Babs. "Do they have the internet?"

"They do," she says.

"So, if I'm a student here," I add, to make extra sure, "I can walk right in and use any of these?"

"As long as a class isn't in session, the lab is open for free study and research."

Ms. Diaz keeps talking, telling me about the classes the school offers and the kinds of programs you can learn to use on the computers.

But I'm having trouble paying attention. Here I won't have to sneak around or limit my time. I can take as long as I need to search the internet for the Ranch's address.

"Shall we?" Ms. Diaz asks after she finishes talking, motioning to the door. She goes out, but I linger for a moment. It takes everything in me not to rush to one of the computers, to get on the internet right this very second.

One of the kids glances up at me, like she's trying to figure out why I'm standing there, gaping at the room.

I force myself to turn away, to go join Ms. Diaz, Mom, and Babs in the hallway.

"When can I start?" I ask as soon as Mom, Babs, and I are outside in the parking lot, walking toward the car.

"Hopefully, next week, from the sound of it," Mom says.

I don't want to wait until next week to get back into the computer room. I mentally cross off the days in my head. At least it still leaves me a good chunk of time before the spring equinox.

"You went from so unexcited that we had to drag you here to eager in three seconds, huh?" Babs nudges Mom. "See? Told you this was a good idea. All she had to do was get a look. It will be fun for Fern to be around so many other kids."

I want to tell Babs she's wrong. That it won't be fun at all. That it's going to be awful, and hard, and I'll probably get sick from all the germs crawling on those kids who don't understand how to properly take care of their health. But I keep my mouth shut.

Because the school has the internet. And computers I can use without Mom breathing down my neck.

And for what I need right now, that's more than enough.

11

Even though Ms. Diaz said I didn't need to take any kind of assessment test, Mom is making me take one that she had Alex print out for us from the internet.

It's basically just pages and pages of questions I don't know the answers to. Well, I know a *few* of the answers—some of the math ends up feeling okay. Certain chores on the Ranch—like figuring out gardening-supplement-to-soil ratio and the animal-feed amounts—require math to do them right. The science part of it also turns out to be okay. Better than okay. There are questions about pollution and the environment and plants that I whiz right through. And the other science questions, the ones I don't know the answers to, are interesting in a way that makes me want to learn more.

But the rest of it?

Not so good. Not so good at all.

"I don't know any of this!" I throw my pencil down in frustration and lean back so hard against my headboard that it smacks against the wall. "Why are you making me do this? She said I didn't have to."

"I want to know where you're at," Mom says. "I want to know how worried I should be."

"Fine." I push the test toward her. "Here."

Mom reaches out from where she's sitting cross-legged at the end of my bed and gathers up the pages. She frowns as she flips through my answers. I slump down lower.

"Okay. Listen. Anything you don't understand at school, I want you to wait until you can ask me, okay? Don't ask the teachers. You and I can work through everything together until you're caught up."

She looks so worried, the way she keeps pushing the hair behind her ears, that it makes me think about the conversation I overheard between her and Babs.

"Or else someone might take me away?"

Mom sits back. "What? What do you mean?"

"When you came into the tea shop, you said you thought someone had taken me. And then, the other night when you were talking to Babs, you said it again. I heard you say you were worried someone was going to take me away."

Mom's face falls. "You heard that?"

"Yes. So what did you mean?"

"It's hard to explain." Mom pauses a long time, like she's searching for the right words. "There's an organization called 'social services.' They . . . expect certain things from parents. And I'm worried that if someone—like a teacher or another parent—sees how behind you are in school, that person might call them. And if social services comes, they might ask a lot of questions. And if they decide I haven't done a good job raising you, they might take you away."

"To where?" I whisper.

"To stay with another family. Until they can figure out if I deserve to have you back or not."

I stare at her. "And they can come get me, without any notice? Like, if I'm just walking around? Or at Babs's shop?"

Mom looks confused for a second. "Oh—no, honey. That's not what—*who*—I was worried about at Babs's. I thought maybe . . . I thought someone from the Ranch had come to get you without telling me."

My heart lifts for a minute. "Wait . . . do they know where we are?"

She shakes her head. "No. I made sure of that. But I still got scared when you didn't answer your phone. Bottom line is I don't want *anyone* to take you away."

I think over everything she's said. The fact that a total stranger from this organization could take me away—just because I don't have the exact "right" kind of education, whatever that means—makes me so angry I could shout. Dr. Ben is right. Mainstream society is all kinds of twisted.

But it also makes me afraid.

Because I don't want to go anywhere, except home to the Ranch. I want to stay with Mom, and I want us to get back to our real family, our community, our people. And I'll do anything to get there.

So I take a breath and point at the test. "Okay. Then tell me what I got wrong."

It takes us an hour and a half to finish the assessment test, and then a while to go through the answers. Like I thought, I did pretty well in science and math, but when it came to questions about history, geography, some critical reading and writing skills . . . I did not do well. Mom keeps telling me that it's okay, that I'll catch up, because I'm smart.

But after finishing that assessment, I definitely don't feel smart.

Next we start on the welcome packet Ms. Diaz gave us to fill out while we wait for my enrollment forms. Before Mom can fill anything in, I grab the pen and write "Fern Silvana" where it says to write the student's name.

Mom stares at it, and I tense up, ready for her to tell me to cross it out and write "Frankie" instead.

But she doesn't. Instead, she asks, "Do you remember why you chose the name Fern?"

Choosing a new name—one that reflects the beauty of nature—is something everyone does at the Ranch, usually a couple of months after getting there. For your first few months, you aren't called anything at all. Dr. Ben says it's so you can "readjust your self-perception." According to Dr. Ben, it's important to strip yourself of your old identity entirely, so you can commit yourself to a new one. The whole community makes suggestions, but at the end of the day you get to pick your own new name.

I'm not sure how the name "Dr. Ben" relates to something in nature, but I'm sure it does. I've always been too nervous to ask, because I bet it's short for something obvious, and I'd feel stupid once it was explained to me.

"Yes," I say automatically. "I chose it because ferns do a lot for the environment. They can be food and medicine for people and animals. They filter toxins and heavy metals from the environment. They're the helpers of the forest."

Mom laughs softly. "No. That's not why. You chose the name Fern because you loved the way ferns uncoil from fronds, like a dancer." She hops off the bed and crouches in a tight ball on the floor. Then she slowly uncurls herself until she's standing straight with her arms thrown in the air, her wrists slightly bent. "You chose it because you said ferns were the ballerinas of plants. Don't you remember how much you loved your old dance classes? You know, I used to love dancing, too."

Now that she mentions it, I *do* remember dancing. I'm pretty sure the kind of dancing I did was called ballet. When I was five and we were living in Brooklyn, I took classes in a basement studio that had a wall of dusty mirrors. I remember the pink shoes and the silky outfit I got to wear.

"I don't know," I say. "Maybe."

"I have an idea." Mom grabs her phone and clicks a few buttons. Music starts. It's low and tinny, but she puts the phone into an empty water glass, which makes the sound louder. It's not ballet music—there's way more shouting and energy to this. Mom bops her head and grabs me by the hands, dragging me off the bed. "Dance with me?"

I resist at first, but she starts to do some ridiculous dance moves and I can't help but join her. The song gets faster and shoutier, and soon I'm out of breath from all the jumping around. Mom shout-sings along to the music. When the song ends, we both collapse on my bed, sweating.

I forgot how good dancing feels. People play instruments at the Ranch, guitars and banjos, but no one ever *dances*. Not like this.

"What kind of music was that?" I ask.

"Punk rock," Mom says. "I got into the scene when I moved to New York City, back when I was eighteen. The person who sang that song is Frankie Bellows. One of my all-time favorites. She has so much . . . power and energy. She's who I named you after."

"Oh," I say, turning this new fact over in my mind. "I didn't know that."

Part of me likes that Mom named me after someone who obviously has so much to say, someone people want to listen to.

But the other part of me . . .

I grab a handful of the bedspread in my hand and twist. "I still want you to call me Fern."

Mom rolls over so she's facing me, propped up on her elbow. A strand of hair is sticking to her sweaty forehead. "Okay. More than anything, honey, I want you to feel free to be the person you want to be. Not the person Dr. Ben wants you to be. Not even necessarily the person I want you to be. So if that's really what *you* want"—she taps me on the chest—"I'll be better about calling you Fern from now on. I promise."

12

A few days later, Mom takes me to see the doctor.

"I don't need to see a doctor. I'm perfectly healthy. Or at least I was," I tell her on the way there. Because who even knows what's going on in my body now that I've been exposed to so many new toxins. "Before you dragged me out here."

"We need to go before you start school. It's been a while, and there are some things you're behind on."

"What things?" I ask.

"Nothing serious," Mom says, but she won't look me in the eye.

The doctor takes my height and weight, feels my neck, and looks inside my ears and in my mouth. Then he leaves the room, and comes back in with a couple of small plastic tubes that are attached to long, sharp needles.

I feel the color drain from my face. I think I know what that is. Medicine. The bad kind that Dr. Ben talks a lot about. If he were here, he'd knock the needles out of the doctor's hand. Honestly, he'd probably punch him in the face to keep him from sticking me with that stuff. But he's not here.

"No," I say. "No, you can't. Please. I won't."

"Not a fan of shots? Don't worry. The anticipation is the worst part." The doctor smiles at me. "A few quick jabs and then it's all over. It'll only hurt for a second."

He comes over, but I thrash, trying to move away from him. "No!"

"I'm sorry," Mom says to the doctor. She won't even look at me. "I'll hold her."

Mom grabs me, and no matter how much I wriggle and move, I can't get away. She's stronger than me. Tears stream down my face as the doctor injects me with whatever horrible things are inside those shots. As soon as Mom lets me go, I push her away from me.

"Why?" I say. "Why did you do that to me?"

"All done. Take as much time as you need," the doctor says, leaving the room as quickly as possible.

"We had to. For you to go to school." Mom holds her face in her hands. She's crying a little, too. "I'm sorry. I'm so sorry. I can't believe what I let Dr. Ben do to you. To us."

I pull the sleeve of my shirt back down. "*He* didn't do anything to me. You did."

An hour or two after we get back to the motel, Mom sits down next to me on the bed. I roll so my back is facing her.

She sighs. "I know this isn't the best timing, but we're about to have some visitors. They should be here any minute, actually."

I don't ask who, but she tells me anyway.

"It's Paul and his daughter, Alyssa. Or Forest and Kestrel, when they were at the Ranch," she reminds me.

"Why?"

"They want to check in on us. They live in Truckee now, which is a few hours north. Like I told you before, Paul was the one who helped us leave."

"Who helped *you* leave," I correct her. "I had nothing to do with it."

"Right," Mom says lightly. "But it'll be fun. We'll go out to dinner. It'll be nice to see some familiar faces, don't you think?"

I don't say anything. I don't want to see either of them. I don't want to call them by their other names or pretend to be happy or thankful that they did anything remotely good for me, when in reality, their "help" has ruined my life.

A few minutes later, there's a knock at our door.

"Ready?" Mom asks me, her eyes bright. "That should be them."

I can't believe she's trying to act like things are fine between us, after what happened today. My eyes are still puffy. My arm aches from the shots, from the horrible, disease-causing soup that is no doubt coursing through my veins. "I'm not going anywhere. I don't feel good."

"Fern, please. Get up. It'll only be for an hour or two."

I don't budge from my spot on the bed. "I said I don't feel good!"

There's a second knock at the door. "Yoo-hoo! Jamie, it's me," comes a deep voice. "Paul."

Mom exhales in frustration before she goes to open the door. Some damp air gusts in, and the room fills suddenly with the salty smell of the ocean. "Hi, Paul. Alyssa—wow, you're so grown up! Come on in. I'm having trouble getting Fern moving." She reaches out and hugs Paul—*Forest*, I think defiantly—and then steps back so they can come into our room.

"I can see why you wanted to land here," he says as they step into the room. "What a great little town. I bet the sunsets here are incredible."

I hug a pillow to my chest and stare at them over the top of it. Forest's bushy beard is gone, and his hair is cut short. And as for Kestrel . . . she looks like an entirely different person. She's got a hoop through her nose, and half of her head is shaved, and the half that isn't is dyed pink. The look of it makes my scalp itch.

"Hey," she says, nodding at me.

"Wow, look how big you got!" Forest says. "It's great to see you, kiddo."

I look between the two of them and don't say anything.

"Come on, honey," Mom says. "Let's go."

"I told you I don't feel good. If I go, I'll just throw up all over the table."

"It's rough at first, isn't it?" Forest says. "But maybe you'll feel better if you let us take you out for a good meal. We can order French fries, maybe. Or, *oh*"—he rubs his hands together, like he's trying to get me excited—"some ice cream!"

"I'm not sure she's ready for that yet, Dad," Kestrel says, touching his arm.

I make sure she can see me scowling at her.

"Fine," Mom says, throwing up her hands. "Fine. Stay. Lock up as soon as we leave, and keep your cell phone on, okay?"

I nod, relieved I don't have to spend a minute longer with these people. These traitors.

Mom turns to Forest. "Oh, but before we leave, I want to give you this." She goes over to our desk, which we're using as our makeshift kitchen, and opens the drawer. She takes out an envelope and tries to hand it to Forest. "It's my first paycheck. It's not enough to cover what you did for me, not even close, but—"

Forest holds up his hands to stop her. "No, no. I won't accept that. Not yet. Not for a long time, okay? We can talk about that much, much later."

I can't tell if Mom looks relieved or upset by this, but she doesn't argue as she puts the envelope back in the desk drawer. She only thanks him.

"Good to see you, hon," Forest says to me on his way out. "I hope you feel better soon."

Once Mom and Forest are gone, Kestrel lingers in the doorway. "You know . . . he hit my dad over the head with a rake. All he did was ask a simple question. But Dr. Ben thought he was questioning his authority, so . . ." She shakes her head. "One of these days he's going to kill somebody. You're lucky you got out."

Immediately, my thoughts go to Rain. He died after Kestrel and her dad left. Do they know? Has Mom told them? I'm certainly not going to be the one to tell her. Because it wasn't Dr. Ben's fault, right?

But I feel strange for a second, a little like the moment right after you slip but you haven't hit the ground yet.

"Do you have a phone?" she asks suddenly.

I nod and tip my chin at my cell phone, which is plugged in on the other side of the room, close to her. As far as it can be from where I sleep.

She picks it up and wiggles it. "Do you mind?"

I shrug. I don't know what she's planning, and I don't really care. She could keep the thing, if she wanted it. She presses some buttons and then sets it back down. "There. Now you have my number. If you need anything or if you have any questions, you can call me anytime."

"Thanks. But I won't."

"Yeah. You might feel that way now. I know I did," she says. "But things will get better for you soon. Or at least I hope they will."

She taps the doorframe twice and then she's gone.

13

When it's finally time for me to start school the next week, I have only two goals.

First, use the computers to research Dr. Ben and see if I can find the Ranch's address.

And second, blend in as much as possible. Don't stick out or give anyone a reason to take me away from Mom, because that would make getting back home even more complicated.

I fail at my second goal almost immediately.

As soon as I step into the hallway, I realize I should have listened to Mom, I should have worn some of my new clothes. I haven't been able to bear the idea of putting any of that stuff on, so I've been washing my clothes from the Ranch twice a week and hanging them to dry from the shower rod. I have the new sweater I made, too, but I don't know if the yarn Mom got me was treated with any chemicals or anything. She claims it wasn't, but who knows if that's the truth? She also got me a pair of jeans, and I know since Dr. Ben wears jeans all the time, they're probably okay, but . . . my normal clothes feel so safe. So familiar and healthy.

I hadn't paid attention to what the other kids were wearing during our first visit, but now that I'm here, alone, it's all I can see. There are a lot of T-shirts, jeans, stretchy black pants. No one is wearing *anything* that looks like my work pants or homemade sweater.

Some of the kids seem to be noticing it, too. I'm getting funny looks as I stand here, waiting for Ms. Diaz to come meet me. A lot of funny looks. Maybe it's also because I don't have the kind of bag everyone else does, the kind that hooks over both of your shoulders and rests on your back. I'm carrying all my stuff in Mom's woven tote bag. The school gave me the textbooks I need, but Mom and I had to go out to get pencils, pens, binders, and paper ourselves. Ms. Diaz said the school would get me set up with a Chromebook—which is a computer—if Mom and I couldn't buy one ourselves, but that it might take a month or two for the request to go through. I hope we're gone by the time it arrives.

I shift my bag self-consciously on my shoulder and turn my attention to the scuffed white floor.

None of this matters, I remind myself. *You'll be out of here before you know it.*

"Fern! Hello!"

It's Ms. Diaz. When she walks up to me with a warm smile, I feel a little bit better.

After she welcomes me officially, she walks me to one of the classrooms. This one has paper star cutouts all over the door, and written on the stars are names. One of the stars, a yellow one, says "Fern Silvana."

My teacher for this class—a class called homeroom—is Mr. Dulbecco. Once everyone is seated at their desks, he makes me stand up and introduce myself.

Everyone stares at me from their seats.

I'm so nervous my whole body is shaking. "I'm—I'm Fern Silvana."

There are some coughs and quiet laughs.

"Sorry," says the teacher. "Can you speak up? I don't think anyone could hear you."

I say my name again, louder. Only then does he let me sit down.

Homeroom is over quickly. Next is a class called social studies, which is in a different room. The seats aren't assigned, so I sit in the back row, my hands sweating. My social studies teacher, Ms. Fong-Hines, makes me introduce myself, too.

Beyond introducing myself, I stay completely quiet for all my morning classes. Words wash over me, and I don't understand most of what anyone is talking about. At the end of each class, the teacher assigns work we'll have to do at home.

Finally, it's time for lunch.

Mom packed me a chickpea salad sandwich on sprouted bread, which is wrapped in paper at the bottom of my tote bag.

I bring it with me to the lunchroom.

Inside, it's loud and busy. Kids buzz and swarm around

certain tables more than others. I see teachers and other adults, but there's so much noise and energy I'm sure none of them will notice if I slip out.

This is my chance.

I hurry down the almost empty hallway to the computer room. I pause at the doorway before going inside. I swear I can almost hear the high-pitched whine of the machines from where I'm standing. Maybe I'm imagining it, but my head starts to ache, probably from the wireless signals. Dr. Ben would tell me to get far away, and fast.

But he would also understand that I *have* to be here. So I force myself forward.

Some other students are here, too, but they're all focused on what they're doing and don't look up as I come in. A few of them are eating, which makes me feel better about deserting the lunchroom.

I slide into one of the empty seats. Luckily, this computer is already on, so I don't have to worry about that.

There are lots of different little pictures on the screen, and each one has words beneath it. Words like "PowerPoint," "Word," and "Trash." I look for one that says "Internet," but I don't find one.

I try to remember what the picture for the internet looked like on Mom's old laptop, the one I used for watching a show about a cartoon pig and her family. *Peppa Pig*—that was the name of it. I remember cozying up in Mom's bed, her laptop in front of us, and feeling happy. Feeling safe. Which is confusing, because TV is really bad for you, so I shouldn't have felt that way, right? I shake my head, trying to get my mind back to the task at hand: finding the button for the internet. But I can't remember what it looks like.

Maybe someone can help me. I look around the room. My eyes land on a girl working a couple of computers away from me. I recognize her—she's one of the girls I followed into Babs's tea shop. The blond one, the one who has the same color hair as Meadowlark.

I walk over to her. She's got big leather earmuff things on, and she's leaning toward the screen, using her pointer finger to click the mouse. At least I know what that is.

She glances up when she notices me standing there and raises her eyebrows, like she's saying, *What do you want?*

I rub my hands on my pants. "Um, hi. I'm—"

She pulls the things off her head. "What?"

I swallow. Why is this so scary? "I'm Fern. I'm new."

"Okay? Hi? I'm Havana. Do you need something?" Then she lifts her nose into the air and sniffs. "Do you smell that? Wow, that's strong. Wait." She leans toward me and sniffs again. "Is that *you?*"

This morning, I rubbed some herbal tincture onto my chest. Thankfully, Mom thought to bring some with us. It wards away germs, which I need in a place like this, which is probably crawling with them. Dr. Ben says we're each our own universe of bacteria, which can be good or bad. Most people don't pay attention to things like this, so they let themselves become infested with bad bacteria. I don't want to go back to the doctor's office again. Not ever. More than anything, I don't want to mess up the balance I achieved at the Ranch. I want to stay good.

And to me the sharp tang of oregano oil and eucalyptus smells nice. Healthy, like home. But by the expression on Havana's face, I can tell she doesn't think so.

I take a step away from her. "No. I don't know. But I was wondering, can you help me with something?"

"With what?"

"How do I . . . I'm trying to look up some information. On the computer. On the internet."

"And?"

This is so much harder than I expected it to be. "How do I . . . do that?"

Meadowlark was easy to talk to from the moment I met her. I asked her loads of questions, because she'd been at the Ranch for a while already and knew a lot more about things than I did when I first got there. Well, except for knitting. But just because this girl and Meadowlark look similar doesn't mean they are similar. Which is becoming more and more clear.

"Um, use Google?"

She says it like it's the most obvious thing in the world. I can't bring myself to ask, so I stay quiet and hope she'll show me.

She stares at me. "Don't tell me you don't know what Google is."

"No, I . . . do," I lie.

"You don't! I can tell. Wow. I've never met anyone

who can't use a computer. What are you—like, Amish or something?"

"No," I say quickly, though I don't know. Maybe I am. I don't know what "Amish" is.

She turns to her screen. "Click on this." She moves the arrow to a little circle that's red, green, and yellow. The word beneath it says "Chrome." A page pops up that says "Google" at the top. "And type whatever you want to look up here. Got it?"

"I think so," I say. "Thanks."

"Wait—" she says as I turn to move away. "You're that girl. The one from the tea shop. With the mom who totally freaked out!"

"Oh. Yeah."

"That was so weird."

"I guess so."

She seems to be waiting for me to say something else, but I have no idea what she's hoping for. So again I stay quiet. Eventually, she says, "Well, okay, then," and slides her ear covers on without another word.

I go back to my computer and use the mouse to click on the circle icon, and up pops Google, just like it did on Havana's computer.

"Dr. Ben." I use my pointer fingers to punch in letters on the letter board. "The Ranch address."

I hold my breath as the results load. The first results are for a Dr. Ben D'Amico, a veterinarian who works with cattle in Texas. But he's much older than the real Dr. Ben, with thinning gray hair and glasses. I keep looking. There are also results for restaurants, hotels, and dude ranches. There are results for other Dr. Bens, too, but none of them are who I'm looking for.

I add "New York State" and "futurist sustainable living community," because those are the words I've always heard the adults use to describe the Ranch.

For the next ten minutes, I click, page after page, but there's nothing that looks remotely like the Ranch listed anywhere.

Sitting back in my chair, I close my eyes and think.

I try to remember everything.

Dr. Ben's last name, for starters. Does it begin with a *W*? I can't remember. Nothing comes up in my head. On the Ranch, there's no need for last names.

In fact, I don't know what Meadowlark's last name is. She's been my best friend for years—she's basically my sister—and I don't know her last name. The realization jolts me in a way I don't like.

Okay, the name thing isn't going to happen, so I try to think of other things to search for that might get me closer. "Old convents New York State" only brings up lists of religious orders, current convents, and articles about amazing places to visit in New York. Looking through the images that come back with that search, I realize that none of the pictures of convents look *anything* like the Ranch.

The market! I scour my brain for details about the farmers market. Did it have a more specific name? Everyone just said "going to the market." We sold things "at the market." Was "the Market" its full name, or was that just what we all called it?

I wish that I hadn't fallen asleep in the taxi. That I'd paid attention to the street names, the turns, everything and anything. I could kick that stupid, sleepy version of myself. I wish I could go back and wake her up.

Then I remember: the parking lot! The one we got dropped off at. They were selling used cars. I squeeze my eyes closed and try to remember: a name, a sign, anything.

But in my head all I can see are the hot-pink numbers written on the car windshields, and the man in the parka who said "Have a good life." to me and Mom.

He knew, I realize. He knew we were leaving. Even a stranger in a parking lot knew, and I didn't.

"Okay." I breathe. It's still something. I type "used car parking lots, New York State."

The computer returns 260,000,000 results.

I want to cry. How am I supposed to sift through all of this?

The bell rings, which makes me jump. It rings at the end of every class, and then again eight minutes later, to make sure we're all in our classes on time. Lunch is over, but I haven't come close to finding what I'm looking for.

Why did I think this was going to be easy?

"You only fail if you stop trying," I whisper to myself.

I still have a few more minutes, so I carefully type "how to find someone's address when you don't know their last name."

Some of the results look immediately promising. I click on one called "Sleuth for Truth," but the information it gives is way too complicated, so I go back.

Then my eyes land on something else. It's a link at the top of the screen, with a box around the word "ad." It says: "Hire a private investigator to find someone (fast)."

A private investigator.

That's one of the things the lady at the post office said I could do to find the address! I click on the link, and it takes me to a page called "Foglamp Investigators."

At the top of the page, there's a drawing of a tall thin building, with a wide beam of light sweeping out toward the sea. It's familiar—a *lighthouse,* I realize.

I use the mouse to move down the website. There's a picture of a magnifying glass, and beneath that, in big black text, it says, "Trying to find somebody? We can help!"

And below that, at the bottom of the page, there's an address. And it's here, in Driftaway Beach. On Moonraker—a street name I recognize from my route to the post office.

The second bell rings, and I scramble to find a pencil to write down the details.

I might not be able to find the Ranch's address, but maybe someone else can.

14

I barely pay attention in my next class.

All I can think about is the little slip of paper, the one with the address for Foglamp Investigators, which feels like it's burning a hole in my pocket.

Then I get to my last class of the day, which is science. I'm early, since the English language arts teacher let us out five minutes before the bell rang. Most of the other students are clustered in the hallway, talking and laughing. A few of them glance over at me. I don't want to talk to any of them, and I don't want to stand there alone, either, so I go inside.

This classroom isn't like any of the other ones I've been in today.

There are plants everywhere. Interesting plants. Plants hanging from the ceiling. There are some I've never seen before inside glass cases that are fogging from the humidity, like mini-greenhouses.

As I move down the row of glass cases, I see more plants, some with exposed ghost-white roots growing in water instead of soil. Some of the cases have rocks and moss and long, slithery bugs crawling in them, and others are filled with water and colorful fish. At the end of the row is the biggest case of them all, made of wire instead of glass. Inside is a chubby rodent-like creature. But "rodent" isn't exactly the right word. This little creature is much cuter than the rats that plague the Ranch's compost piles.

His gray fur looks soft, and his whiskers twitch as he gets closer, like he's trying to get a sniff of me. I hope he doesn't mind the smell of my medicinal salve.

I glance at the little sign.

CHARLES THE CHINCHILLA, it says. And underneath: * *Please check with Mr. Carlson before taking Charles out!* *

"Hey there," comes a voice from behind me. I whirl around. He must be the teacher. He's Black, with dark brown skin and a bald head. His short-sleeve T-shirt has a bright flowery print. He smiles apologetically. "Sorry, I didn't mean to surprise you. I see you've already met Charles. You're my new student, right? Fern Silvana?"

I nod.

"Great to meet you, Fern. I'm Mr. Carlson. Do you want me to introduce you at the beginning of class, or would you rather have a break from it? I bet you've been doing it all day."

"A break. Definitely," I say, and he laughs.

"Right on. I totally get it. No introduction it is. I'm glad to have you in my class. Sit anywhere you'd like."

For the first time all day, I pick a seat in the front row instead of the back.

Mr. Carlson heads to his desk and opens a slim silver computer. His laptop. "You're in luck. We're starting our big 'Science in Driftaway Beach' project today. Most of my students say it's their favorite project of the entire school year. It's certainly mine."

The bell rings, and other kids start streaming in.

Havana is in this class. She walks in with the girl I saw her with at the tea shop. She looks at me and whispers something to her friend, who looks at me, too. Their eyes stay on me as they walk by to sit a few rows back.

So much for blending in. The wool of my sweater feels itchy against my neck. I wish I'd looked up what "Amish" means on the internet. I hope it isn't a bad thing. If it is, will Havana tell one of the teachers? Will it get Mom in trouble?

"Okay, class!" Mr. Carlson cries once the second bell rings. He pumps a fist in the air. "Today is the day!"

Everyone is quiet and paying attention in a way they didn't in my other classes. I find myself leaning forward in my chair.

"As I've mentioned before, my favorite project of the year is the one we'll be starting today," Mr. Carlson continues. "We get to take some of the scientific and environmental principles we've learned so far and apply them to real-life scenarios."

He goes on to explain that, with a partner, we'll be conducting science-oriented projects and experiments around Driftaway Beach. He gives us some examples of projects students have done in previous years. Two students built beehives in someone's backyard, using recycled materials, and they planted all kinds of bee-friendly flowers. Other students set up birdhouses for local nesting birds and recorded how many chicks they had. Another pair of students did a big project where they helped recycle athletic shoes to keep them out of the landfill. One project looked at the local effects of climate change by measuring the erosion of the cliffs along the coastline.

I listen carefully to every word. This is my kind of class.

"All right," he says. "Now that you've gotten the gist of things, you can go ahead and choose your partners."

The class erupts in a frenzy of movement and voices. Before I can turn around in my seat, kids are dragging their desks together, pulling out paper, and talking loudly about ideas. I glance to my left and right, but the kids on either side of me are already partnered up.

Sitting here, I feel something I rarely ever felt at the Ranch. I feel alone.

But then again, it doesn't matter if I make any friends here. I touch the piece of paper in my pocket. Because we won't be here for long.

Someone walking past me bumps into my elbow. I watch as a girl with light brown skin and long black hair marches up to Mr. Carlson at the front of the room.

"Mr. Carlson, I'd like to do my project alone. Can I have your approval?"

He shakes his head. "Sorry, Eddie, but this is a partner project."

"But I already have a very specific idea of what I'd like to do. And I don't need any help."

Mr. Carlson's eyes fall on me. "Why don't you talk to Fern about it?"

The girl turns around and looks at me, her eyebrows knit together. "Are you Fern? Do you have a partner yet?"

"Yes. And no."

"Okay." She comes over to my desk. "To be my partner, you have to agree to do my idea."

"Eddie, that's not how this works," Mr. Carlson calls out.

But I can tell by the determined expression on her face that whatever her project idea is, it's important to her. I'd be happy to do any of the kinds of projects Mr. Carlson gave as examples, and I understand what it's like to have a mission. So I say, "We can do whatever you want."

Her shoulders relax, and she smiles. "Excellent. I'd like to get started today. Can you come over after school?"

"I have to ask my mom."

"Or I could come over to your house," she offers.

"No," I say, thinking of our small motel room. Even I know that our living situation isn't exactly normal. "Sorry."

"Okay. That's fine. By the way, I'm Edwina. Edwina Chattar, but everyone calls me Eddie."

"I'm Fern," I tell her. "Fern Silvana."

"Fern—right. That's what Mr. Carlson said. I like it. You have a weird name, like me."

I frown. "It isn't a weird name. Ferns are amazing plants."

"Sorry," she says. "I didn't mean to be rude. I say the wrong thing sometimes."

That makes me relax, because honestly, I feel like I've been saying the wrong thing a lot lately. "It's okay. I do, too."

"Great. Well, it's nice to meet you, partner." She sticks her hand out to shake mine, but I lean away from it. She drops it immediately. "Not a handshaker? No problem."

"I don't want to get sick."

Instead of giving me a funny look, Eddie only nods. "I understand. I want to be a scientist, maybe even a virologist, so I've read a lot about germs and viruses. I'm a bit of a germophobe myself." She scribbles down her address and phone number on a piece of paper and pushes it toward me. "My house, four o'clock. If your mom says it's okay."

15

When the school day finally ends, Mom is waiting for me outside, still in her housekeeping uniform. It's a nice day, and—like everything in Driftaway Beach—the motel isn't too far, so she must have walked.

"Fern!" she calls when she sees me, waving her arms. "Fernie, hi!"

I go over to her. "Hi."

"How was your first day?" she asks. "Did you like it?"

"No," I say, and her face falls. I feel a little bad, so I add, "I did like my science teacher, though. His name is Mr. Carlson."

The sun is warm on my cheeks but the breeze is cool, with a hint of salt and moisture from the ocean. It feels similar to an October afternoon back home. She asks a lot more questions on our walk back to the motel. Was I confused in my classes (yes), do I have any questions for her about my schoolwork (too many to count), did I meet anyone (kind of).

"I have to do a project with this girl, Eddie. Actually, she wants to know if I can come over today at four."

Mom unlocks the door to our room and pushes it open. "Where does she live? Do you have a phone number so I can call her parents and make sure it's okay?"

The first thing I notice when we walk in is a little leaf in a glass of water sitting on the windowsill. The edges of the leaf are mottled green, but the center is a brilliant pretty pinkish purple.

"What is that?" I ask as I give her the slip of paper Eddie gave me with her parents' phone number on it—but not before I double-check to make sure it's the right slip of paper, not the one I wrote the private investigator's details on.

Mom takes out her cell phone. "Oh—there's a nursery just down the highway. They had the most gorgeous begonias, and they let me have a cutting. I went during my lunch break."

I gently run my fingers along the ridges of the begonia leaf as Mom calls the number Eddie gave me. Mom loves plants. She's had a green thumb since before we moved to the Ranch. I know she loves being assigned greenhouse duty the most; it's where we prep our seed trays and grow the vegetable starts for our garden. Sometimes she's late to meals because she spends so long tinkering in the greenhouse.

Once she hangs up, she says, "All set. They're right in town, on Main Street. Do you want me to drive or walk with you? I have a few more rooms to do, but if you wait until my shift is done—"

"No," I say quickly. "I can walk by myself."

"Okay," Mom says, but there's doubt in her voice. I haven't gone out for a solo walk since the tea shop incident. "But I want you to go directly there, and to text me when you get there. I'll pick you up when you're ready."

"Mom—"

"Those are the rules."

"Fine," I say. "I'll walk directly there and text you as soon as I get there."

But that's a lie. Because I'm planning to make a stop first.

The office for Foglamp Investigators is on Moonraker, one of the streets I had to turn on to get to the post office. I walk up and down the street twice before I find it. Or at least I hope this is the right place. It has two square windows, the blinds drawn, and a wooden front door. Only then do I notice a small picture of a lighthouse that matches the one I saw on their website. Below that is another sign that says OPEN.

I take a deep breath and go in.

It's dim inside, and small. There are two desks with computers on them and some tall metal cabinets along the far wall. Sitting at one of the desks is a white man with gray hair and a thick gray mustache.

He stares at me as I walk inside. "Hi. Are you lost?"

"No." My voice is shaking, so I clear my throat and try again. "No—I don't think so. Is this Foglamp Investigators?"

He's still looking at me like he's convinced I'm in the wrong place. "Yes. . . ."

"I found your website. You can find people, right? Or find an address?"

"We can do that, yes," he says.

"Can you find someone even if I don't know their last name?"

"Depends on what other details you can give me. But usually, yeah." He gets up from his desk and goes over to the window, stretching two of the blinds apart with his fingers to look outside. "Is there a parent or an adult with you?"

I lift my chin. "No. It's just me. Please. This is extremely important. Like, life-changingly important."

He doesn't look entirely sure about this whole thing, but he does sit back down at his desk. "Okay, well, why don't you start by telling me who or what you're looking for, and we can go from there."

"I'm looking for an address," I say.

Then I tell him everything I know. That it's not an actual ranch but that we call it "the Ranch." That there's a big stone-and-wood building surrounded by acres of land in the northern part of New York State. That about thirty of us live there, give or take. I tell him about the vegetable gardens, the orchards, the greenhouse, pigs, chickens, sheep, and goats. And that there's a long driveway, a big metal gate, and a tall wooden fence around the whole property. That the man who's in charge is called Dr. Ben, and that he's who I'm looking for specifically.

As I talk, he jots down notes on a piece of paper, but stops when I get to the part about Dr. Ben.

"And do you have a last name?" he asks. "That would make this a lot easier."

I shake my head. "I don't know. I can't remember. We don't use last names. But—I think it used to be an old convent. The building, I mean."

He jots that down. "Great. That could be very helpful. Can you give me any other identifying details beyond that? What town this place is in? Names of any local businesses?"

"I don't know," I admit.

"What do you mean, you don't know?" He checks his notes. "You lived there, right?"

"Yeah. But I didn't leave the property. Not until we *left* left, but it was dark and I . . ." My face flames. "Fell asleep in the car."

"For how long?"

"I don't know. For at least an hour or two, maybe more."

"No, I mean, how long did you live there without leaving the grounds?"

"Oh. Six years."

He whistles, long and low. He slaps his notepad against his desk. "And you're sure you want to go back to this place?"

I stare at him. I hope he can see the conviction burning in my eyes. "More than anything in the world. 'This place' is my home. The people that live there are my family."

"I don't know, kid." He spins his pen in his fingers. "What kind of 'family' keeps you at the same house for six years straight?"

"It's complicated. It isn't . . . it isn't like that. It wasn't just a house. Most of us stayed on the property because there wasn't any reason to leave." I try to remember the words

Dr. Ben uses to talk about what the Ranch is. What it means. "With climate change and war and all the other bad stuff in the world, people need to learn how to live in small communities that can take care of themselves. That's what we were doing. Please. I just want to go home."

That seems to get him. "Okay. All right." He thinks for a minute. "I have enough that I can probably find either the place or the guy—this Dr. Ben. If I find one, I'll likely find the other."

My heart sings. "Really?"

"I think so, yes. It isn't entirely by the books, but I can help you. But listen, since you're a minor, there can't be a legally binding contract, unless you get a parent to sign off on it."

"No," I tell him. "No, I can't do that."

"Okay. I've worked with a few teens who've needed help and couldn't go to their parents, so I get it. But like I said, this'll all have to be a handshake deal, okay?"

"Yes. That's fine." Then I think about my tiny calendar in the back of the book Mom gave me. Every day I have to cross off makes my chest feel a little tighter. "How long will it take you?"

"That depends on how soon you can pay me," he answers.

He's talking about money. Of course. Money was something I never, ever thought about on the Ranch. But out here, it's a part of everything.

"How much will it cost?" I ask.

"For research projects, I charge fifty an hour, plus a base

project fee of three hundred dollars. My guess is this'll probably be a few hours of research at the least, so a fair price will probably shake out to be six to seven hundred all in, more or less."

"Six to seven hundred *dollars*?" I say. "That much? To find an address?"

That's way more than I have, seeing as I currently have zero dollars. It feels like an impossible sum. My lower lip starts to quiver, and I know by the hot feeling in my nose and eyes that I'm about to cry.

"Hey, hey. Whoa. Don't cry." He sighs and rubs his face with his hands. "Listen. If you can get me three hundred flat, I won't charge you for the actual hourly work. I can tell this is important to you. You get me three hundred, and I'll get you the information you need."

Three hundred dollars. Three hundred dollars is all that stands between me and the Ranch. Me and Mom finally going *home*.

Somehow, some way, I can find three hundred dollars. I *will* find it.

"Okay." I extend my hand. For this, I'm willing to risk germs. "It's a deal."

16

I basically run all the way to Eddie's house to make up for lost time, the investigator's business card tucked safely in my pocket.

On the card is his name—Ron B. Tully—his phone number, and his email address. He told me to email him if I think of anything else that might be helpful, because he doesn't like using the phone for non-emergencies. When I asked how to do that—how to email him—he said that if I didn't have email, I'd have to set up an account. It was clear he was done talking at this point, so I said goodbye and left. So now I have to figure out how to do that.

When I get to the address Eddie gave me, I'm kind of surprised. Because it doesn't belong to a house or an apartment. It's a shop, and it's called Spirit of the Sea.

I double-check the address to make sure I'm in the right place. According to the number on the building, I am. I text Mom to let her know I've arrived safely.

This door has a bell that tinkles when I push it open, like the one to the tea shop.

"Hello?" I call. "Eddie? Are you in here?"

But no one answers.

The shop is full of sweatshirts and T-shirts on metal hangers, hats, posters on the walls, and clear plastic bins filled with small pieces of plastic in the shape of lanterns, lighthouses, and a woman wearing a white dress. I don't know what half this stuff is, but everything—and I mean *everything*—is Spirit of the Sea–themed.

The poster above the T-shirts is of an old-timey black-and-white photograph of a lighthouse. The view of the coastline stretching out around it is familiar to me. This must be the lighthouse that burned down where the motel is now. Something about that sends a shiver down my spine. The poster next to it is the same one hanging above Alex's desk in the office. The one of the ghostly figure with a glowing lantern, standing on top of the bluff.

"Hey."

I turn to find Eddie standing next to me. "Sorry. I forgot to explain that there's a separate entrance to our apartment. We live upstairs, above the shop. Ready?"

Before we can go anywhere, a woman hurries over.

"Hi there. Do you need any assistance, or is my daughter helping you?"

She's got an accent I've never heard before. I think she's speaking English, but I have to listen hard to understand what she's saying.

"Mom, *no*," Eddie says. "Fern's not a customer. She's from school."

She and Eddie don't look much alike. Her mom's got tons of freckles on her pale white skin and blondish hair that's threaded with silver. She's wearing flowy clothes, and around her neck is a necklace with a red crystal.

"Oh, how lovely! Great to meet you, Fern."

She comes in for what appears to be a hug, but I dodge away and flick my eyes to the floor. "It's nice to meet you, too. Sorry."

"Fern doesn't like germs," Eddie explains.

"Oh! Apologies. I'm a big hugger, and sometimes I forget to ask. I won't do it again."

I pull the sleeves of my sweater down to cover my hands. "It's okay."

Eddie's mom smiles at me. "Any interest in learning more about the Spirit of the Sea before you go upstairs, dear?"

"Mom, stop. She's here to do a science project, not to shop." Eddie widens her eyes and motions for me to follow her. "Come on, Fern. Quick."

I shrug helplessly at Eddie's mom before I follow Eddie down an aisle, toward a door in the back of the store. "Where is your mom from?"

"You mean because of her accent? Scotland."

"Oh." I think Scotland is in Europe, but I'm not sure which part. Yet another thing to look up when I'm back at school.

The narrow stairs pop and squeak as we walk upstairs.

"Speaking of my mom, I'm sorry," Eddie says. "Actually, I'm sorry about both of my parents. They're obsessed."

"With what?"

"Anything slightly paranormal. And right now it's the Spirit of the Sea. If they try to rope you into talking about it, pretend you have to go to the bathroom. That usually works."

The stairs lead to a big open room with wide-plank floors and simple furniture. There's a tall potted tree sitting in front of one of the windows. I like the feel of the space immediately.

"Dad?" Eddie calls. "I'm here with my science partner. We'll be in my room!"

A short, slender man with black hair and light brown skin like Eddie's pops his head in from behind a door. "Hi, science partner. I'm Eddie's dad. You can call me Dev. Welcome. Let me know if you need anything, okay?"

He doesn't have an accent like Eddie's mom. He talks like me and Eddie. An American accent, I guess?

"We won't," Eddie replies. "Thanks, though."

I give him a small wave before I follow Eddie down a narrow hallway.

"Tuna? Tuna!" Eddie cries as we go. "He's my cat," she explains over her shoulder. "He's shy, so he probably won't come out while you're here. I'm going to check the bathroom, though. He likes to hide behind the toilet. One sec."

I stand in the hallway and wait for her to come back. The walls are covered with family photos of the three of them. Eddie's taking a while in the bathroom. I can still hear her banging around and muttering for her cat, so I look at the pictures more closely. Lots of them are recent, but in some of them—in the ones where Eddie is little—there's another girl, too. She looks about our age in the photos, so she must be a lot older than Eddie. She looks like Eddie, except her hair is wavy, and she has deep dimples where Eddie has none. She's not in any of the more recent photos, though. Sisters, maybe? I wonder if she's old enough that she's moved out and lives on her own now.

"No luck," Eddie says, coming out of the bathroom. Her eyes dart to the photo I'm looking at and then away again. "He's like a ninja when he wants to be. Hopefully, you can meet him next time. Come on. My room's this way."

Eddie's room is at the end of the hallway, and it's tiny but cozy. Her bed is tucked in the corner and has a big fluffy comforter. There's a plant with vines cascading down from its spot on top of a tall wooden dresser, and a pretty glass ball is hanging in the window above a comfortable-looking chair. I can't take my eyes off the ball—it's all different colors, and it catches the sun, spraying rainbow drops of light all across her walls and ceiling.

"What is that thing?" I ask. "Hanging in your window. It's so pretty."

"That? That's a fairy orb."

I want to know what a fairy orb is, but I don't ask. So I just repeat, "It's pretty."

"Pretty—but stupid, if you actually believe in it," she scoffs. "Like my parents do. Because fairies don't exist. And neither does Bigfoot, the Loch Ness monster, or, most importantly for our current purposes, the Spirit of the Sea."

"Oh. Okay." Beyond what little I know about the Spirit

of the Sea from the plaque Mom read, I have absolutely no clue what she's talking about. I make a mental note to look up "Loch Ness monster" and "Bigfoot" at school tomorrow.

Luckily, it doesn't seem like she's expecting more of a response from me, because she goes into her closet and starts rummaging around. "Which brings us to the reason we're here today: our science project."

Eddie comes out of the closet with a giant piece of cardboard. She flips it around and presents it to me. At the top it says "Disproving the Existence of the Spirit of the Sea with the Scientific Method. Project by Eddie Chattar."

"Oh, let me add you." She grabs a pen from her desk and adds "and Fern Silvana" next to her own name.

"Anyway," she continues, "we moved here because my parents want to prove the Spirit of the Sea is real. Just like they made me move to Ireland to look for fairies. And to northern Canada to live in a camper van for eight months when they were looking for proof that Bigfoot exists." She wrinkles her nose. "It smelled like old socks. Tuna *hated* it."

I frown. "Wait. So you want to prove the Spirit of the Sea *isn't* real? I thought you said your parents are trying to prove it *is* real."

"They are. *I'm* not." Her eyes burn with intensity. "And if I—we—can find a way to prove, scientifically, that the Spirit of the Sea doesn't exist, then maybe they'll finally stop going around the world chasing fairies and ghosts. They'll finally have to face some hard proof, and that will make them realize *none* of that stuff is real, so we can stop moving. And we can . . . stay." She fiddles with the edge of her board. "I like living here. My grandparents live in San Jose. It's the first time we've ever lived close to them."

"But if you prove she isn't real," I say, "wouldn't that just make them want to move on even sooner? Wouldn't proving that she's real be the thing that makes them want to stay here for good?"

"But she's *not* real, and that's the whole point. Sometimes bad things just happen. Not because of anything supernatural."

I have no idea what she means by that last part, but I can tell my questions have deflated her a little. She flops onto her chair. "What else am I supposed to do? I want to stay here, and this is the best plan I have. It's the *only* plan I have."

That, at least, I understand. It's funny to think Eddie's working to stay in Driftaway Beach, while I'm working as hard as possible to leave. But I understand why. I understand how much it sucks to move all the time. To be new everywhere you go, to never stay anywhere long enough for people to *care* if you stay or go. Which is one of the biggest reasons I want to go home to the Ranch. I know in my bones they care that we left, that they miss us and want us back.

I feel bad for her, but I'm still disappointed this is her big idea for Mr. Carlson's science project.

"So that's all we'd be doing?" I ask. "For the project, I mean."

"Yes," Eddie says defensively. "Why? Don't you like it?"

"No, it's— I was hoping we'd be doing something to help

the environment. Like the examples Mr. Carlson gave in class."

Eddie frowns. "But you said you'd do my idea."

"Yeah, but . . ." I trail off. I want to be able to tell Dr. Ben I was doing important work, even while we were gone. "I don't know. I wanted to do something good for the planet."

Eddie moves her mouth from side to side, like she's thinking. "Well, Mr. Carlson offers extra credit for anyone who goes out and picks up litter around town. If you collect a certain amount, it adds up to a free A on a test. That's environmental. And it might help you catch up, grades-wise, in the class."

"He does?" I don't care about grades, but I do care about all the trash I've seen around Driftaway Beach, strewn on the roads and sidewalks.

"Yeah. You can borrow gloves and a trash picker from him, so you don't have to touch any of it. You can ask him about it tomorrow."

"Okay. Thanks. I will"

"Great. So we can do my project—no problem, right?"

I bite my bottom lip. It would be easy to say yes, sure, whatever you want. But that's something the Fern who doesn't take up space would do. The Fern who'd be too nervous to do her rite two years early.

Put yourself out there, I tell myself. Be a leader. Not a follower.

"You know, I actually need help with something, too. So maybe if I do your project with you—"

Eddie catches on fast. She nods and basically finishes my

sentence for me. "I can help you with something, too! Anything. What do you need?"

I think about what Ron B. Tully said. "I need help getting my own email."

"You don't have email?"

I shake my head. "I don't really know a lot about that stuff. Like, technology and computers, I mean."

"Interesting. Then, yeah, of course, I can help you set one up. That's easy-peasy."

I steal a glance at her. She isn't looking at me the way Havana did in the computer lab. "You don't think I'm . . . Amish?"

She laughs. "I mean, unless you're part of a religious group from rural Pennsylvania, then no."

"No," I say. "Is that what Amish is? I'm not that."

"Don't worry, even if you were, I'd get it," she says. "The way I've grown up isn't exactly normal, either. Do you need anything else beyond email? Because that should only take a couple of minutes to do."

I think about the paycheck Mom gets every week from the motel. "Yeah. I need help finding a job."

"Hmm. That might be tougher."

"Oh!" I say. "Do your parents need help? Downstairs?"

"My parents need all the help they can get," she mutters. "But not in the shop. They're only the managers. The owner lives in San Francisco, and he's the one who makes all the hiring decisions. Don't worry," she adds when she sees my face fall. "We'll think of something."

We decide to work on the science project first and set up my email after.

Eddie explains what the scientific method is once she realizes I've never heard of it. But she isn't mean about it. I write it all down in the notebook I brought with me as quickly as my hand can fly over the page.

According to Eddie, the scientific method happens in a series of steps. Those are:

(1) Pose a question.

This one's easy, since we already have that. Our question is, "Does the Spirit of the Sea exist?"

(2) Form a hypothesis.

Eddie says a hypothesis is a kind of opinion. "But it's based on facts," she tells me. "For instance, there's never been clear evidence that ghosts exist. So my prediction—and our hypothesis—is that the Spirit of the Sea isn't real."

(3) Test the prediction with experiments.

"Our main experiment," Eddie says, "will be data collection and observation. The data collection part will be talking to locals about it. We should each find people to talk to over the next week, and then compare stories. The more incon- sistencies, the better. And for the observation part, if we can observe the ghostly figure of the Spirit of the Sea, maybe we can find a way to show someone's faking it. Or that it's an il- lusion, created by fog and moonlight or something. See what I mean?" I don't exactly, but I write it all down.

(4) Analyze the data we've collected from our experiments and draw a conclusion.
(5) Share our results with Mr. Carlson and the rest of the class.

"Based on my research so far, most reported sightings occur on dark, foggy nights."

"Oh, yeah," I say, remembering what Mom read to me on the ocean path. "It says so on the metal plaque. By the ocean."

"Exactly." Eddie points to a calendar hanging on her wall. "We can't always plan for fog, but the darkest nights are moonless, right? And the next moonless night is two weeks from now. We can collect our first bit of observation data then." She sits back. "Honestly, if we succeed, I bet we'll make the newspaper. Everyone in this town is obsessed with this stupid con."

By the time Eddie's done explaining and I'm done writ- ing, my fingers are cramping and my stomach has started to grumble. Loudly.

"Sorry." I press my hand against my stomach. "I didn't eat lunch."

"Want to grab a snack?" Eddie asks. "I could eat something, too."

I think about Babs, and how she said she'd give me free food whenever I want. Maybe that offer would extend to Eddie, too. I haven't seen Babs since we went on the tour of school last week, and Mom said all that stuff about how I should pay, so I'm not sure if her offer still stands.

"Want to go to Birdie's? My mom and her are . . ." I trail off, not sure how to describe it. We aren't family or in community together. And they don't seem like friends, especially not after how annoyed Mom got with Babs during the school tour. So I say, "They know each other from a long time ago."

"Sure. I love Birdie's. That's so cool you know Babs. From what I can tell, she's more like the mayor of Driftaway Beach than the actual mayor." Eddie grabs her laptop and slips it into a bag. "I'll bring this with me. I'm pretty sure Birdie's has Wi-Fi, so we can set up your email when we get there."

After calling Mom and making sure it's okay—I have to text her when we get there, and she tells me she'll be there to pick me up in forty-five minutes exactly—Eddie and I go to say bye to her dad.

He only waves and tells us to have fun. He doesn't make Eddie promise to text every ten seconds to check in. His face doesn't crumple with worry at the idea of us leaving the house.

I should tell Mom she can relax a little bit.

17

On our walk to Birdie's, the sun is setting. At the Ranch, it felt more that the light was seeping out of the sky. The trees were all around us. It felt safe, but they also kept out the sky. Here it's like . . . it's like the world is going through a transformation. Every sunset is different. Sometimes it's nothing but foggy grayness that turns to darkness, whereas now the sky is bright pink. And then a minute later, it's orange. The block we're walking down is soaked in this golden light that makes even the pavement look beautiful.

As we walk, Eddie tells me more about some of the places she's lived. Eventually, she asks, "So it's just you and your mom, huh? You must be close."

It's funny to think about, but there was a time when Mom was my everything. Eddie's question brings a slice of a memory back. I'm six, and it's Sunday morning. We called them lazy days. We'd get muffins or donuts and eat them in bed and watch as much TV as I wanted, and we could stay in our pajamas all day. Some lazy days felt like we were the only two people in the world. Like no one else mattered except me and Mom.

But being that close wasn't good on the Ranch. There can only be one leader in a strong community, one north star, or else people get confused. Which meant that after we moved to the Ranch, Mom couldn't be my everything anymore.

"We used to be," I finally say. "But it's different now."

Even though it's supposed to close in the next hour, Birdie's is busy when we get there. As soon as Babs sees us, her whole face lights up.

"Give me two seconds," she says to us as she whisks by with a huge green teapot and six matching teacups balanced on a tray. "I always save a table for my VIPs."

"Wow! It's so cool to be a VIP," Eddie says to me. "I've never been a VIP anywhere."

Another word I don't know to add to my ever-growing list. But "VIP" seems like it's a good thing, so I don't ask what it means.

Soon Babs leads us to a spot by one of the front windows and puts down two large menus on the table. "Ignore the prices, girls. Get anything you want. It's on the house."

Eddie grins at me.

"Do you have any more of those croissants?" I ask hopefully once we've taken our seats.

"Not right now, I'm afraid. I usually sell out of them by eleven. But I have something better. How do you feel about petits fours?"

I'm about to tell her—to admit for what feels like the ten millionth time—that I don't know what that is, when Eddie asks, "What's a petit four?"

And I could hug her.

"Oh, you're in for a treat. Your pastry education is about to begin. Tea as well, girls?"

"Chocolate truffle for me, please," Eddie says.

"Great choice." Babs jots it down on her notepad. "Fern? How about you?"

I look at the menu. There are so many kinds of teas on this list—at least fifty. There's chamomile, but there are also flavors like chestnut, forest berries and rose hips, peppermint mocha, white peach, spiced citrus, black strawberry. . . .

I'm about to say chamomile tea, because that's what we drink at the Ranch, but when I open my mouth, that's not what comes out.

"Can I try the frozen mango tea, please?" I ask.

Mango used to be my favorite fruit. When we lived in Brooklyn, there was a fruit stand near our old apartment we'd get mangoes from. Sometimes the man we bought them from would carve one up for me in the shape of a flower and put it on a wooden stick, so I could eat it as I walked. If the mango was ripe, its yellow juice would run down my wrists and make my hands sticky.

But you can't really grow mangoes in New York State, and since we mainly eat what we grow on the Ranch, I haven't had a mango in a long time.

Babs jots down my order. "It comes blended with evaporated milk. That okay, sweets?"

I bite my lip. I should say no and get the chamomile. It's like there's a war going on inside my head. Then again, we made milk powder on the Ranch from our goats' milk, so that has to be what "evaporated milk" is, right? And mango is just fruit. The sugar in mango is natural. So I nod, but immediately my stomach starts to hurt a little, like my body understands I'm making the wrong decision. I almost call Babs back to change my order, but she's already out of earshot.

Across the table, Eddie takes out her computer. Her fingers fly over the keys. "Email time."

She shows me what to type to get to the place—to the website—where my email will be. She explains that I have to create an account, starting with a username and password.

"What do you want your username to be?" she asks me.

"I don't know," I tell her. "What do you think?"

"You could do something fun, if you wanted." She scrunches up her face, thinking. "It can sort of be like . . . your thing. Something you're interested in or a hobby. Mine's 'soccergirl0505' because my birthday's May fifth, and I love watching soccer with my mom. So . . . what do you want yours to be?"

I try to come up with something. I'm good at knitting, but I don't love it. I like ferns, obviously, and growing food, and making sure I live a life that doesn't negatively impact the earth. I used to like to dance, to do ballet, like Mom said, but I honestly don't even know if I like that anymore.

"I don't know," I finally say. "I'm sorry."

"You can just make it your name, too," Eddie offers.

"Okay," I say, relieved. "Let's do that."

"Do you want any social media accounts?" she asks. "I could get you set up for those, too."

"No." I don't know much about what you actually do with social media, but I do know that it's bad. Then, repeating something Dr. Ben says all the time, I add, "That stuff is like anesthesia for your brain."

"I'm probably on TikTok too much," Eddie admits. Then she grins. "But it's so fun."

We get my email set up, and Eddie's showing me how to send an email, and how to check for new emails, when Babs comes back to our table.

She puts a small teapot in the shape of a chicken in front of Eddie, plus a teacup with a feather design. I don't have a teapot—mine comes in a tall frosted glass, and the drink is orange and foamy.

Petits fours, as it turns out, aren't made from just flour and butter, like croissants. They're colorful little cakes. They're square and so small at least two or three could fit in the palm of my hand. They look like they might have artificial dyes in them.

"These are lemon cream." Babs points at the yellow ones. "And the pink ones are raspberry. Sorry it took me a minute to get together. It's a busy one today. Enjoy!"

"It *is* busy in here, isn't it?" Eddie sits up straighter and then waves her hand in the air. "Babs! Hey, Babs! Can you come back for a second?"

A few of the tables glance over at us. I shrink down in my seat.

Babs comes back. "Yes? Everything okay?"

"Sorry to bother you. But do you think you could give Fern a job? She's in the market for one."

I want to sink deeper into my chair. No—I want to sink into nothingness. I'm sure my face is the color of a Brandywine tomato.

"That so? As much as I'd love to, I can't hire anyone younger than sixteen." She smiles at me. "But don't worry. Your food here will always be free."

I'm embarrassed Eddie asked her like that, but I'm also disappointed at her answer. Truth is, Babs was probably my best shot at getting a job. "It's fine. Forget it."

Babs hesitates for a second, like she's about to say something else, but then another table calls for her. "I'll be back to check on you in a bit. Enjoy."

"It was worth a shot," Eddie says. "I'll keep thinking. For now, let's eat."

I take a small sip of my frozen mango tea. It's delicious, one of the best things I've ever tasted—but it's sweet. Way too sweet for it to be all from the mango.

"Try one of the cakes," Eddie says, her mouth full. "I mean, the petits fours. The lemon ones are *so* good."

I hesitate. It would probably be rude if I didn't at least *try* one, right? Babs did give them to us for free, after all. And wasting food is the worst thing you can do.

I choose a lemon one and take a bite. This is sweet, too. This icing, all this sugar . . . My stomach churns. Not because the food is bad—it's so good. It's because *I'm* bad.

I'm bad, I'm bad, I'm bad. I'm weak.

I lean over and spit the half-eaten cake onto my plate.

Eddie stops midchew and stares at me. "Are you okay?"

"Yes I— Sorry." My cheeks flush, and I crumple up my napkin to cover the half-chewed bite. "I didn't like it. You can have the rest."

I take a shaky sip of my ice water. It's so easy to fall off the path. I have to be better. Stronger.

Eddie happily drags the plate of cakes toward her side of the table, eating the last of the petits fours in a few big bites. She closes her eyes. "*So* good." When she opens them, she says, "So, this place you're from. What was it like? Other than not having technology."

"It's . . . it's the best place I've ever lived." I'm not sure what else to say. Because how do I explain the early-morning birdsong, the patter of rain against the roof, the way all of us spend our days together, working toward the same goals? With the knowledge that even if the future gets scary, we'll be safe and okay and able to take care of ourselves, of each other? "It's hard to explain."

Eddie nods sympathetically. "You miss it, huh? I understand. Moving sucks."

"We didn't *move* here," I say. "We're sort of . . . visiting. We're going back."

"Oh, I didn't realize." She hesitates. "But . . . are you sure? I used to think that about Edinburgh. That's where I was born. I always thought we'd move back." She shrugs. "But it never happened."

"Yes, I'm *sure*."

"Okay, sorry. I really do understand," Eddie says. "How you feel, I mean. It's hard to move. It's especially hard to move again and again and again."

We sit in silence for a minute, and then Eddie's phone pings. When she pulls it out of her bag to check it, she groans. "It's my mom. The store got a shipment, and she needs my help unpacking."

She stands up and slips her laptop back into its puffy case. Once she's all packed up and about to leave, she stops. "I didn't mean to offend you, by the way. Sorry if I did."

"It's okay," I say.

I watch her go. She was being so nice to me, but I feel . . . angry. Not at her, just in general. At myself, maybe.

18

Once Eddie's gone, I check my phone to see where
Mom is.

Running 15 minutes late! says her text. *Let's see if you
recognize me. ;)*

I reread it a few times. I have no idea what she means.
Let's see if you recognize me?

"Not a fan of the mango tea? Want to try something else?"

It's Babs. She's standing next to the table, looking at my
unfinished drink with concern.

"No. I mean, yes, I was a fan. I just— My stomach hurts."

"A cup of ginger or peppermint tea might help," she offers. "I have both kinds."

"No, it's okay."

"If you're sure." She tucks her little pad into the pocket
of her lacy apron. "Also, I had an idea. As per your friend's
question."

I glance up at her. "About the job?"

"That's right. Come with me and I'll show you."

I stand up to join her.

"Johnno," Babs calls, to a man in a black shirt who's clearing off a just-vacated table. "You got the floor? I need five."

"No prob, boss," the man says back.

I follow Babs through the kitchen, outside past where the garbage bins are kept, and around the corner to a narrow alleyway between Birdie's and the store next door. Babs goes to a door and unlocks it.

We go up a rickety set of stairs and enter a wide room, roughly the same shape and size as the tea shop below.

Babs motions around. "Welcome to your potential job."

I'm pretty sure it's an apartment, but all I can see are boxes and white sheets draped over furniture. A skylight in the ceiling turns the light the color of dirty dishwater. It—and everything else here—looks like it could use a deep cleaning. "Does someone . . . live here?"

Babs laughs. "No. At least, not for a long time. We had a tenant when we first bought the building, but they moved out years ago. Birdie and I had big plans of expanding the shop. We were going to make this floor all about high tea, you know—make it real nice, real fancy. But after she died, I didn't have the energy. Or the desire." She flips up the edge of a wilted cardboard box stacked on a table next to her, and peeks inside. "So, it's become my storage area. But I've been thinking, maybe it's time to dust off the dream and make it a reality. No better time than the present, right?"

I look around again. I see a couple of broken teapots, a table from the tea shop, with one of its legs lying on the floor next to it, and boxes of old books and magazines.

"So, what do you want me to do?"

"Right. Of course. The shop's well staffed, and like I said, I can't officially hire anyone under sixteen. But what I really need help with is clearing this place out. Organizing it. Anything you think can be salvaged or sold, keep it in here. And anything that needs to go to the dump, pile in that room over there." She points to a doorway. "Once you're finished, I can come and take everything away, and we can try to sell what's left. Have a tag sale, maybe. Make an event out of it."

I don't know what a tag sale is, but that doesn't matter right now. "And you'll . . . pay me for that? For organizing and cleaning up?"

"I was thinking ten dollars an hour. That sound fair?"

I do the math in my head. Ten goes into three hundred thirty times. So to get what I need, I'll have to do thirty hours of work. With thirty hours of work, I'll have enough money to find Dr. Ben. To write to him and get him to bring us home.

"That sounds great," I say.

"I'm so glad. It's going to make it so much easier for me." She glances around, her eyes landing on a long plastic paddle leaning against the wall. "Lots of this stuff was Birdie's. It's difficult for me to go through any of it."

"I'm sorry," I tell her. "And I'm sorry she died."

"Me too, sweets." Babs is still looking at the paddle, but she seems far away. She stays like that for a long moment.

Then she turns to me with a smile, and I can tell by her eyes she's here again, here in the room. "She would have *loved* to meet you. Birdie and your grandma are probably drinking margaritas in heaven, looking down and talking about what a fine kid you are."

It's a weird mental image. Dr. Ben says heaven isn't real, but I kind of like the idea of it. I fiddle with the edge of my sweater. I shouldn't care. And I don't, I tell myself. I'm just curious. "Why haven't you been back to see us? Since last week?"

Babs sits down on a creaky wooden chair. Part of me worries it's going to buckle underneath her—not because of her, but because one of the chair legs looks like it could use a good tightening. Ash taught all the fifteen-and-unders basic carpentry, and I can tell when something needs attention.

"Your mom asked for some space," Babs says. "While you two get settled. She's always wanted to do things herself, you know that? Her whole life. Gracie—your grandma—never had to ask her to do anything when she was a kid. Push in her chair, do the dishes, clean her room. She just *did* it."

That sounds like Mom. She's always been independent. Dr. Ben once said something about how resourceful she is, and that we should all strive to do our work like her. Hearing him say that was probably the moment I felt proudest to be her daughter.

Babs goes on. "But it's not all her. Sometimes I also . . . push. I push too hard, too fast, too often. I try to take the reins. So I'm trying to give her room to breathe. To settle. I don't want to lose her again. Or you."

I shift guiltily and don't say anything. If Babs knew *why* I wanted this job—to leave Driftaway Beach—then she probably wouldn't have offered it to me.

"Anyway! Suffice to say I'll be happy to have you around more, and to start getting this place cleared out. Birdie's high-tea expansion, coming right up!" She checks her watch and stands. "Poor Johnny's probably drowning. I should get back down."

"Yeah, me too," I say, checking my phone. I have a new text from Mom, saying that she's outside. "My mom's here."

Babs and I go down together, and I wait as she locks the door to the second floor.

"Can I start tomorrow?" I ask. "After school?"

"Sure. I love the enthusiasm." Babs wiggles a key off her key chain and hands it to me. "Here's the spare. The toilet doesn't work up there, so if you need to go, come down and use the shop's. And check in with me when you get here tomorrow." Babs points down the alley, the opposite way we came in. "If you go that way, it will spit you out on the sidewalk. Say hi to your mom for me."

"I will. And thanks." I lift the key. "For the job."

Babs winks. "See you tomorrow, honey."

I go the way Babs pointed, and it takes me to the sidewalk by the front of the shop.

Mom's there, waiting, exactly like she said she'd be.

Except I have to do a double take, because it's not Mom. At least it's not the Mom who walked me home from school today.

164

19

She looks *totally* different.

"Your hair," I choke out. "What did you do?"

Her long brown hair is now cut short, up to her ears, and she's got bangs, too, short little bangs that hit halfway on her forehead. But the biggest change of all is the color— her hair isn't brown anymore. It's black. So black it's almost purple.

She touches it self-consciously. "I thought I could use a change. I guess I'm trying to find my way back to myself. And before you start, I didn't use chemicals. I used an all-natural dye, so don't worry."

She seems to be waiting for me to say something else about it, but I don't. We start the walk back to the motel together. Thankfully, it's dark out, but even so, I can barely look at her.

"Babs gave me a job," I tell her stiffly. "Organizing the second floor of Birdie's. There's a ton of stuff up there. She wants to expand the shop."

Mom stops walking and stares at me. "She gave you a *job*? Was that her idea?"

"No. It was mine."

"Why do you want a job?"

"You have one. Why can't I?"

Mom thinks about it for a moment. "Well, I suppose that's fair. But I don't want you spending all your time there. No more than an hour a day, okay?"

"What?" I say. "Why?"

I was planning to do at least two or three hours a day. One hour a day means it'll take me *thirty* days to make enough money.

"I don't want it to interfere with your schoolwork. And we have a lot of catching up to do. Together."

"What about the days I don't have school? Can I do more then?"

"I want you to use the days you don't have school as days *off*. Not working. In fact, I don't want you working every school day. So it's an hour a day, four days a week, or nothing."

Four days a week! I almost shout. That means . . . that'll take me almost two months!

But she means it, I can tell. And I have to admit it, she's right about the catching-up part. I still have all my subjects to do for homework today, except for science. Or *we* do, because there's no way I'll be able to do it on my own. Plus, if I can get the address in two months, I'll still have enough time to get us home before the spring equinox. It's not ideal, but it's enough.

"Fine. One hour a day, four days a week."

We start to walk again. I keep stealing glances at her hair, and she notices.

She tugs lightly on a newly black strand. "Come on. It can't be *that* bad."

I can tell how much she wants me to like it.

And if I'm being one hundred percent honest, the strange thing is that I do. Somehow it fits her face better, and it makes her green eyes pop. She looks beautiful.

But I know Dr. Ben isn't going to like it. He says it's important to embrace the natural way our bodies were meant to exist in the world, which means no piercings, no dye, no tattoos, no pills or medicine.

"Honestly? It makes you look kind of . . . fake."

"Ouch" is all Mom says back.

I shrug. "You asked."

We walk the rest of the way in silence. I feel bad for not being nice, but I feel worse that she's changing so quickly into someone I barely recognize, while I'm remaining true to myself. To our values.

I hope the dye fades before it's time to go home.

My second day at school goes pretty much the same as my first one.

I'm confused through most of my classes and have trouble understanding what the teachers are talking about. I stay quiet, even when I want to ask a question, because I want to avoid calling attention to myself. Which is also why I don't use any of my herbal health salve in the morning. Before school, I even picked up one of the new tops Mom got me, a light blue, feathery-soft shirt, and held it against my chest. But I still can't bring myself to wear anything except my sweater from the Ranch.

As a compromise, I put on a pair of jeans from the bag. They're a little tighter and stiffer than my work pants. It's going to be hard to get used to them.

It's not until it's time for Mr. Carlson's class that I feel like I can let my guard down. I get there early again, and this time Mr. Carlson is already there. Today he's wearing a button-down shirt with big flowers on it, and it's bright pink.

He smiles when he sees me. "What up, Fern?"

"Hi, Mr. Carlson. I wanted to ask you . . . Eddie told me yesterday you offer extra credit?"

Mr. Carlson's eyes light up. "Yes! My trash-collecting program. Come check this out."

He walks me over to a poster hanging by the door. At the top it says, "Mr. Carlson's Class Cleans Up." Below that, there's a chart with a column of names. "I keep track of how much trash everyone collects. Like Eddie said, it's extra credit, so it's totally optional. But if you're interested, I can add your name to the list."

I nod my head hard. "I am. I'm definitely interested."

"That's great." He goes over to a closet and takes out a few things from inside. He shows me a long metal pole with a grabby claw-thing on the end, a strange little object that looks like a compass, and a handful of plastic bags.

"This is what I call the 'clean-up kit.' I ordered all this stuff in bulk, so there's enough for everyone. This is a trash picker," he says, pointing at the long metal pole. He shows me how to clamp the handle so the end of it opens. "The plastic bags are all donated by students, for the actual garbage collection. And this is a scale." He points at the compass-thingy. "I measure extra-credit points and graph the bar chart by weight. Hang the bag of litter or bottles or whatever you collect on this scale, and it'll tell you how much you got. It's honor code, so just mark down the weight and dispose of the litter appropriately. I'll keep all this up front for you until it's time to leave for the day so you don't have to lug it around. Cool?"

"Cool," I agree. I think about all the litter I've seen, strewn on the sidewalks around town.

I can't wait to get started.

Over the next week, I settle into a routine.

It feels good to have a clear-cut schedule again. At the Ranch, the days and seasons are mapped out—predictable. I didn't realize how adrift I'd felt by not having a schedule to build my days around.

On the way to school I pick up trash. It takes me about twice as long to walk there now, so I leave early to give myself time to scour the sidewalks as thoroughly as possible. Mom walked with me the first time, but it was making her late for work, so she said I can go alone if I stay out of the street. I've noticed that the same group of motorcycle riders comes to have coffee in the parking lot a few times a week, and they've started waving and saying good morning to me. They're intimidating but friendly.

The school is inland, away from the ocean, but if I have extra time, I take the oceanside path and then circle back. Every day the ocean looks and behaves a little differently. Some days it's angry, smashing itself against the cliffside below the fence so much that it rises high, drenching the path with water. Other days it's calm and steady, so smooth it's almost a reflection of the sky. Even though it's out of my way, I like to make sure this path stays as clean as possible, so none of the garbage washes out to sea.

So far I've collected over eleven pounds of litter. Cigarette butts, crushed soda cans, scraps of plastic bags, candy bar wrappers, a smushed box of half-eaten French fries.

Our school has three bins for waste—one for compost, one for recycling, and one for landfill trash—so when I throw it away, I separate it. This last step usually makes me late for my first class, but it's worth it to know that every bit of litter I gather won't blow into the ocean, and that not all of it will go into the landfill.

During the school day, I do my best to stay quiet and as invisible as possible in all my classes, except for science. Everything I learn in Mr. Carlson's class feels like information that might be useful back home.

And then, four days a week, I spend exactly one hour on

the second floor of Birdie's after school. Right now, I'm only sorting. There isn't as much stuff as I thought, but I hate thinking any of it will be thrown away. I've got a pile for books and boxes of magazines, a place for plates and chipped teapots and other things from the tea shop, and a whole area for furniture that needs to be fixed. There are some things that really are beyond repair—a rusted pot with a splintered handle, a box of books so damaged by water they're mildewed and hard to read. I put the ruined things in the small room Babs showed me, to be thrown away. And then there are some things—an orange life vest, that one long paddle, a pair of plastic goggles, a lantern with cracked glass—I don't know how to categorize.

After I leave the tea shop, Mom and I do homework together.

Usually it takes us all evening, because Mom struggles with some of the work, too. She was able to check out a laptop from the public library for three weeks. I'm not thrilled to have it in our room, and if I'd known you could just borrow a computer for free like that, I probably wouldn't have agreed to go to school at all. But I do have to admit it's useful to have around, especially for homework (and for checking my new email, to see if Ron B. Tully has sent me anything). Science is my favorite subject—we're studying bacteria right now—and I also don't mind my spelling homework, either. At least with spelling, the correct answers are always right there on the page.

We take Friday off since we have all weekend to do my homework, so Mom decides to head to the library as soon as her shift is over.

"Why have you been going to the library so often?" I ask her.

"I like to study there. It's quiet and peaceful. You should come with me. You'd like it."

"Study for what?"

She sits on her bed as she pulls her shoes on. "I never finished my last year of high school, so I'm trying to pass a test called the GED. And then if I can pass that, I could maybe even try for a college degree. But I'm starting small."

All of this is news to me. Everything she just said is stuff that sounds like it would take a really long time. "What do you need a college degree for?"

"I was thinking. . . ." Mom pauses. "I'd like to study botany. Which is basically a fancy way of saying plant science." She explains it a little bit more, saying how she could learn about chemistry and fungus and how plants interact with their environment on the cellular level. As she talks, her eyes have this bright light to them, and I feel confused. Botany sounds amazing. Botany sounds like the kind of thing that's in perfect harmony with what we do on the Ranch. Could she study botany at college and live at the Ranch at the same time? Is there even a college nearby? Would it be enough to get some books on botany to add to the Ranch's library?

"Anyway," Mom continues, "that's a long way off. GED first. Do you want to come with me this time? You could choose some books, just for fun."

"No, thanks." I lift up *Firestride*, the book Alex lent me. "I have this."

"Oh! That's great. Is it any good?"

I shrug. I've been putting off starting it. But I know I should at least try, because otherwise Alex will suspect I wasn't telling the truth about why I broke into the office. I've been avoiding him so he doesn't ask how I'm liking it, but I can't avoid him forever.

"I'll pick up some dinner on the way back." Mom pats the door. "Lock up after I leave, okay? All three locks."

"I know," I groan. "You say that every time."

As soon as she leaves and I've locked the door, I lean back against my headboard and open the first page of the book.

I read *Firestride* all night.

I read through dinner, and I read until Mom tells me to turn off the light so we can both go to sleep.

I end up finishing the book—the whole book, despite how long it is—on Saturday night. When I'm done, I close my eyes and hug it to my chest.

In this story, the planet where the dragon-people live is precious. They're trying to keep outsiders from drilling into the heart of their earth, because the fiery magma at its center has special, magical properties. They're trying to live in a way that keeps their earth alive.

I have trouble falling asleep, because I can't stop thinking about Mom wanting to study botany, or why this book couldn't be on the shelves of the Ranch's library. Even though it's set on another planet, it left me wanting to protect my planet even more. It also makes me want to be brave, like the characters. It makes me want to fight even harder for what's right.

And no matter how I try to think about it, I can't figure out what about this book is bad or misguided.

The next morning I wake to a hand on my shoulder.

Mom's still in her pajamas, but she's got a flat white box in her hands. "Psst. Wake up, sleepyhead."

I sit up on my elbows. "Mom? What time is it?"

"It's eight. You slept in." She wiggles the box at me. "I got donuts. It's cold and rainy out, so I thought . . . maybe we can have a lazy day."

Donuts. Sugary, artificially dyed donuts. First her hair, and now this?

"I don't want to eat those. And I don't want to have a lazy day."

"I just thought— It used to be our thing."

"No. I don't want to."

"Why not?" Mom asks.

I try to collect my thoughts, to figure out how to explain why this feels so wrong. It's like she's choosing to remember only the good stuff from our lives before the Ranch. Like she's suddenly trying to sell me on the idea that our lives before were great and our lives at the Ranch were bad. "We didn't live a perfect life before the Ranch. We barely even lived an okay life. So why are you trying to make it like it used to be?"

She stands there for a minute, like the air's been sucked out of her. "Okay. Fine. No donuts. I'll go see if Alex or Dina want these." Then at the door, she pauses, her hand on the knob. "You know, just because it wasn't a perfect life doesn't mean there weren't perfect moments."

As soon as the door closes, I almost call her back. But I don't, because we aren't that mom and daughter anymore. If we want to stay meaningful and equal members of the Ranch's community, we can't be. And if that isn't what *she* wanted at some point, too, then why would she have ever taken me to live there in the first place?

On Monday I go to the motel office before school. I wait by the brochures as Alex checks out two guests, and then as soon as they leave, I go over to him.

"I *loved* it," I tell him, sliding the book across the desk.

His whole face breaks open in a huge smile, and he leans forward, putting out a palm for a high five. I slap it.

"I can't tell you how happy it makes me to have another *Firestride* fan around here. My dad doesn't understand why I love these books so much. The author is so talented." His cheeks go a little pink. "I'm actually working on a story that's, like, deeply inspired by her work."

The words come back to me: *She thrust her sword into the loamy earth.*

Suddenly, I realize those papers I saw on the desk when I broke in to use the computer—those were pages of a book.

His book. The only other person I've ever known who's written a book is Dr. Ben.

"You're writing a book? Can I read it?"

His blush deepens. "I mean . . . it's not finished. I need to work on it more before it's ready for outside readers. Well, no—a lot more." He laughs and rubs his face with his hands. "Honestly, it's pretty terrible."

"If it's anything like *Firestride,* I'd love to read it."

"Okay. Then, yeah. Cool. But in the meantime, here." He scribbles on a piece of paper and passes it to me. "These are her other books. They're all incredible, but nothing quite matches up to *Firestride.* In my opinion."

I tuck the note in my pocket. "Thanks."

I turn to leave, but he says, "Hey, also . . . Speaking of my dad, he got back from Manila yesterday. He wanted to know if you and your mom wanted to come over for dinner tonight. He's resting now, but said he'd love to meet you both."

Mom and I have been cooking almost every meal on our hot plate in the motel room. Mostly we've been eating simply—soups, grains, boiled eggs, and vegetables, that sort of thing. I've had afternoon snacks at Birdie's a few times, but the idea of eating a real meal outside of our motel room sounds pretty nice. "Sure. I'll ask my mom."

"Cool."

Then he makes the hand signal they use in *Firestride,* the one that means you're a part of the secret resistance group— that you're a protector of the planet.

With a smile I make the sign back to him.

20

It's lunchtime, but I'm in the computer lab.

Every school day I come in to look up words. "Amish." "Bigfoot." "VIP." "Tag sale." "Marzipan." I like looking things up here instead of on the laptop Mom borrowed from the library, because this way I don't have to explain myself to her if she sees what I'm searching. Here I have privacy. Sometimes I also look up descriptive words I haven't heard used on the Ranch. Words like "irrelevant." "Bewildered." "Exonerated."

But today I'm not looking up anything. I'm emailing Ron B. Tully at Foglamp Investigators, because I remembered something while I was collecting litter on my way to school earlier.

The Econo Lodge.

The name popped up out of nowhere, like my brain was annoyed I hadn't remembered it yet. It's the name of the motel we stayed at that terrible first night after leaving the Ranch. We drove there in one day. That must be helpful information, right?

After sending the email in a moment of excitement, I get a response five minutes later. It says,

OK, thx. How long had you been driving for? RBT

I think about it. I don't know how long we were in the taxi, since I was asleep for most of it. But we drove from the used-car lot basically from sunup to sundown. So, at least ten hours, I write, if not more.

He pings me back right away.

OK. It doesn't help all that much, because the search radius is still big. But I'll add it to the file. Will begin more research once I get payment. RBT

I sink back in my chair. I've only done five hours of my thirty. I still have $250 to make before he even begins.

"Hey. I was looking for you at lunch."

It's Eddie. I jolt up, scrambling to close my email.

She slides into the chair next to mine. "So, as of this morning, I'm up to seven interviews about the Spirit of the Sea. I discovered some conflicting beliefs, which is great, because conflict makes for great data. For us, at least. I was hoping to compare my interviews against yours."

She looks at me hopefully. Shoot. I totally forgot.

"Oh. I—I haven't done them yet. I've been busy. Working. But my mom and I are having dinner with two locals tonight, and I can interview them over dinner."

Eddie sighs. "I guess that's okay. I just don't want us to fall behind on the project."

"We aren't behind," I tell her. "Some groups haven't even selected their topics yet. If anything, we're ahead." But this only makes her frown, so I add, "I promise I'll do the interviews tonight."

"Okay. Thank you. But hold on. You said 'working.' Did you find a job?"

"Yeah. With Babs."

"She changed her mind? That's great!"

"Kind of." I explain to her about the second floor full of stuff, about how Babs wants to expand the tea shop, and about some of the furniture I'm hoping to fix.

"Can I come see?" Eddie asks.

I'm a little surprised she wants to. "Sure. I'm there four days a week. Why don't you come tomorrow, and we can go over the Spirit of the Sea stuff then?"

"Great. I'll be there." Eddie pauses. "Do you think Babs might give us more free food?"

I smile. "I don't see why not."

Today, social studies is my last class.

I was able to get one of the seats close to the window. Outside, the sky is blue and bright sunshine drenches the parking lot, which is lined with tall, skinny palm trees. They look like they'd sooner belong on the *Firestride* planet than they would back home. They sway slightly in the breeze, and

I can almost feel the tickle of it on my face. I'd much rather be out there than in here.

". . . Fern?"

Ms. Fong-Hines, my social studies teacher, is looking at me expectantly. So are some of the other students.

"Um, yes?"

"I asked what you thought about that?"

My face burns. I didn't hear what they were talking about. Even if I had, I probably wouldn't have had anything useful to say. "I'm sorry. I don't know."

Ms. Fong-Hines presses her lips together. "I'd like to see more participation from you, Fern. You haven't asked a single question since you've been here."

The disapproving way she's looking at me sets off alarm bells.

Because what if she mentions something to Ms. Diaz? What if she talks to one of my other teachers, and they realize I don't say anything in any of my classes? Is that enough of a red flag to get Mom in trouble?

I don't look out the window for the rest of class. I listen hard, trying to figure out when would be a good time for me to raise my hand and ask a question or give an answer.

Right now we're talking about a group of men called the Founding Fathers. There are a lot of names, so I pick one at random. I raise my hand.

Ms. Fong-Hines immediately points at me. "Yes, Fern?"

"Who's George Washington?" I ask.

The entire class bursts out laughing, and Ms. Fong-Hines frowns. Immediately, it's obvious I've asked the wrong thing.

My chest feels tight. I don't know what else to do, so I smile a big, goofy grin and add, "Just kidding!"

Ms. Fong-Hines's frown grows deeper. "I like my students to take my class seriously, Fern. Please see me after the bell rings."

It takes a while for the rest of the class to settle down after that.

My talk with Ms. Fong-Hines is uncomfortable. She tells me about the standards of behavior she expects. I stand there and nod and say I'm sorry, because I know I can't tell her the truth. That I wasn't joking with my question. That I really don't know.

Finally, after a warning, she lets me go.

When I leave her classroom, three of the other students are there, clustered together. One of them is Havana. There's a boy with a buzz cut and light brown skin—I think his name is Robbie—and another white girl who has shiny stuff on her lips and always sits next to Havana.

As soon as I see them, I can tell they've been waiting for me.

The girl with shiny lips nudges Havana. "Ask her."

Havana takes a small step forward and tilts her head at me. "So, who is George Washington, Fern?"

"One of the Founding Fathers," I say, repeating what I heard in class. I rub my palms against my jeans.

"Yeah, but what else?" Robbie asks.

I stand there and don't say anything. I wrap my arms around myself.

Havana turns to the other two. "Told you she wouldn't know."

"Oh my God," the girl with shiny lips says. "You were right. I can't believe it. You really don't know who George Washington is?"

Again I say nothing.

"Where are you even from?" Robbie asks.

I swallow hard. "I'm not Amish, you know. I've never even been to Pennsylvania."

Havana laughs. "You don't know George Washington was the first president of the United States. I've known that since I was, like, three. You might not be Amish, but you are kind of ignorant. I don't say that to be mean. I just want to help you. The school offers tutoring, you know."

When I don't say anything to that, either, she turns to the other two. "Whatever. Come on. Let's go."

I wait right where I am in the hallway until they've disappeared.

Mom comes to walk with me after my work hour at Babs's.

"You didn't need to come," I tell her as I lock up. "I know my way back."

"I know. But I was finished with the rooms, and I like walking with you, so . . ." She shrugs. "You're stuck with me. How was your day?"

"Why do you care?" I mutter.

"Hey." She stops to face me. "Don't talk to me like that. You haven't said one nice thing to me in days. I was asking you a simple question."

I throw my arms out. "I had a terrible day, okay? And the reason I had a terrible day is because you forced me to come to this place, to this school, and I don't want to be here!"

Mom takes a step toward me. "Then tell me about it. Maybe I can help. Please. Please, just talk to me."

I start toward the motel. "No. Forget it."

Now Mom is the one to throw her arms up. "Fine. Have it your way, then."

For the rest of the walk, we don't talk. Not until Mom raises an eyebrow and says, "You'd better be more polite at dinner with the Reyeses tonight than you're being with me. Or else there'll be consequences."

I don't respond. I just smolder.

Mr. Reyes looks like an older version of Alex, with graying black hair that's buzzed down short. His eyes are a warm brown, and he smiles a lot.

I try to focus on their answers when I ask them what they think about the Spirit of the Sea. They're more eager to talk about it than I thought they'd be.

"A lot of our motel guests actually come to visit Drift-away Beach because of her," Mr. Reyes tells me. "It's a big mystery. There's even a tour company that does midnight ghost tours. We have their brochure in the office, if you're interested."

"Maybe," I say. Honestly, I wasn't all that interested in the Spirit of the Sea when Eddie pitched the project idea to me, but knowing that lots of other people are fascinated changes things a little bit.

When I push, both Alex and his dad admit they don't think she's real, but they're happy the myth exists because it's good for tourism. (Alex guesses the glowing light on the bluff is caused by the moon reflecting off fog.) I also try to focus on the food, which is delicious and fresh. We eat chicken with steamed rice and vegetables in a light, salty sauce.

Despite all this, I can't stop thinking about the word Havana called me. "Ignorant." It was a vocabulary word we did in ELA last week, so I know exactly what it means. That she thinks I'm uneducated. Unintelligent. Stupid.

After dinner, Mom and I make the short walk back to our room from the Reyeses' apartment.

Mom bumps me with her shoulder. "Hey. Will you talk to me now? About what happened today? You seemed really upset earlier."

Lots of things cycle through my head. I feel stupid, and angry, and embarrassed. I want to know if anyone out here has called her ignorant. Or why she never thought to tell me some of the basics of American history. Or history in general. She could have taught me things while we were working in the greenhouse together, or while we hiked the perimeter of the Ranch, like we did on some nice days, for exercise.

Dr. Ben said we shouldn't focus on the past, but it always felt to me he meant more along the lines of our own personal pasts, not history itself. Wouldn't knowing about the good and bad things that have happened in history help us from making the same mistakes in the future?

So why wasn't I taught any of this? Is it Mom's fault? Or Dr. Ben's?

But it feels like asking those questions would either start a fight or a longer conversation I don't want to have. Instead, I ask, "Can I come to the library with you tomorrow? After we do my homework?"

She reaches out and puts her arms around me. Not only do I let her, but I hug her back.

After a minute, she pulls away and gives me a kiss on the top of my head. "There's nothing I would love more."

21

I forgot I invited Eddie up to the second floor of Birdie's until I hear the creak of the wooden steps the next afternoon.

"Hey! Fern?" she calls out. "You up there?"

"I'm here," I call back. I'm kneeling on the floor, re-assembling a chair I took apart. It's the wobbly one Babs sat on while she was showing me the space. When I told Babs I wanted to see if I could fix some of the furniture, she gave me two boxes from her garage.

"Birdie was the handywoman, not me," she said. "This belonged to her. I don't know what half of it's meant for."

Thankfully, it looks like Birdie knew what she was doing. There's a lot of good stuff in here. There's a bunch of well-cared-for hand tools, sandpaper, a bag of screws, nuts, and bolts, plus a lot more. It's more than enough for me to do some basic repairs.

When Eddie reaches the top of the steps, she stops and looks around. "I had no idea this was even up here."

I flip the chair so it's upright and sit on it to test its sturdiness. It's solid as can be. All I had to do was remove its legs and clean and tighten its screws and washers. And now it doesn't need to be thrown away.

"Babs has been using it as storage."

Eddie looks inside boxes, and touches things I put on the big table because I haven't categorized them yet. She stops at the cracked glass lantern. "Whoa. This is old-school. I think this is one of those old-fashioned lamps, the kind that uses kerosene."

"It is." We had some of them back on the Ranch, just in case our solar panels failed. They aren't very environmentally friendly, but in a pinch they provide a lot of light. I haven't decided if I can repair the glass yet, or if there's any way to salvage the parts. It's just one of the many random things Babs has stored up here.

Eddie sets the lantern back on the table and goes over to the long paddle leaning against the wall. "I didn't know Babs kayaked."

A kayak paddle. So *that's* what it is. I remember how Babs's eyes lingered on it the day she showed me the space. "I think it belonged to her wife, Birdie. She died."

"Oh." Eddie leans the paddle back against the wall. "How?"

"I don't know." I feel bad I haven't thought to ask.

"Sorry. That was a stupid question. I actually hate that question, so I don't know why I asked it." She flips her backpack around, so it's on her front, and unzips it. "Where should I get set up?"

"Right here." I pat the chair I just fixed, and then drag over a large cardboard box of books for her to use as a desk.

She takes out her laptop and her science notebook and as she gets organized, I start sanding the top of a small side table that has water stains and scratches. When I'm finished, I can restain it with coffee or black tea and rub it with mineral oil for an all-natural finish.

"So," Eddie says, fingers poised on the keyboard of her laptop. "Tell me about your interviews."

I recount all the things Alex and his dad told me about the Spirit of the Sea the night before. Eddie seems particularly interested in Alex's theory, the one about the moonlight and fog.

Eddie interviewed Ms. Diaz and a person named Jared H., who Eddie says works at the Seaside Bean Café, the coffee shop I pass every day on my way to school. Eddie called him a "barista." I've picked up paper cups off the sidewalk from there. According to Eddie, Ms. Diaz believes in ghosts, and says it's possible the Spirit could be real. Jared thinks it's a big hoax.

If I were the one taking notes, I'd jot them all down messily. But Eddie puts them into a very organized file on her computer called a spreadsheet, highlighting pieces of the interviews that are contradictory.

"This is a great start," Eddie says. "If she was real, don't you think we'd see more shared beliefs about her?"

"Sure," I say as I sand out a particularly deep scratch. "I guess we would."

"We should conduct some more interviews. And you're still free to do the nighttime observation this weekend, right? There's going to be no moon on Saturday night. My dad said he'd come, too, so we'd have an adult with us as we make our observations of the bluff."

"What time would it be?" I ask.

"I think later would be best, so there's less light interference. So maybe ten? Eleven?"

I stop sanding and look over at her. "P.M.?"

She nods.

There's no way Mom will let me go out so late. We have the bolts on our door locked by nine at the latest. As soon as the sun goes down, she gets jumpy. She wasn't like that at the Ranch, not that I can remember. "I don't think my mom would let me do that."

"Hmm." Eddie leans back in the chair, and I'm super proud when it doesn't even creak. "Well, what if you came over for a sleepover?"

"A sleepover?"

"Yeah. Like, you'd come spend the night at my place. Then we could do the observation together. It would be totally safe and chaperoned by my dad. An important outing for the sake of science."

A sleepover. It would be nice to have a night off from sleeping in the same room as Mom. Although I have no idea what she's going to say. "Well . . . okay. I'll ask."

"Great." Eddie snaps her laptop shut and gets to her feet. She goes over to one of the windows and drags a finger down the glass. When she turns, I can see gray dust on her finger-tip. "What this place needs is a 'right good scrubbing,' as my mom would say."

"I know. I haven't gotten to that part yet."

"I could bring over some cleaning supplies, if you want."

I immediately think of the toxic chemicals the motel uses and shake my head. "You don't need to do that."

"I want to. Babs wouldn't even have to pay me," she adds quickly. "But only if you want company."

The company would be nice. I do need a broom, and maybe a mop and some rags. If she brings chemicals, I could tell her Babs doesn't want us to use that stuff. In a pinch, we could just use water.

"You'd do that?" I ask.

"Sure. I like it here. It can be, like . . . our clubhouse." She holds up her hands like she's framing a picture. "The location where two brilliant young minds finally disproved the existence of the local legend, once and for all!"

I laugh. "Okay. Sounds good to me."

Eddie drops her hands. "Are you hungry? I wouldn't say no to some tea and cake right about now."

My hour's just about up anyway, so I stand. "Yeah. Let's go."

According to Mom, the library is a ten-minute walk in the opposite direction of the main little downtown.

As we go, Mom hums a song with a funky beat. She's wearing a new black coat I haven't seen before, with silver buckles and studs on the shoulders. It looks kind of like the jackets the bikers wear. It matches her new hair. It's a chilly evening, and I have on my white knit hat. I don't see why she had to get a new coat when she had a perfectly good one already.

When I say so, she says, "I know. But I saw this in the window, and I couldn't resist. It reminded me of a jacket I had when I was younger." She plucks at one of the buckles. "Plus, it's secondhand. Buying used helps keep clothes out of the landfill. I could take you to the store and you could choose some things for yourself. If you wanted."

I think about it. I know I don't need more than I already have, but my sweater from the Ranch is starting to pill, and the constant washing in the sink has been annoying. Having a few more options might be nice—especially if I get to pick them out myself. And it *will* keep them from clogging the landfill.

"Okay," I say, surprising myself a little. "That'd be nice. Thanks."

Mom smiles and lifts her shoulders in a happy way. "Great. We can go this weekend."

"Oh," I say. "Speaking of this weekend, the girl from school I told you about—Eddie—wants to know if I can sleep over on Saturday."

I didn't think Mom could look any happier, but she does. "You were invited to a sleepover?"

"Yeah. Is that okay?"

"Better than okay. But I'd like to come meet her parents in person, instead of over the phone."

"Sure," I agree. I'll just have to hope Eddie's parents don't spill the beans on our late-night observation plans. "That's fine."

Mom reaches out and squeezes my hand. "I'm thrilled you're settling in so well. And so fast. It's better than I could have ever imagined."

"I'm *not* settling in." I tug my hand back. "I'm making the best of a bad situation."

"But it isn't that bad being here, is it?" Mom asks softly.

I think about it. I think about meeting Eddie and Babs. About Mr. Carlson's class, the sunsets, the new words I'm learning, the Pacific Ocean and the comforting push and pull of its waves. But I also think about Meadowlark. I think about how *right* life feels on the Ranch, with its set rhythms. With a community I never had to wonder if I was a part of, a place where I never felt stupid or ignorant. I think about all the green and the sway of the forest all around. The safety of it.

"No," I admit. "But it isn't home, either."

Mom sighs. "No. I guess not. Not yet, at least."

The library building reminds me of school in that it's ugly and surrounded by a big parking lot. Like everywhere else in Driftaway Beach, I wish there were more trees, more grass, more *green*.

But inside, it's totally different. The ceilings are soaring and high, and there are rows and rows of books of all shapes, colors, and sizes. The Ranch's library could probably fit onto a single one of these shelves.

I can't stop staring. "There are so many books."

"That's a public library for you." Mom points at a set of gray-carpeted stairs. "I'll be upstairs, in the adult-education study room. Keep your cell phone on, just in case, and stay inside the library, okay? Once you've picked out some books, come up and sit with me." She points to the left. "The children's area is over there."

Once Mom and I part, I go the way she pointed. There's a big sign that says CHILDREN'S AREA hanging from the ceiling, and beneath it is a woman sitting at a desk. The librarian, I'm guessing.

I go up and stand in front of her.

"Hey there." She looks up from her computer screen. "What can I do for you?"

She's got pale white skin and a shaved head. Tattoos snake up both of her arms, and she's got lots of silver piercings in her ears and nose. There's even one on her lip. Her name tag says, "Hi. My name is Wren."

But now that I'm standing closer, I'm not actually sure if Wren is a she or a he. I mean to ask for some book suggestions, but instead a different question slips out.

"Sorry, are you a girl or a boy?"

The librarian—Wren—raises an eyebrow. The left one. The one with two silver hoops threaded through it. "And how, pray tell, is *that* any of your business?"

The librarian is angry. Or annoyed. It must have been a rude question. On the Ranch, there are more women than men, and all the women keep their hair long and the men grow out their beards, so it's easy to tell everyone apart, even when they wear the same kind of clothes. That's the way Dr. Ben likes it. The rules are so different out here.

"I'm sorry. I'm ignorant," I say, using Havana's word. "It means I don't know a lot of things."

The librarian's face softens. "Hey, it's okay. Neither do a lot of people."

And then Wren goes on to explain they go by "they," not "he" or "she." That it's a gender-neutral pronoun, because they identify as gender-fluid. "There are two boxes society tries to put you in when it comes to gender, and I don't fit in either one. A lot of people don't."

I'm surprised we haven't heard more about this on the Ranch. Dr. Ben is always telling us we should write our own rules, especially when it comes to things society tells us.

"I didn't know you could do that," I say. "It makes a lot of sense. Thank you for explaining it to me."

That seems to be the right thing to say, because now Wren is grinning at me. "It's funny. Kids seem to grasp this concept a lot faster than adults. So how can I help you?"

"I need to learn."

Wren taps their pen on the desk. "About . . . ?"

I sigh, thinking of the way the entire class laughed when I asked who George Washington was.

"Everything," I say.

Wren's grin widens. "Then you've come to the right place."

I have a big stack of books when Mom and I leave the library an hour later. One of them is called *The Big Book of Just About Everything: What You Need to Know to Get By*. Wren told me it has information about, well, everything. Facts about history, science, religion, geography, important poets and writers— "the works," they said. I also took out two more books by the author who wrote *Firestride* and put one "on hold." Apparently, some books are so popular you have to wait in line behind other people to check them out.

On the walk home, my books tucked safely in Mom's big tote bag, I remember the question I'd been meaning to ask her.

"Mom?"

"Yeah, honey?"

"How did Birdie die?"

"It happened a long time ago, when you were a baby. It was an accident. She was a big outdoorswoman. Has Babs mentioned that to you?"

"A little," I say.

"Well, she loved kayaking. She'd go most mornings, if memory serves. She even did whitewater kayaking. I think she was well-known in the community, because she was one of the oldest women who kayaked competitively. But one morning she took her kayak out to sea, and she didn't come back."

"What?" I glance over at her. "Did they find her?"

"No. Or at least the articles I read about it said they never did. Only her kayak paddle, but never her. I—I've actually never talked to Babs about it."

"You didn't talk to her after Birdie died?"

Mom looks pained. "No. And I regret that. But I was so wrapped up in my own life at that point. I was young and stupid. We hadn't talked in so long, and I thought Babs wouldn't want to hear from me." She isn't looking at me. "But I should have reached out. Obviously, I should have."

For the rest of the walk home, I think about Birdie, lost at sea.

And I won't mention it to Eddie, but a small part of me hopes the Spirit of the Sea might be real. For Babs's sake.

22

Wait. Be patient. Have patience. All good things in life require it.

These are things Dr. Ben says *all* the time. He says it about the tender vegetable starts in the garden, about waiting for the chicks to become old enough to lay eggs. About waiting for the sharp bite of winter to soften into spring.

And I'm trying to have patience—I am. But now that my calendar counting down to the spring equinox has more and more *X*s, it's getting harder. I'm only halfway through my thirty hours for Babs—I counted the money I have hidden in the back of the book Mom gave me, the one with my calendar in it—and I have $140. It'll be $150 after I finish my hour today.

I do the math in my head as I trudge up the steps to Birdie's second floor after school. Including today, I'll have worked fifteen days so far, which means I have fifteen hours left before I make the money I need. That's a month of work, since I can only come in four days a week. And then who knows how long it'll take Ron B. Tully to track down the address? And then how long will the letter take to get to Dr. Ben?

What if all this time away has rewritten Dr. Ben's memories of us? His memories of *me*? Of all those things he said about the kind of person he thinks I can be? What if I write to him, and he rips up the letter and throws it away? What if I never get to talk to Meadowlark ever again, and she never finds out what happened to me? Or where I went? Or why?

Every time I go down this path of "what if," my chest gets tight and my mind spirals out.

I'm trying to have patience. I'm trying to focus on the work.

At least having *The Big Book of Just About Everything* has been helpful for distraction's sake. Because in the few days since I checked it out of the library, I'm having trouble tearing myself away from it.

I read while I gather trash on the way to school. (Or at least I *tried,* until I tripped and skinned my knee.) I read at lunch now, instead of going to the computer lab, and I read past bedtime, which is pushing me to sleep in a little later than sunrise.

So far I've learned about a woman named Cleopatra, who ruled Egypt as queen when she was only eighteen.

I've learned about the founding of America, the Constitution, and the thirteen original colonies.

I've read about sea animals and honeybees, and all about a beautiful piece of math called the Fibonacci sequence.

As I read, I imagine each piece of information is like a

petit four, dissolving on my tongue. (Even though I only had one small bite, I haven't been able to stop thinking about those sweet little cakes.)

But I learn other things, too. Painful things. I learn about the terrible things early settlers did to America's Native people. I learn about slavery, the Civil War, and the Tulsa Race Massacre. Those facts don't dissolve like sugar. Those truths hurt.

I'm taking a quick break, sitting beneath the best window on the second floor of Birdie's, reading, when I hear a loud knock downstairs.

"It's open!" I yell.

Maybe it's Babs. She usually isn't here on Fridays, but sometimes she drops in. I immediately feel guilty because I should be working every minute I'm up here, not reading.

I'll work an extra ten minutes, I tell myself. I don't want to cheat Babs, because honestly, I don't think she'd notice if I read the whole time, anyway. She hasn't really been checking in on my progress. Mostly she comes up with a mug of tea or a plate of tea sandwiches. My favorite are the cucumber–cream cheese sandwiches on whole-grain bread. She's noticed, too, because that's mostly what she brings now. Sometimes she brings croissants, but only whenever there are any left over from the morning rush.

I hear the creak of the door, the crunch of feet on steps.

"It's me!" calls a voice I immediately recognize as Eddie's. "Cleaning crew, reporting for duty."

I flip my book closed and stand up.

When Eddie reaches the top of the stairs, I'm amazed she made it all the way up. She's got a broom, a mop, two buckets filled with supplies like rags and spray bottles, and a big glass ball dangling around her neck, like a necklace. She's breathing hard.

"Help," she says, her voice strangled.

I rush to take some of the supplies from her. "Did you walk all the way over from your apartment like this?"

"No. My mom dropped me off, thankfully."

Once she's disentangled from all her cleaning supplies, I point at the glass ball. "Is that the fairy orb? From your room?"

"Yes. I mean, no, it's not the one from my room. It's another one. We have, like, a hundred in boxes."

She takes it off and hands it to me. Even the light from the room's dirty windows makes it sparkle. Now that I'm looking closer, this one has more bluish green hues than the one hanging in her window.

"My mom insisted. She said it'll bring us protection as we work." She points at the window where I'd been reading. "Maybe we can hang it there?"

I grab the stepladder, as well as a hammer and a nail or two. It takes us ten minutes, but once we have it hung, it sprays droplets of colored light everywhere, bringing life to the room.

"It'll be even better once we clean that window." Eddie tosses me a pair of gloves. "Here. If things get gross."

I put them on, and then go to see what kinds of supplies

she brought, ready to tell her we won't be using any of it. But much to my surprise, most of it is in glass bottles, with words like "environmentally friendly" and "nontoxic" printed on their labels.

"This is so much better than what they use at the motel," I tell her, looking at the ingredients in one of the spray bottles. It's mostly words and plant names I recognize.

"This? Oh, yeah. My mom's into the whole all-natural thing. Farmers markets, homemade soap—that sort of stuff."

It feels good to be doing something productive with someone in easy, comfortable silence. As Eddie and I clean, I feel happy-warm on the inside. She has music playing from her phone, and for the next thirty minutes we scrub, dust, and sweep. And she's right—as soon as we clean the main window, the room brightens up, and the droplets of light from the fairy orb glow even stronger. The window faces south, and I bet it would be a great place to have a little indoor herb garden. Mom's been visiting the nursery more regularly; I wonder if she could get me some herb plants. Maybe Babs would consider offering homegrown herbal tea as part of her fancy tea setup here. Suddenly, I can imagine this space as so much more than just a dusty storage area.

The music briefly stops as Eddie's phone pings. I recognize it as her text sound. She takes off her gloves to see who it's from.

"My dad," she says as she texts something back. "My grandparents got here earlier than expected for dinner, so he wants to come get me. I can tell him we still have more to clean."

I stop to look around. The floors aren't nearly as gritty, and the windows in the main room are now letting in almost double the light. We need a taller ladder to get to the skylight, but it feels so much fresher in here.

"You should go hang out with your grandparents," I tell her. "We've already done so much."

"And we can do even more next time!" She motions at all the supplies she brought. "I can leave these here, if that's okay with you."

"Sure." I glance at the fairy orb, which is catching and spraying blue-green light across the freshly mopped floors. "And please tell your mom thank you for the present. I love it."

"You can thank her yourself tomorrow. Okay, I should go down to wait for him outside. See you tomorrow!" She shoves her phone in her pocket and then comes over to me, throwing her arms around me in a hug.

I freeze. She immediately withdraws. "Oops. Sorry. Forgot about the germ thing."

And then, before I can say anything else, she bounds away from me, down the stairs.

I rub my shoulders. I wish I had a moment to tell her I didn't mind, that I was just surprised. Meadowlark used to surprise me with hugs all the time. It's one thing to be hugged by your mom, but it's an entirely different thing to get hugged by a friend.

Because that's what Eddie is, right? A friend?

Or are we just classmates and project partners? I'm not

sure. On the Ranch, everyone is your family, so you never have to wonder about stuff like this. I try to imagine her and Meadowlark hanging out together, but I can't. They're like two separate universes. I don't know under what circumstances they'd ever collide, and something about that makes me feel incredibly sad.

Thinking about Meadowlark hurts. I miss her more than I miss my bed, the green of the forests all around the Ranch, the manure-and-fresh-hay smell of the barn. I guess you can be homesick for a person even more than for a place.

As I'm standing there, lost in thought, I hear the door open again, and the familiar thump of feet.

"Forget something?" I call out.

But it isn't Eddie—it's Babs.

Her cheeks are red and she's huffing like she's been running. "Fern, I wanted to—" She stops near the stairs and looks around, blinking. "Wow, honey. It looks amazing in here. I don't even think it was this clean when there were tenants living here."

"Thanks," I say. "Eddie came over with some cleaning supplies and helped me. We still have to do the other rooms."

"Fantastic." She uses the back of her hand to wipe sweat from her brow. "Listen, can I steal you for a few minutes? I want to show you something. But we have to move fast."

I think again about the ten minutes I spent reading instead of working. "I still have to finish up my hour."

She waves me off. "I'll pay you for the full time. This'll be worth it. Leave your things but grab your sweater."

I've only gotten one sleeve on by the time Babs has sped back down the stairs. When I stop to lock the door, she waves me off again, and says, "No time! Come on!"

Now I'm really curious. Babs pumps her arms as she walks, going so fast she's almost running. Since her legs are so long, I have to jog to keep up with her. She nearly bumps into multiple people on the sidewalk. She doesn't slow down, but she does shout apologies over her shoulder.

She takes me to the road that runs along the water, across from the post office, where the Spirit of the Sea plaque is. But then, instead of going right or left, she walks beyond the statue, to a set of wooden stairs I hadn't noticed before. They're hidden from view if you're standing on the sidewalk, so you have to walk around the plaque's tall metal stand in order to see them.

"Where are we going?" I ask.

"To the beach."

I glance down the stairs—and there *is* a little beach. I hadn't thought there were any beaches close to town, given the way the land seems to abruptly end and become ocean. I'm amazed I haven't noticed it before. Then again, it's tucked in, as hidden from view as the stairs leading down to it. It has dark, almost black, rocky sand, and it can't be more than a block long. It's shaped like a crescent moon, facing the ocean. With the bluff rising in the background, it could be a scene from another planet entirely.

The wood stairs are damp and rickety, but Babs plummets down them, hanging on to the railing, occasionally calling for me to hurry.

When we reach the beach, she motions me forward, right to the edge of the surf. She's puffing so hard her cheeks are red and inflated.

"I had no idea this was here," I say.

"There are lots of little secrets in Driftaway. Now look."

She points to the ocean, her arm making a straight line in front of us. And then she hands me a pair of binoculars.

At first, I don't know what I'm looking at.

And then I gasp, because a huge shape rises out of the water, and then smacks back down with an incredible splash.

I squint. "Is that—"

"A whale," Babs says. "A gray whale. It's the beginning of their migration season. I think there are two of them. A mother and a calf, if I had to guess. See the smaller one, in front?"

I keep watching—and I do see two distinct shapes. Both of them, even the baby, are so big it's kind of like watching parts of the earth itself moving.

"Gray whales make one of the longest migrations of any mammal on earth. Amazing, aren't they?"

I nod and pass Babs the binoculars, so she can take a turn. Even without them, I can't take my eyes off the ocean, off the whales. Geese and other birds back home migrate for the winter, and I liked catching a glimpse of them traveling in their flying vees, but it was nothing like this.

"How far do they travel?"

"Ten to twenty thousand miles, if you can believe it."

That's far. So far. "Do they ever get lost?"

"The whales? Sure they do. But you don't have to worry about those two." She nods at the water. "They're exactly where they're supposed to be."

I go back to watching them. "This is one of the coolest things I've ever seen," I tell her in a low voice.

Because it is. Their size, the way the water turns white and frothy when they come out and smack back down—it's like magic.

Babs glances over at me. "Your face looks just like Birdie's did when she watched the whales. She loved when the whales visited. That's what she called it. We used to come and watch them together, even if it was only for a couple of minutes in the middle of a service rush. Customers knew how much she loved them, so they'd always come in with news if they spotted any movement." She turns back toward the ocean. "It's nice to have someone to watch them with again."

A small voice—so small it's almost not there—tells me, *You never would have seen this if you had stayed at the Ranch.*

And I'm not sure I like the way it makes me feel to know that.

We stand there for a long time, long after the whales have gone on their way.

23

"Ah, Fern, look at you! What a bonnie jacket!"

Eddie's mom leans forward to touch the cuff of my coat as she greets us at their apartment's front door on Saturday evening.

I don't know what "bonnie" means, but from the way she's smiling, I think it's a compliment. "Thanks. I got it today. At the secondhand shop."

I also got some unbleached cotton shirts and a new (but used) pair of shoes. The jacket is my favorite thing we found. It's a cream color and has a soft fluffy collar. It feels and looks like I'm wearing a cloud.

"Oh, the one on Springer? I love that place. My dress is from there!" She turns to Mom. "You must be Fern's mum. I'm Fiona. Would you like to come in? Dinner's on."

Mom tucks a strand of her dyed-black hair behind her ear. "I'm Jamie. I don't mean to intrude. I just wanted to stop by and say hello in person."

"Dev is cooking. He always makes enough for an army."
She laughs. "Won't you stay for a bite or a glass of wine?"

"I shouldn't—"

"Oh, why not? You're new. And we're new-ish. We could both use a friend, eh?"

Mom glances at me, like she wants to see what I think. She looks so hopeful. I don't really want her to stay, but the idea of her going back to our motel room to eat dinner alone from the hot plate makes me feel sad. She's been alone so much. When I'm at school or working with Eddie on the second floor of Birdie's, Mom is alone. And even though she hasn't said anything to me, I can tell it's been hard on her. So I say, "I don't mind."

"Okay." She smiles. "Then, sure. Thanks."

As soon as we step into the apartment, I smell onions, garlic, tomato, spices. It's the smell of curry, and the aroma immediately transports me back home. We have big pots of curry and rice pretty much every week at the Ranch. But somehow Eddie's dad's curry smells richer and deeper and better. Like he's turned the volume up.

Eddie and I settle on the sofa, waiting for dinner to be ready. With the smell of curry and the adults laughing and the pots clanging, I can shut my eyes and feel like I'm back home. The familiarity is both comforting and painful.

When dinner's ready, Eddie's mom asks, "Do you want to eat with us at the table?"

"No," Eddie says. "Fern and I will eat in my room. I want to show her something."

Eddie's dad—Dev—serves each of us a huge scoop of vegetarian curry over fluffy white rice, and sticks a piece of flatbread called "roti" on the side. The steam wisping off it smells so good I almost take a bite standing there.

Once we get to her bedroom, Eddie stops in the doorway. "Oh, Tuna! You came out!" She puts her bowl down on her nightstand and goes to pick up a slate-gray cat from her bed. He wriggles a bit at first, and then relaxes into her arms. "Isn't he so cute?"

I'm about to reach out, to ask if I can pet him, when I realize . . . he doesn't have any eyes.

I snatch my hand back. "What—what happened to him?"

"Oh, don't worry. Nothing horrible. He was born without them." She gives him a kiss on the top of his head. "He was also the runt, which is why he's so small. Tuna, meet Fern. Fern, Tuna."

"So he's blind? How—how is he alive?"

"I don't understand what you mean."

"I mean, why didn't someone kill him? When he was a kitten?"

"Kill him?" Eddie repeats slowly.

I can tell I said it wrong. "Or . . . was he a stray?"

She shakes her head stiffly. "No. Our neighbor's cat had kittens."

"Oh. Well. Even so, it's kind of a miracle he survived."

"I still don't understand what you're getting at," Eddie says. She's holding Tuna even closer now.

"I'm just saying it's a miracle he didn't starve to death.

Most of the time, it's more humane to kill them than to let them die from hunger."

Dr. Ben had explained that to me, almost two years ago. Like Tuna, a kitten in one of the barn cats' litter was born without eyes, and was having trouble nursing. He wasn't gaining weight like the other kittens were.

I'd begged to help with the kittens. I was ten, and I thought I'd get to play with them, change their bedding, and check to make sure the mom cat had enough fresh food and water.

So when Dr. Ben told me we were going to kill the blind kitten, I wasn't prepared.

"What?" I'd said. "No."

Dr. Ben got down onto one knee and put his hand on my shoulder. "In the wild, this kitten would die. This is the natural way of things. Putting it down now will only eliminate its future suffering. It's important that you bear witness to this, Fern. I want you to see with your own two eyes that death is a part of life."

"But I don't want to," I'd said, and immediately started to cry.

Dr. Ben nodded. "I know. Sometimes the most humane thing to do can feel like the hardest. But it's what's right. Bring the kitten into the barn when you're ready and we'll take care of it together."

As soon as Dr. Ben left, my whole body shook. I held the sweet kitten in my arms. The runt. I kissed her soft head again and again.

That's when Rain came over and said, "Hey. Give her to

me. I'll make up an excuse so you don't need to see it happen, okay? He shouldn't have put this on you."

I wanted to fight him, to say I was strong enough to handle it, but the truth was, I wasn't. After I handed over the kitten, I ran back to the dorms and cried for hours. The next day I felt embarrassed at how I'd acted, that I hadn't been stronger and able to handle it. It's strange to think that only a couple of months later, Rain was gone, too.

"Tuna is very healthy." There's an edge to Eddie's voice that wasn't there a minute ago. "He eats more than any other cat I've ever met. And he's fast. He loves to play. We had to feed him formula with a dropper when he was little, but that's it. He's a totally normal cat. He's better than normal."

"Even though he's blind?" I ask. "And the runt?"

"Yes," she says, even more stiffly. "Even though he's blind. And the runt. He's perfect. I'm going to go get some water."

She takes Tuna with her, hoisting him under one arm. He meows in protest. She disappears from her room for a long time.

While she's gone, I can't stop thinking about the little blind kitten from the Ranch, with the creamy dot of fur on her forehead. What if we'd formula-fed her, like Eddie said? Would she have learned to pounce fearlessly, if we'd given her the chance? To chase mice by scent?

I think about Rain, too.

He's been on my mind a lot since we left the Ranch. We weren't close or anything. The moment with the kitten was one of the few times we talked like that. If we ever did talk, it was usually about the animals or what was for dinner. A casual joke here, a comment about the weather there. Our lives didn't intersect all that much. Me as a kid and him as a teen, almost an adult. It's strange that I've been thinking about him *more* as time has passed since he died, not less. I didn't realize it could work that way.

"I'm sorry," I say, once Eddie finally returns. I know I upset her, and I don't want to ruin the one friendship I have here. "Things were different on the Ranch. And I can tell I'm wrong about Tuna. I never should have said that."

She stands there for a long moment, like she's deciding how to respond. I hold my breath.

And then, as if on cue, Tuna saunters into the room and jumps up onto the bed. He lets out a long meow, and then settles in, right against my thigh.

Eddie laughs a little. "Well, Tuna's clearly forgiven you, so I guess I should, too. Let's eat. There's also something I want to show you."

She sits cross-legged on the floor with her computer. I'm expecting her to pull up research or a plan for tonight's observation of the bluff.

But instead she goes to YouTube. "Do you like BTS?"

I take a bite of the curry. It's cold by now, but I don't care. I'm just happy Eddie isn't mad at me. "I don't know what BTS is."

"*Who* they *are*," Fern corrects me. She grins as she presses play. "And oh, are you in for a treat."

As it turns out, BTS is a Korean music band. Eddie calls it "K-pop." The music fills me with a feeling I'm not familiar with. Like I'm excited and hopeful about *something*, but I don't even know what that something is. Mom would love it. I wonder if she can hear it from the other room.

At the Ranch, no one sings in other languages, because everyone only speaks English. I close my eyes and try to imagine what it would be like if we could knit to music like BTS, instead of thoughtful silence. If I could knit to music like this, I think my patterns would be funky and chunky and full of life.

Eddie seems less interested in the music and more interested in telling me the long backstories of all the members of the band. I don't mind. She gets just as excited talking about one of them, Jungkook, as she does about our project for Mr. Carlson's class.

Mom leaves around eight-thirty. Her cheeks are flushed, and she seems a little unsteady on her feet, but happier than I've seen her in a while.

Around ten I start yawning.

"Want to watch a movie?" Eddie asks. "Or some TV? It might help keep us awake."

But I shake my head. Using computers at school—and letting Eddie show me a couple of music videos—is one thing. But watching TV for fun is something else entirely. Television is worse for you than white sugar. "Can I read instead?"

"Oh. Sure. Do you mind if I watch something?"

"Go ahead."

Eddie sits on her bed with her computer on her lap and Tuna

next to her, and I curl up in her armchair to finish the last few chapters of *Veil of Sampson*, one of the *Firestride* author's other books. Eddie keeps laughing softly at whatever she's watching, and she's got these little twinkly lights that reflect off her fairy orb. It's so cozy. I rest my head against the side of the armchair.

At some point I must fall asleep, because around eleven-thirty, she shakes me awake.

"Hey. Fern. You ready?"

I sit up, yawning. What I really want is to nestle deeper beneath the fuzzy blanket in her comfortable chair and go back to sleep for the rest of the night.

But Eddie's eyes are wide and bright, and she's already got her coat on, so I force myself to my feet. Knowing Mr. Carlson will be impressed with our commitment to the scientific method helps, too.

"Hey," Eddie says as I'm getting my coat and shoes on. "Did you know you talk in your sleep?"

"I do?"

Eddie nods. "You were talking about little cakes. I *think* you said petits fours, but you were pretty mumbly."

"Huh," I say. No one's mentioned that to me before. Meadowlark never said anything. Have I always talked in my sleep? Or is Mom somehow starting to rub off on me? I had no idea I did it, too.

As we walk down the quiet streets, Eddie's dad seems as bleary-eyed and tired as me. He's got three fold-up chairs and a few blankets slung over his shoulder, and a warm winter hat pulled down low on his forehead.

Next to me, Eddie chatters nonstop. She's got a flashlight and a notebook, so we can make our observations.

We set up our chairs on the little beach where Babs and I watched the whales. We're not the only ones here. There are a few other small groups—some with chairs like us, others with blankets and thermoses of hot drinks. They're all facing the bluff.

Eddie's dad sets up his chair away from ours, to "give us a little space."

He comes over to give us some supplies, but before heading back to his own seat, he stops. "I'm so happy you wanted to do this, Eds. It's fun, right? Maybe we'll see something. If I can manage to stay awake."

Eddie's eyes dart to me. "Yeah. Maybe."

After a big yawn, he stoops to kiss her on the forehead, and then turns and makes his way across the sand. When he's settled in his chair, Eddie says under her breath, "Just so you know, they don't know what my project is. I mean, *our* project. That we're trying to prove she *doesn't* exist. Could you maybe . . . not mention it?"

"Your secret's safe with me." Then I nod my chin at one of the other groups. "Are they all here for the same reason as us?"

"Yeah. I told you. People are obsessed. Including my parents."

I remember what Alex and his dad told me at dinner. "Have you done the ghost tour?"

"Twice," Eddie says. "My parents dragged me both times. It's total mumbo jumbo, though. Nothing checks out, absolutely nothing scientific about what they claim. But people eat it up."

Once we've settled in, each of us with a blanket tucked in around our laps, I turn to Eddie. "So now what?"

"Now we wait." She's got her flashlight off, so I can only see the outline of her face in the darkness. "Look for anything strange. A light. Or, better yet, a light that *isn't* strange and can be explained by natural phenomena."

I crane my neck back. The bluff rises in front of us, black against the navy-blue sky, which is dotted with both foggy clouds and faint stars.

We sit there for a while. One of the other groups gets up and leaves. Eddie's dad starts to snore. Eddie's got a pair of binoculars she trains on the bluff every few minutes. The waves pound and hiss, and every now and then I feel a cold mist as the wind pushes the ocean spray toward us.

"My parents want to believe she's real so much." Eddie's voice is low, barely even a murmur. "I think they want to believe in the Spirit of the Sea more than any of the other weird make-believe things they've been chasing."

"Oh?" I'm focused on the bluff, not on Eddie. Maybe my eyes are getting more and more tired, because the darkness has become almost fuzzy. "Why?"

"My sister died."

I turn away from the bluff, toward her. Suddenly, I remember those pictures in her hallway. The ones with the older girl in them. "What?"

"My sister. Her name was Skye. She drowned when I was

only two. She was eleven. We were at Loch Ness when it happened, on holiday. You know, of Loch Ness monster fame?"

For once, I actually do know what she's talking about. The Loch Ness monster is one of the things I looked up at the computer lab.

"Anyway," Eddie continues. "It was sort of . . . a freak accident. She was a great swimmer. And it's a lake, so it's not like there was even a riptide that could have pulled her away from shore. And I think it messed with my parents' heads. Because they became obsessed with the idea that it was the Loch Ness monster that'd done it." She rubs her face. "We moved out of our apartment in Edinburgh to stay near the lake. When they couldn't find any proof, we went to Ireland to find the fairies. And so on. It's like . . . it's like they think that if they can prove something impossible exists, then something impossible happened to Skye, too. It's like they're looking for some reason. Some explanation. But sometimes people just die."

It all comes out quickly, quicker than she usually talks. Like the words have been on the tip of her tongue for a long time, and it feels good to let it all out, like a rush of water.

"I'm so sorry. About your sister." I try to imagine losing Meadowlark. *Losing her* losing her, not just being unable to see or talk to her. She's not a strong swimmer, so she mostly avoids the pond and the rowboats, even though I love being on the water. When I go out, she likes to wait for me on shore, somewhere in the shade, because her pale white skin burns so easily. When I get back, she'll have braided flowers together so we can have matching flower necklaces or crowns. They only ever last an hour or two before they wilt and fall apart. I try to imagine what life would be like if she died. It hurts so much I immediately have to stop thinking about it.

"I bet you miss her a lot," I add.

"I don't know. I was so little. I think I miss the *idea* of her more than anything else. I miss being able to do all the things sisters get to do together. I can tell my parents aren't the same without her. And I guess I miss the version of who they were before she died, even though I was too little to know what that even was. If that makes any sense at all."

"It does," I tell her.

As we continue to sit there, waiting for something that may or may not appear, I find myself telling Eddie more about the Ranch than I mean to. Maybe it's the darkness or the fact that she confided in me. I tell her about our schedules, about the way life is structured, how Dr. Ben oversees it all. I tell her about how I was chosen to have my rite of passage early, but that we left before I was able to do it.

I even find myself telling her about how humanity is off course, how we're overconnected, overstimulated, undernourished. That we're hurtling toward environmental collapse, societal collapse, and that the Ranch isn't just a model of a sustainable future, it *is* the future. It offers protection and safety. The words are big and adult, but I know them as well as I know the curves of my own face. Dr. Ben has said them so many times it's like they're a part of me now.

Eddie asks a lot of questions. She seems most interested in what we're not allowed to do.

And before I can even think about what I'm saying, I confide it to her—all of it. How I'm trying to get us back. How I'm working to pay someone to help me find the address.

"That's why I needed the job," I tell her. "And the email address."

"Wow. That's . . . Wow. Are you sure you want to go back? It sounds intense."

"I'm sure," I say, with as much force and meaning as I can gather up. "It's my home."

She's quiet for a long moment. "It just seems weird. I don't know. Why hide away from the world when you can help change it instead?"

I don't have anything to say to that.

A little while later, Eddie sits up in her chair, rigidly straight. She shakes my arm. "Fern! *Look.*"

She passes me the binoculars. It takes me a second to get them right for my eyes. When I do, and the view comes into focus, I let out a surprised breath. I blink hard a couple of times to make sure I'm truly seeing what I think I'm seeing.

Because at the top of the bluff I see a light through the fog. The way it wavers is like a lantern or a candle. It's hard to see any real details with the fog and the darkness, but I swear I can almost see the shape of a person. A person in a long white dress.

It's not a trick of the light. . . . The shape I'm seeing is definitely a person. Or the ghost of a person.

"She's real," I gasp. I press the binoculars hard into my eyes. If only it wasn't so grainy, so far away.

Eddie pulls them away from me by the strap so she can look again, too.

"No. It's not real." I've never heard her sound so fierce. "It's someone *pretending*. A human being. This is great, Fern. This is so great! This means we've observed some proof that our hypothesis is right. This is an elaborate hoax. Now we have to figure out who it is and why they're doing it."

I remember what it said on the plaque Mom read aloud. That the bluff is inaccessible by foot. "But there aren't any paths to the top, are there?"

Eddie shakes her head, binoculars still pressed against her eyes. "Technically, no. But I bet you can *climb* the bluff. Maybe that's how they're getting up there. If we can figure out a way to do it, we can go up there early one night. And then we can catch whoever it is."

"That sounds dangerous. And probably impossible, too."

Eddie lowers the binoculars, her face splitting into a grin. "The only thing that's impossible is that what we're seeing is a ghost. Now we just have to prove it."

"Okay," I say.

Though I'm not convinced.

Looking with my naked eye from down here, on the beach, all I can see is that bobbing, wavering light. It flickers in and out. I imagine hundreds of years of sailors, lost at sea. I think of Birdie. And I like the idea that there will always be someone—or a ghost of someone—beckoning them home, no matter how far they've drifted.

24

<<<<<

The next day, Sunday, Mom and I make a plan for the whole day. The library is our first stop, since it's only open until noon.

I already finished reading all the books I checked out, which Mom could hardly believe, but I'm ready for more. I want to read more science fiction. I want to learn more about Egypt, the Civil War, and whales, too. I'd love to check out a book about whales.

I want to know more about everything.

When I say that to Wren at the library, they laugh. "Let me see what I can find for you."

Not only do they get me more books—including one about whales with full-color glossy pictures—but they have a brilliant idea, too. I complained about not being able to read while I walked to and from school or when I was cleaning the second floor of Birdie's.

Wren slides something over to me. It isn't a book. It's a

little plastic-metal thingy, with a pair of headphones. "Allow me to introduce you to the miraculous audiobook."

The thing Wren gives me is called an audiobook player, with books already downloaded on it. Someone reads the text aloud so you can walk, clean, or do all sorts of other things while reading—I mean, listening.

"This is the best thing ever!" I tell them, and they laugh.

Before going up to join Mom, I want to ask Wren about one more thing.

"Wren?"

They don't look up from their computer screen. "Yes, young scholar?"

"Does the library have books or anything about the Spirit of the Sea?"

Now Wren looks up. "Ah, the local myth. You've gotten sucked in, too, I see. Folks love her here. I moved here from San Francisco a few months ago, and I'd never heard of her. But I was amazed at how many people come and ask about her every day. So much so, the library has its own little table for it. It's in the adult section, right by mythology."

I thank them before going to check it out.

On the table there are a couple of books, a stack of pamphlets, and some clipped-out magazine articles encased in plastic.

I skim one of the articles. A part of it sticks out to me:

Driftaway Beach, California, isn't your typical
"haunted" town. Visitors don't come to this small

seaside community for spooky thrills; they come to be comforted, drawn in by what the Spirit stands for—that she can bring the restless souls of lost loved ones back home. Some of the visitors make shrines, leave flowers at her statue, or give small offerings to the sea. Some are widows or widowers, others are people with relatives or children who have gone missing. People who desperately want to find their way back to those they love. They come to Driftaway Beach, and hope the Spirit of the Sea can help them.

I read the words again and again.

I know Eddie and I are trying to prove the opposite—that the Spirit of the Sea is a big fake, an imposter.

But I'm exactly like those people the article is talking about. All I want is to find my way back to the people I love.

I wish there was a light for me in the darkness. Held up by someone who wanted to help me. A light to guide me home.

After we leave the library, we head back to the motel to grab supplies, and then we go to the beach. I want to show Mom, since I'm not sure she's seen it yet. Part of me also wants to see if any of the magic or ghostliness is still there from last night, though I'd never admit it to Eddie, who's still convinced we'll discover who's faking it, and, as she puts it, "blow the cover off the whole thing."

We bring a blanket and a packed lunch. I bring the book

on whales plus my trash-picking supplies, since even in the darkness I noticed there was some debris on the beach.

It's overcast but warmer and less windy than it's been the past couple of days. With my new coat on, I don't even need to wear my hat.

"I completely forgot this was here," Mom says as we make our way down to the beach.

We're not the only ones here. There's a guy throwing a ball for his dog, which enthusiastically plunges into the freezing cold water to go get it. He waves hello as Mom spreads our blanket on the sand. Mom immediately takes out her books to study, since she's decided she wants to try taking her first GED practice test this week. Even though I brought a book, too, I'm more in the mood to move around and do something. Plus, a lot of garbage washes up on the shore. It's much more obvious in the daytime.

There are pieces of old fishing lines, nets, bottles. I even find half of an old bike helmet. The fishing lines are heavy and soggy, so it feels a little bit like cheating, since Mr. Carlson measures it by weight. But litter is litter.

Once I've done three, maybe four passes back and forth, I use the portable hanging scale to weigh it, and then I go to show Mom my haul.

"Look," I say, almost breathless. I drop three garbage bags next to the blankets. "This is twenty-five pounds."

She looks up from her worksheet and smiles at me. "That's amazing, hon. Great work."

I had to weigh the bags separately, because the hanging scale only goes up to fifteen. I haven't told Mr. Carlson yet, but my secret goal is to collect one thousand pounds of garbage before Mom and I go home. It's a big goal, but I want to leave Driftaway Beach better than it was when we arrived. Cleaner. I want to help keep the ocean clean, too, so the whales can make their long journey as safely as possible.

Hopefully, this will help Dr. Ben see that us being away wasn't totally wasted time.

I am worried about Mom's hair, though. The dye is still black as ever and doesn't show any signs of fading.

When I get to science class on Monday, Mr. Carlson says, "Fern! Come check this out."

Something beeps as he moves out from behind his desk.

"Oops, one sec." He stops to check a little machine attached to his belt. It looks like a cell phone. I haven't noticed it until now. He presses a button. "I'm diabetic," he explains when he sees me looking. "This is my insulin pump. It's been acting up the past two days."

I look at the little contraption again. "Is that—medicine?"

"It sure is."

"What would happen if you didn't have that?"

"Well. Specifically, I would fall into a coma, and then there's a good chance I would eventually die. But don't worry," he says when he sees my face. "With this, I'm perfectly fine.

The marvel of modern medicine, eh?" He moves toward the clean-up poster on the door. "But look. This is what I wanted you to see."

Next to my name, the bar is longer than anyone else's in the class. By . . . a lot. And he hasn't even added my big haul from this weekend yet, because I haven't told him about it.

"You've been here a fraction of the time everyone else has, but you've gotten pretty much double the amount of litter off the streets. Pretty rad, Fern."

"I want to collect one thousand pounds," I confess. "That's my goal."

He holds out his hand in a fist. I stare at it. I know how to do a high five, but I don't know what to do with a fist.

He laughs at the expression on my face. "Bump me back."

"Oh. Right." I make a fist of my own and bump his.

"But seriously, I'm impressed. You have great initiative."

I fiddle with the straps of my bag. It's a backpack, not Mom's tote. We picked it up at the secondhand shop. It still feels weird on my shoulders. "I don't want the whales to choke."

"Me neither." He thinks for a second. "You know, there's a great program you might be interested in. It's a youth marine biology day camp. I help them out sometimes. I feel like you'd be a great fit. You get to study whales and other sea life, and learn about ocean conservation."

My days are already full—too full, honestly, with working for Babs, reading, and homework—but I would figure *something* out if it meant I got to spend more time learning about whales and the ocean. "When is it? Is it during the week or on the weekend?"

"Oh, it's not until summer," he says, and my heart drops.

Summer. If things go according to plan, we'll be gone by then.

"I'll print out some information about it and give it to you tomorrow."

I tug on my backpack straps again. "Thanks."

I go over to sit down at my desk, feeling like I'm about to cry. Not only because I won't be able to see the whales up close. I'm thinking about how if Mr. Carlson lived on the Ranch, he wouldn't be allowed to take his medicine. He wouldn't be allowed to take his medicine and he would probably die.

Eddie's question rings in my ears: *Why hide away from the world when you can help change it instead?* Maybe I can start by changing some things back at the Ranch.

On Tuesday morning, Mom won't get out of bed.

I must have been extra tired last night, because I went to sleep early, and I slept in later than usual. Mom was studying at our little desk, and the soft light and the sound of her pen scratching against the paper lulled me to sleep. And now it's almost seven, which means her shift starts in less than ten minutes.

I touch her shoulder. "Mom? It's time for work."

"I need a day." Her voice sounds croaky and broken. "Just one day."

"One day for what?"

Her words are so muffled I barely hear them. "To do nothing."

"Mom? What's wrong?"

She burrows deeper under the covers. "I failed my GED practice test last night. How will I ever go to college if I can't even pass a practice GED test that a teenager should be able to understand? I'm thirty-six, and I live in a motel room with my daughter."

I guess I'm not the only one who's felt ignorant out here. I could say, *We can go back. We can go back today.* Right now she might even be receptive.

But I also know how hard she's been studying. She's stayed up late, woken up early, gone to the library day after day. She's been working at it so hard the skin beneath her eyes has become blue and bruised. And all because she wants to learn more about the science of plants. About botany. I think about the new little herb garden I've started on the windowsill at Babs's, thanks to her.

I sit on her bed and put my hand on her shoulder. "Can't you take another test?"

"I can. But I'll probably fail it again. I don't know if I'm cut out for this. For any of this."

"For any of what?"

"I don't know. . . . Life. Because what does it say about me if I can't seem to make it work *anywhere*?"

I hover there for a minute. I'm not sure what to do or

say to help her feel better. She's supposed to be cleaning the rooms, and I don't want her to get in trouble.

So first I go to the office.

Alex is there this morning. "Hey, Fern. What's up?"

"Hi." I wring my hands. "I'm sorry to bother you, but my mom's sick. I don't think she can clean today. Could Dina do it?"

"Dina's not around today, but please, tell her not to worry. I'll take care of it. My dad was going to be doing some inventory, but he can take over desk duty."

I'm not sure what we've done to deserve the Reyeses being so good to us, but I'm grateful they are.

"Thank you. Thank you so much."

Next, I go outside and use my cell phone to call Babs.

"Babs," she says, instead of "Hi" or "Hello."

"Hi, Babs. It's Fern."

"Hiya, sweets. Everything okay? It's a little early for a phone call."

"Yeah. Sorry." I grip the phone tight. "I think something's wrong with my mom."

Babs is immediately serious. "Wrong? Wrong how?"

"Just . . . wrong. I don't know. She's sad. She failed her practice test, and she's saying weird stuff."

"I'll be right over."

I know Babs is usually at Birdie's no later than seven-thirty for an eight o'clock opening, when they do tea-and-pastry takeaway. "But . . . what about the shop?"

"The shop can wait."

Five minutes later, Babs pulls up in her car. I'm outside, sitting on the low wall separating the walkway between rooms and the parking lot. It's sunny today, with an almost summery breeze. She comes over and gives me a kiss on top of my head. "Okay, reinforcements are here. Let's go see what's up."

Back in the room, the lights are still off and the curtains drawn. Mom is a lump beneath the blankets.

Babs goes to sit on the side of Mom's bed and brushes her hair away from her face like Mom always does for me. "Jamie? What's going on, babe?"

Mom says something back, but I can't hear her from where I'm standing. Babs turns to me. "Do me a favor and wait outside for a minute, will you?"

I nod and slip out the door. Instead of sitting on the wall, I make my way over to the far edge of the parking lot, to the fence.

"Morning, Fern," Tank calls out. He's one of the bikers. He's got a thick mustache, lots of faded tattoos on his neck and hands. He introduced himself to me the other day, saying he'd noticed me with my trash picker. He held up a plastic bag that looked half-full, and explained he'd made the group go around the parking lot that morning, grabbing anything they could find that wasn't supposed to be there.

"If a little girl is taking care of business," he said, "we figured we should probably help out, too."

He's got a newspaper with him today, spread out on the seat of his motorcycle. It looks like he's working on a puzzle.

I wave hello.

I swing my feet through the middle part of the fence and sit on the bottom rung of wood, hanging my arms over the top. The morning light winking off the surface of the water is so bright I have to squint my eyes. When the breeze shifts so it's coming from the ocean, it feels almost icy cold in comparison to the sun-warmed air. I listen to the sound of the waves lap against the shore and the drifting conversation as Tank and his friends talk and joke with one another.

Babs comes back outside five minutes later and leans on the fence next to me. "Okay. You know what I'm thinking?"

"What?"

"Today is a perfect day for the three of us to play hooky."

"What does that mean?"

"No school, no work." She grins. "A little adventure. Your mom's getting changed right now, and we've already called you out of school for the day."

"What are we going to do?"

"Well . . ." Babs stretches out the word. "We're only a half hour away, but I don't think you've seen the Golden Gate Bridge yet, have you?"

I shake my head. I've seen pictures of it, though. There's a big mural of it at school in the main hallway. It's a funny name, because the bridge is reddish orange, not gold.

"Then I have the perfect plan. First, we need supplies."

When Babs says "supplies," what she means is a whole box of pastries and a jug of iced tea. After she tells her employees to take the day off, she leaves a note on the door of Birdie's—it says, *Closed today for an unexpected adventure— sorry for the inconvenience! —B.* Then we load the food into the trunk of her car.

Mom's sitting in the front seat and still hasn't said much. But at least she's out of bed and dressed. I hope Alex won't be mad if he realizes she's not actually *sick* sick. I hope whatever Babs has planned makes her feel less sad.

We inch up the coast toward San Francisco. Babs says it *should* take only thirty minutes, but because of all the cars on the road, it might take longer.

"Rush hour," she grumbles.

When we finally reach the Golden Gate Bridge, I press my nose against the car window. I've seen the mural of it at school every day I've been there. But there's something about seeing it in person—the way the arches soar, how the reddish orange contrasts against the blue of the sky and the blue of the ocean—that amazes me.

Mom's looking, too, and Babs notices. "Been a while, huh?"

Mom nods. "No kidding."

But the bridge is only the beginning of the amazing things we see. Babs takes us to a place called Muir Woods. After parking, the three of us follow a map she gets from the ranger's office. There are paths through a forest, but it's unlike any forest I've ever seen before. These trees—Babs tells me they're redwoods—are bigger than I imagined a tree could ever be. I've never felt so small in my whole life.

There are other people here, but their voices are hushed as we make our way along the raised wooden paths.

I walk with my neck craned so far back I trip over my toes a couple of times.

Babs catches my arm the third time so I don't fall. "Beautiful, huh? Some people call it 'Nature's Cathedral.'"

And I get it. Because it feels sacred here. My heart is beating slower, and if souls are real, then my soul is calmer here, too.

Mom stands next to me. "Some of these trees are between six and eight hundred years old. The oldest tree is over one thousand."

I can hardly wrap my brain around it. I try to imagine the things they've seen. What they've survived.

As we walk, Mom seems to come more and more alive. She tells me about their root systems—that even though the trees can grow over three hundred feet high, their roots barely go down a dozen feet in the ground. She says they survive by extending outward in a shallow layer, intertwining with the roots of the trees around them.

"They literally hold each other up," she explains. "Isn't that amazing?"

After an hour or two meandering through the redwoods, Mom sharing a bunch of different facts as we go, we turn to make our way back to the parking lot.

"You know," I say to Mom, "I bet most teenagers wouldn't know *any* of that stuff."

Mom slips her hand into mine and squeezes.

We make a couple more stops. We go into San Francisco and walk along the beach, which has a view of the bridge. It's windy but warm, so Babs puts down a blanket and lays out a bunch of pastries and cups for the iced tea. She brought some petits fours, too. I hesitate, looking at the pretty little cakes. Maybe a tiny bit of sugar is okay. In moderation. Honey is a kind of sugar after all, right? Maybe I can eat petits fours sometimes and still be healthy. So I take one, and I eat it slowly, trying not to feel too guilty. I savor every bite.

"Do you think the Spirit of the Sea is real?" I ask Babs while we eat.

She unwraps a muffin. "Oh, well, I think that depends on your definition of 'real.' "

Mom rolls her eyes. "Babs."

Babs chuckles. "Who knows if she's real or not? But it is something I choose to believe in."

I think about this the entire drive back to Driftaway Beach.

Dr. Ben says there are truths about what society is doing to the world we have to accept. That it's not a question of believing, it's a question of accepting.

I guess I never realized what—or *who*—we believe in could ever be a choice.

25

After school the next day, Mom gets a weird phone call.

When the phone rings, she pushes up off her stomach from my bed. "Intermission."

We're doing my math homework. We're on functions right now, which I barely understand, so I'm glad for the brain break. I throw my pencil down and roll onto my back as Mom answers the phone.

"Hello?" There's a long pause, and I watch as the color drains from Mom's face as she listens to whatever the person is saying. Her eyes flick to me. I sit up on my elbows.

"Why are you calling me?"

I hear a voice on the other end, but I can't make out the words. Mom turns her back to me. "No, I don't want to— No. Stop. Stop calling me. Don't call this number again."

She hangs up and throws the phone onto her bed, like it's hot to the touch.

"Who was that?" I ask. My heart starts to beat really fast.

"No one. It doesn't matter."

I stand up. "Who—"

The phone starts ringing again. Mom ignores it as she slips on her shoes, goes and grabs the car keys. I glance between her and her phone. She clearly doesn't want me to know who it is. So I lunge for it.

But Mom's too fast. She grabs the phone first, silences it, and sticks it in her pocket. "Stop! Get your stuff together. We're going to Babs's house for dinner."

On the way over, I try a few more times to figure out what's going on, but she's so distracted she barely hears me. My own thoughts bounce around wildly. Maybe it was someone from the Ranch. Maybe someone found a way to reach out to us. If I'd only grabbed the phone a little faster, if I'd answered the call, I would know.

Babs's house is on a street with a lot of small houses set very close to one another. I've only been here once before, on a quick trip to pick up some tools. Her house is pale yellow, with a covered porch and tidy garden out front.

We park in the driveway, and Mom hustles me out of the car. When Babs answers the door, I can tell she's surprised to see us.

"My two favorite ladies! Did we have plans I forgot about?"

"No. Can we come in?" Mom asks.

Babs steps back so we can get by. "Of course! What did I do to get so lucky for a drop-in visit? Everything okay?"

"Fern. Math." Mom points at my bag. I start to protest, but she doesn't stop pointing until I begrudgingly unload my homework on the coffee table. Then she turns to Babs. "Can we talk for a sec?"

Mom and Babs go outside. A weird, anxious feeling is buzzing inside of me. When they come back, Babs claps her hands together. "Sleepover at my house tonight, you and me! Pizza, movies, staying up too late, eating candy into the early hours of the morning, what do you say?"

"I have school tomorrow. And I don't eat candy. Or watch TV."

Babs widens her eyes at me. "No TV? No *candy*? What kind of kid are you?"

"A healthy one," I tell her, but my mind's on Mom, on that phone call. On who it might have been.

"Okay, fine. No candy. No movies. Maybe some games, then."

I don't want to play games or have a sleepover. I want to talk to Mom, to demand answers. "Did my mom leave?"

"Yes, but she's coming right back. She went to grab your pajamas and your toothbrush."

Ten minutes later, there's a quick honk outside. I abandon my homework and jog out to meet her. She rolls down her window and holds out a duffel bag for me.

I cross my arms, not taking it from her. "Who called you? Was it someone from back home?"

Mom squeezes her eyes shut. "Please, Fern. I don't have time to get into it right now, okay? AT&T closes in twenty minutes. We can talk about it later. And I need your phone."

"My phone? Why?"

"I'm going to get us new phone numbers."

"No. Why should I? Why do we need new numbers?"

"Fern, it's not a request. Give me your phone or you're grounded. That means no Eddie, no working at Babs's."

"That's so unfair!" I cry.

"Life's unfair," Mom replies.

I go inside to get my phone, and when I come out again, I basically throw it at her. I go back into Babs's house without saying goodnight.

Babs makes us dinner and helps me with the rest of my homework at her kitchen table. She's got a different teaching style than Mom. She thinks all her thoughts out loud, gets frustrated even faster than I do, and goes through at least six pieces of scrap paper with her huge, messy handwriting.

I sleep on the couch, since Babs uses her guest bedroom as her office, and the twin bed is covered in stacks of loose papers. She wanted to get it organized and cleared off for me at first but kept getting sidetracked by missing invoices from Birdie's or notes she'd left herself.

"The couch is fine," I tell her. "Really."

Babs sighs and drops a stack of papers on the bed. "I'm sorry. As you've seen from the shop, I'm a bit of a pack rat. I'll make it a priority to get this cleared out. Just in case you want to come over for any more sleepovers."

She directs me to the laundry room down the hall to grab blankets and pillowcases. And . . . whoa. She really *is* a pack rat. There are piles of clothes everywhere—folded on top of the washer and dryer, on the floor, and scattered around the room in white plastic baskets. One basket is filled only with colorful patterned socks, and another basket is propping the door open, piled high with dirty white laundry. The dress or skirt or whatever it is on top has about six inches of dirt, dust, and grass stuck to the hem. My fingers itch to pluck off the bits of stray grass and throw the whole load in the washer for her, but I'm suddenly so exhausted I can hardly keep my eyes open. I find the extra blankets and pillowcases in the cabinets above the dryer and take them back into the living room.

Babs makes me a nest on the couch. Everything is soft and comfortable, maybe even better than my bed at the motel. Even so, it takes me a long time to fall asleep. I don't know what to think. Because if it *was* someone from the Ranch . . . all I can think about is how close I was. If I'd only reached out faster. I could have snatched the phone, locked myself in the bathroom, given our address, and this whole thing would all be over.

But at the same time, that would mean Mom was telling me the truth. That someone at the Ranch does have a phone. Multiple someones, even. And if she's telling me the truth about *that* . . .

After school, Eddie comes back to the second floor of Birdie's to help me finish cleaning.

We're pretty much . . . done. Everything is organized in neat piles. I've fixed the furniture that could be fixed. But I still have ten hours of work before I can make my final $100. So somehow I have to figure out a way to stretch this out.

"I checked the weather," I say as we clean. Mostly we're going around, halfheartedly dusting ledges that don't need to be dusted. "It's supposed to be foggy next weekend. Maybe we can have another sleepover and stake out the beach again."

"Yeah. Maybe."

I've been distracted all day thinking about yesterday's phone call, which is probably why I'm only now noticing how strange Eddie's been acting. She's barely looked at me, and she's been giving single-word responses, when usually she's a fountain of bubbly thoughts and ideas.

"Are you mad at me or something?" I ask.

She turns her back to me to clean invisible dust off the sparkling fairy orb. "No."

But she sounds mad or upset or . . . something. I don't know. "Are you sure?"

"Yep."

Suddenly, it hits me. I'm so stupid. She must be mad I'm getting paid and she's not. I'd offer to share my earnings with her if I didn't need mine so badly.

"Is it that you aren't getting paid for this?" I sweep my hands around the room. "I'm sorry I didn't think of it before. We should ask Babs if she'll pay you, too. You deserve it for all the work you've done."

"No—I—it's not about money." She still won't look at me. "I don't need Babs to pay me. Getting to have free tea and cake at Birdie's is more than enough. And I . . . I like hanging out with you."

I feel relieved, but secretly I know I'm still going to ask Babs if she'll pay Eddie for the hours she's helped. Knowing Babs, she will. "Then is something else wrong?"

Eddie stands there for a long moment. She's hesitating, like she's weighing something in her mind. I almost think she's not going to say anything, but then she blurts out, "Why don't you like it here?"

"What?" I'm thrown by the out-of-the-blue question. "I—I do like it here."

"No, I mean, why don't you want to *live* here? Like, permanently? It's not so bad here. It's nice here."

"Yeah, but it's not my home," I say. "It's different. I've told you this before."

"All that stuff you told me," she says, "on the beach. I don't know. This ranch place sounds like a bad place to live. This guy's ideas . . . He seems kind of dangerous."

Her judgment is so heavy it's like it whacks me over the head.

"What do you know?" I say back. "You've never been there."

I know the Ranch isn't one hundred percent perfect. Neither is Dr. Ben. I'm realizing that more and more. But even if I disagree with what he does sometimes, I know he makes the decisions he does because he wants the best for us. And the Ranch is a good place to live. It's the safest, most stable home I've ever had. The safest and most stable future I'll ever have.

"I—I overheard our moms talking about it. About some of the stuff your Mom said happens there. And . . ." Eddie tugs and pulls on the sleeve of her sweater. Her eyes are firmly on the floor. "I think, Fern—I think it's a cult."

I stare at her. I hate that Mom was gossiping about our lives. And what's worse is I have no idea what the word "cult" means, and I don't want to admit that to her. "What are you talking about?"

She goes over to her backpack, unzips it, and pulls out a few sheets of paper. I catch a glimpse of the first page—it's printed-out text, which has been highlighted here and there. "Our moms used that word. In their conversation. After what you told me that night on the beach, I started doing some research. And I have some questions for you."

I don't know why I feel so angry all of a sudden, but I do. "What if I don't want to answer? I don't owe you anything."

Eddie's finally looking at me now, and her eyes are pleading. "Please?"

Whatever stupid research she's done that might suggest the Ranch is a bad place to live is wrong, so I'll answer her even stupider questions honestly to prove it. "Fine."

"Okay. First. Do you consider the ideas and beliefs you've learned within your group are the way forward in solving the problems in the world?"

"Yes," I answer. Because the answer to that is obviously

yes. Maybe not all of the world's current problems, but definitely its future problems. It shouldn't be a surprise that living more closely with the land, in a self-sufficient community, is the right way to survive.

"Have you thought that if only everyone understood these beliefs, the world would be a better place?" Eddie reads.

Again I nod. For obvious reasons. But then my mind flashes to Mr. Carlson's insulin pump, to Tuna. To Rain. But maybe . . . maybe not *everything*. Maybe not every single belief would make the world a better place. I start to feel a little queasy.

"Do you ever feel bad or guilty for not behaving the way the group says you should?"

I think about the sweet mango tea, the blue clothes, the books and stories I've read. "I mean, sometimes, yes. But that's my fault."

Eddie keeps going. "Is there a leader of your group who's above the law?"

An image of Dr. Ben's face flashes in my mind.

"I don't want to do this anymore." My face is burning. "In fact, I think you should leave."

Eddie lowers the papers. "I'm just trying to help. I wanted to show you—"

"No," I say fiercely. "You don't know what you're talking about. When we agreed to do your project, you said you would help me with what I needed, too, but you lied. Because this—whatever you're doing—is the opposite of helping me.

If you can't hold up your end of the bargain, I'm done helping you with your part. Figure out if the Spirit is real on your own. I don't want anything to do with it. I'm done."

Eddie goes extremely red in the face and throws the papers on the ground. "Fine!"

"Fine!" I shout back.

I slump to the floor as soon as she's gone. I feel shaky with anger. Everything she asked me spirals in my mind. From the look on her face, my answers were exactly what she was expecting. But I don't understand why any of that is so bad.

I stare at the papers on the floor in front of me, the questions she printed out, that somehow suggest the Ranch is a bad place to live. I know I shouldn't. But I know if I don't, the word she used—"cult"—will burrow deeper in my mind, like a splinter.

So I reach forward, grab the papers, and begin to read.

26

School is worse now that Eddie and I aren't talking. I can't even look forward to science anymore, because it's our one class together.

We'd also started eating lunch together every day in the lunchroom. But I don't want to see her after our fight yesterday, to have to avoid her and go sit somewhere by myself, so instead I go to the computer lab, like I used to.

For the entire thirty minutes of lunch, I search online for more information about cults. But the more I read, the more I'm certain that's not at all what the Ranch is.

The definitions say cults are mostly formed around religious beliefs and practices. There isn't much religion on the Ranch. Meadowlark's mom wears a faded gold cross under her shirt, but I only know that because Meadowlark told me once. So if there's no focus on religion, then the Ranch can't be a cult, right?

But then there's another definition, the third definition. It says, "a misplaced or excessive admiration for a particular person or thing."

That one I read again and again.

Is my admiration for Dr. Ben excessive or misplaced? The thought makes me feel itchy and uncomfortable. No—it makes me mad.

Because no. It isn't. I admire him for good reasons. For the right reasons. Don't I?

I have the sudden urge to talk to someone about this. I take my phone out of the bottom of my bag. But when I go to my contact list, only Mom's new number is there. Everything on my phone was wiped after Mom took our phones in, including Alyssa's—I mean, *Kestrel's*—phone number. I squeeze my eyes shut before shoving the phone back in my bag.

It's for the best.

The outside world is getting into my head. Making me question things. Exactly like Dr. Ben said it would.

As I've been searching, I've also had my email open in a different window. I see a (1) appear on the tab, which means I have a new email. I click over to read what it is. It's from Ron B. Tully.

Hey, kid—Are we still on for this? I'm starting to book up for the next couple of months. I'll need payment ASAP if you still want me to search for your person/ place of interest. RBT

That's when it hits me: I'm running out of time. Recently, I've felt the creeping sense that it's all been taking too long, that working for only four hours a week hasn't been cutting it. Getting this email is like a truth-punch to the face. I'm losing momentum. I'm losing my focus. Suddenly, the quiet hum of anxiety I've been feeling floods over me.

I reply right away.

Yes. We're still on. I'm going to try to get you the money by Monday.

Fern

"Babs? Can I talk to you for a minute? Upstairs?"

It's Monday. Babs was out of town this weekend, so this is the first chance I've had to talk to her in person since I got Ron B. Tully's email. I've caught her as she's going from one of the tables to the kitchen. I wouldn't have asked if it was busy, but there are only a couple of tables with customers today. The rest are empty.

Babs does a sweep with her eyes over the tea shop and seems to come to the same conclusion, because she says, "Sure, sweets. Give me five, and I'll be right up."

As she promised, I hear the steps creak as Babs stomps upstairs a few minutes later. Now all I have to do is work up the courage to ask to be paid in advance for my remaining hours.

But the minute she steps onto the landing, she whistles and looks around. "Done already?" She immediately starts checking things out, running her hands over some of the furniture I've restored, and looking through the piles I've made. She catches sight of my little potted herb garden on the windowsill beneath the fairy orb Eddie gave me. "Look at this! How wonderful!" She leans down to smell the thyme. "There's *life* up here again. I can't believe you finished so fast. It looks so great, Fern."

"Finished? No, I—I need to work on it more."

"On what?" Babs asks. "You're all done here, babycakes. And you've done an amazing job."

I can't help it. I start to cry.

Babs immediately looks concerned and comes over to me. "What? What's wrong? What's going on?"

"I was hoping to have the job for a little longer. To, you know, make some more money."

"Oh, honey. Come here." She scoops me up in a big hug. Her arms and chest are soft. She releases me and pats my back. "Listen. How about we have that tag sale next weekend?"

"Can we do it this weekend?" I ask.

Babs shakes her head. "I'm co-chairing a fundraiser this weekend to turn that vacant lot across the highway into a community garden, and I have a million things to do for it. But next weekend, it's me and you for the tag sale, sweets. We can share the profits."

A community garden sounds amazing. I'd love to hear more about it—a lot more about it, actually—but I have a bigger concern right now. I don't have two more weeks to wait. "Could you . . . I kind of need the money soon. Could you pay me a hundred dollars in advance?"

"What? Why do you need money soon? Is something going on?"

I can't tell Babs what I actually need the money for. She'd never give it to me. And she'd tell Mom right away.

So I lie.

"I want to get something for Mom. As a surprise. Before . . . she takes the official GED test. It's a study packet, but it's expensive."

The lie feels bitter in my mouth. On the Ranch I never lied. I always told the truth.

Babs palms my cheek. "Oh, you sweet thing. I'm sure your mom wouldn't want you to do that. I bet she'd want you to spend your hard-earned money on something for *you*."

"It's also for me. Helping her with this is what's best for both of us."

At least I'm not lying about that.

"Well, then, if you're sure. Then, yes. Of course I'll front you." She reaches into her pocket and pulls out a faded leather wallet and opens it up. "I went to the ATM yesterday, so I should have enough. . . . Yep." She counts out five twenty-dollar bills. "One hundred, right here."

I take the money and fold it carefully in half before tucking it into my pocket. "Thanks, Babs."

"You got it. I can't wait to get rid of some of this old crap. And then I'll find you something else to do, if you want. Your mom said you knit. Maybe you can give me lessons."

I haven't knit anything since that first sweater I made

when we got here. The other one I started is still half finished in the bottom of the dresser. I should force myself to get back to it, so my skills don't get rusty. "Oh. Yeah. Sure."

"I can make flyers for the tag sale tonight after I close up the shop. Maybe you can help pass them out around town."

"Of course."

She ruffles my hair. "You're a good kid. Want to come downstairs for a bite?"

"No," I tell her. "I have something I need to do."

"Three hundred dollars even."

I'm back at the Foglamp Investigators office. I counted—and recounted—the money and put it in a Lighthouse Motel envelope. I hold it out for Ron B. Tully to take.

He looks at me for a moment before he takes it from me. He counts through the stack, wetting a finger with his tongue each time he goes to flick a bill. I try not to make a gross-out face. He must be happy with the amount, because when he finishes counting, he tap-taps the edge of the envelope against his desk. "I've got to be honest with you, I'm surprised you're following through. I thought for sure you wouldn't get the money together." He motions for me to sit down. "Let's go over the details again."

We run through everything one more time. I tell him about the schedule of the farmers markets, the name of that first motel Mom and I stayed at, and every detail I can think of when it comes to Dr. Ben and the size and shape of the Ranch's land.

"Okay." He leans back in his chair. "I have a few other things to take care of before I turn my attention to this, but hopefully I'll have something for you by this weekend. Stay tuned."

27

I stay tuned for the rest of the week. I stay tuned through the weekend, but no matter how many times I check my email, there isn't anything from Ron B. Tully. I almost call him—I dial his number at least three times on Sunday morning—but then I decide against it. He doesn't seem like the kind of person who likes to be rushed. Especially by a kid.

On Monday (still nothing), Mr. Carlson's face lights up when he sees me walk into class. I'm early, as usual—partly to avoid bumping into Eddie in the hallway but also because I was hoping to hold Charles the chinchilla for a couple of minutes before class starts.

"Fern!" Mr. Carlson says. "I have something to show you. Come around here real quick."

He motions for me to come stand next to him, behind his desk, so I do. He points at something on his laptop screen. It looks like a list of names. I bend closer and squint at the screen. My name. I see my name. Fern Silvana, Driftaway Beach, CA.

"What is this?" I ask.

Mr. Carlson is beaming now. "This organization is an environmental nonprofit that focuses on kids who are going above and beyond for their communities. Every year they ask teachers to nominate students they think are setting an exemplary standard. You've only been with us for a short while, but you've blown me away with what you've accomplished already with your commitment to cleaning up Driftaway Beach." He points over at the clean-up bar graph on the back of the classroom door. My bar is so much longer than all the other students' that he had to add two extra pieces of graph paper next to my name. "You were selected as a candidate, which means you'll be up for a scholarship to pursue environmental action. You could use it for whatever you're most interested in."

"Like the marine biology camp?" I blurt out. I can't help it. "The one with the whales?"

"Exactly." The first bell rings, and my classmates start to stream in. "We can talk about it more if you're interested. All you'll have to do is write a short essay about what 'environmental stewardship' means to you."

For the rest of the day, the nomination and the essay are all I can think about. After class, Mr. Carlson explains that "stewardship" means taking care of something. So, in this case, taking care of the environment and the earth. Sometimes, back at the Ranch, it felt like we were only taking care of ourselves and our small patch of land, using it to prepare for a difficult future.

But I want to take care of things beyond just me. I want to take care of the ocean, so the whales can keep making their long migrations safely. I want to clean the beaches and the streets, to leave things better than when I got there. I don't just want to hide away from it, like Eddie said. I want to jump in feetfirst.

When I get back to our motel room, there's a large, thick yellowy-brown envelope leaning against our door with a Post-it note on it.

For Fern—

Here it is: my finished book! Well, no. It's a finished draft. The tenth draft. Really more of a first draft, though. No worries if you hate it. It's probably bad. In fact, you don't even have to read it. You can burn it if you want. Anyway . . . enjoy?

Alex

I pull out the stack of papers from inside the envelope and read the first lines:

Sometimes a feather is the only thing that can save you.
Katerina Heralda knew this for the worst possible reason.

I slip the pages back into the envelope and hug it to my chest.

"Fern?" It's Mom's voice. "Is that you?"

"Yeah," I call back. I push open the door.

She's sitting cross-legged on her bed, her GED notes spread out in front of her. There's a new plant in a sunny yellow pot on the nightstand between our beds. She must have stopped by the nursery again today. She smiles when she sees me. "How was your day?"

"Mom? Is the Ranch . . . is it a cult?"

Mom stares at me, her smile fading. "Where did you hear that word?"

I think about the strange phone call she got, the surprise trip away from the Ranch in the middle of the night, her worries about social services coming to take me away. I think of all the things Mom has tried to hide from me since we left the Ranch. I think about how confused I feel about where I'm supposed to be. About where I want to be. And I feel myself getting angry.

"Are you ever going to explain anything to me?" I explode. "Or are you going to treat me like I'm six years old for the rest of my life?"

Part of me hopes she'll explode right back, so we can have a big shouty fight, so I can get some of this terrible fizzing energy out. Or maybe she'll get tense and tell me I'm too young to understand and to drop it. But she doesn't do either of those things. She closes her eyes and breathes.

"You're right," she finally says. "I owe you a lot more answers and explanations than I've given you. I—I didn't think you were ready. Babs wanted me to talk to you about it right away, but I wanted to wait until you were more settled, more open to talking. Maybe I should have explained this earlier. I don't know. I don't know if I'm just constantly screwing up. Which seems to be a theme in my life." She rubs her face, and then pats a spot next to her on the bed. "Come. Come sit."

I go and sit, farther away than the spot next to her. I still have Alex's manuscript hugged against my chest.

"Sometimes," Mom begins, "when you're very lonely or confused, people show up in your life, and at the time it can seem like a lifeline. That's what happened when I met Ben. I was a high school dropout, a single mom. Both of my parents were already gone, so it wasn't like I could have moved back home to live with them. I was confused and lonely and over-whelmed. I couldn't seem to make things work anywhere we went. We were moving constantly."

"Yeah," I say. "I remember."

"I thought every new place we moved to might be the key. Might have the special thing we were looking for. Like every new place we lived, there was a chance I could reinvent myself and be the kind of person with a hundred friends who were always around for dinner, who loved you. But every place we moved I was just myself, but lonelier. The only thing that changed was the scenery. Then the winter before we moved to the Ranch, I got pneumonia. Do you remember that?"

I search my mind, but it all comes back fuzzy. I kind of re-member a time when Mom couldn't get out of bed and had a scary cough that rattled in her chest. I remember spending a lot of time watching TV, eating whatever snacks I could find in the kitchen, and playing by myself. "Maybe. I'm not sure."

"I couldn't take care of you. And I had no one to call, because we were in a new city with no one to help us. When I woke up, the burner on the stove was lit. I'd been too sick to cook, so you'd tried to make something for yourself. A dish rag was sitting too close to the flame, and it had started to smoke." She winces. "Even now I get sick to my stomach thinking about it. Something terrible could have happened. And it was at that moment I knew I had to make a change. A *real* change. I was so lost. I felt like I was failing you as a mother. First, I thought maybe I'd try to track down your father. Maybe getting to know him would give you—us— some stability. But I realized that was almost impossible. I didn't even know his last name." She stares at her hands. "And that's when I met Ben. At a bar, of all places, on the one night I'd asked a neighbor to watch you so I could go blow off some steam. He told me about his community upstate, and invited us, and it was just . . . It felt like fate. A place where we could live off the grid with other people, where we were 'working toward a better earth,' he told me. But it wasn't." She shakes her head, like it's hard for her to keep going. "It didn't end up being like that."

I think of our chickens, the goats, the furniture we built from trees we cut down ourselves. I think of the clanging pots, our giant compost heap that turned back into fertile soil, the cozy nights knitting for the farmers market, the green trees and fresh air. Never having to worry about money or fitting in.

"It's *exactly* like that," I say back. But even I can hear the sliver of doubt in my voice. Because I also think of the rules. The way Dr. Ben decides everything for everyone. The way you can't leave the property without permission. Or take medicine, even if you're a diabetic and would die without your insulin pump. Or get bottle-fed, if you're a small blind kitten with a white dot between your eyes that only needs a little extra love to become a pouncing, lively mouser. Or how you might even die because of something Dr. Ben puts you through.

"I know there are people out there doing it for real," Mom says. "Living off the land in the right way. In a loving way, where community means community and not control. But with Dr. Ben, it all got . . . twisted. And eventually I found out he wasn't exactly who I thought he was."

"What's that supposed to mean?"

And as soon as she begins talking, I wish I'd never asked. She starts saying things about the Ranch and about Dr. Ben's past that can't be true. Her words pound like waves. She says he's never traveled to half the countries he says he's been to. That he's not a doctor of any kind at all. That he's done bad things to people and been arrested for it. She calls him a "grifter." I don't know that word, but I can tell by the way she says it that I don't want to learn it.

"Just—stop." I almost cover my ears with my hands. "You're lying."

"I'm not," she says sadly. "And when they called the other day—"

"So I was right? They called you? Someone from the Ranch called?"

Mom swallows. "Yes. It was Iris on the phone." Iris, who was so frail and sick. Mom shakes her head. "I was stupid to trust her so easily. I thought she might want help, for her cancer. I thought she might feel differently about it all, after what happened to Rain. But apparently that makes it all the worse, because we're the first ones to leave after what happened to him. Based on what she said, it sounds like they're eager to make us come back. And I'm scared about what that means they might do."

I try to take in everything. "Do they . . . do they know where we are?"

"Honestly, I don't know," Mom says. "I did everything I could to make sure they wouldn't find out. But I need you to know I didn't take you away just because I felt like it. I took you away because I needed to protect you."

"Protect me from what?"

"From him. He makes himself the center of your world. He makes you give up everything you know and think and love, and live exactly his way, according to his rules, his dogma, under his thumb. He asks everyone who comes to live there to 'donate' all their worldly possessions. Every single person there gave their savings to support the Ranch. So, yes, sure, we sold some honey and vegetables and sweaters, but that didn't cover the cost of things. Our combined savings—which he took control of—did. And all that travel? All those 'lectures' he was giving? He goes on trips for himself. I know for certain he just went to Florida one time. On vacation."

I'm shaking my head, faster and faster, but she keeps talking. "He takes, Fern. And he takes. He takes and he takes until you feel like you have nothing left, until you're no one, and the whole time he makes it seem like he's giving." Her voice breaks. "When Rain died . . . it woke me up. I know I've made mistakes. But I'm your mother. And like I said, I needed to protect you."

"But . . . *you* chose the Ranch," I say. "You took us somewhere to live where you didn't have to be my mom anymore."

I didn't even know I felt this way, but as soon as the words are out, I can't believe I didn't see it before. It's like I've removed the thought from deep inside myself, like a splinter, and am holding it toward her in the palm of my hand. Like I'm saying, *This. This more than anything is what hurts the most.*

"Oh, honey."

Mom comes over and pulls me into a hug. "I'll *always* be your mom. And I didn't know it would be like that. Not before we went. And for a while . . . I thought it was worth it. I thought the stability was worth me giving up my full claim on you. After everything I'd put you through, I thought maybe I didn't deserve you anymore. But I *love* you. Just as fiercely as I did when you were little. More, if that's even possible. And I want to be the mom you deserve."

I push my face into her shoulder, and it only takes a few seconds before her shirt is damp. I thought having this conversation would make me feel less confused, but it's done the opposite. I feel like I've been wrung out and squeezed dry. "Can we stop talking about this?"

"Yeah." Mom kisses my hair once before she lets go of me. "Of course we can. But from now on, I'll be open with you about anything and everything. No more secrets. I promise."

For the rest of the night I can't stop thinking about everything Mom said. About the Ranch, about Dr. Ben. It doesn't feel like it can be true, but why would Mom lie about it? How could my gut be so wrong about this?

Every thread I pluck at seems to unravel something else. I think about how when you're scared, it's hard to think straight. And maybe Dr. Ben wanted us to be scared all the time on the Ranch, about what might happen to the world, so we wouldn't think straight. So he could think for us.

But no. No, that can't be true, can it?

Once again, I think about the definition I found online. "Misplaced admiration." How can someone who's doing so much good for the world also be doing things that are so bad?

261

"Hey."

Eddie's standing at the entryway to the lunchroom the next day, like she's been waiting for me. Her voice is so quiet I almost don't hear her. When I catch her eye, she seems hopeful. She's clutching her lunch bag in her hands. Like maybe we might talk, or I might say hey back, that we might pretend we never fought and go eat lunch together. And part of me wants to.

But another part of me can't. Because maybe I would say something about my conversation with Mom yesterday, about how confused I am, and Eddie would nod and say, *Told you so,* and I couldn't bear it. So I pretend I don't hear her and keep walking past, with my eyes straight ahead, until I get to the computer lab.

When I open my email, I have a new one. It's from Ron B. Tully. Finally!

I open it up.

Fern, Pretty sure this is your place. I went down a bit of a rabbit hole here; the property has been tied up in a legal dispute since late 2012, and then an additional case was opened in 2018 about adverse possession. One "Benjamin Wozniacki" was listed as the defendant. Basically means he doesn't own it; he's squatting. I suppose that means you all were. It was never a convent, for the record. It was a private hunting estate built in the 1970s.

I have absolutely zero clue what most of that means, although the piece about Dr. Ben not owning the Ranch sticks out to me. I always just assumed he did. I don't know what "squatting" means, and for once I don't really want to know. Below all that, there's an address.

33 State Rte #812, Croghan NY 13327

Let me know if it's the right place. I can do a little more digging if need be. RBT

Fingers shaking, I go into Google and type in the address.

Nothing comes up immediately, so I go to the Maps page. I don't have to look at my fingers anymore as I type, which is helpful for making this go faster.

It says there's a "partial match."

Eddie showed me how to look around Driftaway Beach using the little yellow-person feature. So I click on that, and dangle the person above State Route 812.

Then I drop him.

The view changes—and I almost gasp.

I'm staring at the metal gates of the Ranch. It is undeniably the Ranch.

The picture shows a blue sky, the trees full and green. This photo must have been taken during summer. I keep looking. I click back into the body of my email and stare at the address, until I've memorized it.

This is what I've wanted since the day we arrived in Drift-away Beach. No—since the moment the cold gates snapped behind me, metal against metal.

This is what I've worked for.

I should be racing up and down the hallways, shouting hallelujah! Or hooray!

But I only feel sad and empty.

28

School is closed for something called "professional development" on Thursday, so I head out with my gear for an afternoon of litter collecting. Mom asked for the day off a while ago, just in case I needed her.

"Are you sure you don't want company?" Mom asks when I tell her my plans. "We could do something, go somewhere. Is there anything you want to do? We could go back to San Francisco. Or oh—to the Marin Headlands. They've got a beautiful view of the ocean. Even more than here, if you can believe it."

"No. Thanks, but I'm good." What I really want is to be alone, outside, clearing my head.

She pats my cheek. "In that case, I'll stay in and study. But if you change your mind, I can abandon my notes, okay?"

As soon as I click the door shut behind me, I feel a rush of relief. It's a beautiful day, with a light chill in the air. The sea is calm; my mind is anything but.

Since I got the Ranch's address, I've been carrying around

the letter I wrote all those weeks ago in my pocket. Except now it has postage and an address on the front. When I re-read it, it seemed like an entirely different person wrote it.

I'm not sure if I should send it or write a new one. Wait or send it today.

Anger feels bad. It feels like poison or a well-honed knife. But I think this bone-deep confusion feels worse. Anger lets you focus. But this? This uncertainty? It's like my mind is a tornado, and it's impossible for me to pluck out a single thought from the spiral of wind.

I go up and down almost every street in town. Jared, the barista Eddie interviewed from the Seaside Bean Café, waves and holds up a finger when he sees me outside their wide front windows, telling me to wait one second. He started no-ticing me cleaning up a week or two ago, and ever since, he's brought me hot chocolate whenever he sees me. I feel guilty about drinking it, but I also don't want to be rude, so I always do. It doesn't hurt that it's so, so good. Jared told me they melt down real bars of chocolate to make the base, which is why it's so rich and thick.

I text Mom before I head down to check the beach. I comb it side to side twice, weigh what I've got, and then trudge up the stairs to throw everything out. I'm still not ready to return to the motel, so I go back down to the sand and just sit.

The wind has picked up a bit, so the waves are choppier and it's a little colder. I strain my eyes, hoping for another gray whale sighting.

If I see a whale, I tell myself, touching the letter in my pocket, *maybe that means we should stay here a little longer.*

I keep watching for the next two hours, but I don't see anything except water, sand, and sky.

It's starting to get dark out by the time I get back to the motel. The curtains of our room are drawn, but light glows from inside. Mom is in there, waiting for me.

Something inside of me releases. Because I'm glad she's there. I'm glad it's her waiting for me.

The glowing light of our room's window beckons to me. And it feels . . . good. Warm.

"Hey, Mom," I call, pushing open the door.

She's at the little desk, with a bunch of stuff spread out in front of her. She smiles at me. "Hey, you. Good haul today?"

"Nine pounds," I tell her. "The beach was really clean, so it was mostly stuff from around town. Are you still studying?"

"No. Come over and look," she says. "There's something exciting I want to show you."

I go over to the desk. I look at all the papers and pictures spread out in front of her. There are printouts, flyers, books. They're all about Reno, Nevada.

"What is this?"

She motions at the room. "Well, obviously we can't stay here forever."

"At the motel?"

"At the motel, yeah, but Driftaway Beach, too. I realize I

haven't always been open with you about my thinking, so I want to be open and honest with you going forward. And the fact is, California's too expensive for us, honey. Reno is great, and it's not too far. I got a job offer, even though I haven't completed my GED yet. It's a small business, and the owner was a high school dropout himself. He understands. Even though bookkeeping isn't exactly the field I'm interested in, it's a great opportunity, with benefits."

"What? No." I back away from her. "No, I thought—"

"We can still come back and visit. I promise."

"Have you talked to Babs about it? Maybe she can help us."

Mom winces. "It's complicated with Babs. She's going to tell us to stay. She always wants to fix everything. She'd probably put herself into debt helping us. But I'm sure it'll be a relief to her once we're gone. I don't want to burden her."

Suddenly, I realize staying in Driftaway Beach was never an option. If we don't go back to the Ranch, we'd just be starting the cycle all over again. Sure, maybe Mom and I could be more like we were before, but now the rest of the truth is staring me in the face. It would *all* be the same. The "There's a good job" somewhere else. No roots. No community. Car rides, empty apartments, and packing up our belongings again and again.

"But all that stuff you said . . . No. I don't want to do this again. I don't want to have to keep moving. Please, Mom."

"We won't." Mom grabs my hands. "I promise you. We'll settle for real this time. We can make a life there. We just can't afford it here. I'm so sorry."

"Then let's go *home*," I beg. "To the Ranch."

"That's not our home," Mom says softly. "It can't be. Not anymore."

I close my eyes, but all I can imagine is the blurry view from the car window as we move to *another* new place. With everything going by so fast that I can't hold on to any of it.

The next morning on the way to school, I take a detour. I stop outside the post office, open the slot to one of the blue mailboxes, and slip my letter inside.

29

Somehow time is both crawling and speeding by at the same time.

Babs had something come up, so she called to see if we could push our tag sale to next weekend.

"Sure," I told her over the phone. "That's fine."

At this point, other than wanting to pay her back, it doesn't really matter to me if we have the tag sale at all.

I spent Saturday walking around town, changing the date on all of our tag sale posters.

Sunday stretched out so long and empty I was actually relieved to go to school on Monday.

I know it's that I'm waiting. Waiting to see if someone from the Ranch tries to contact us. Apparently, it can take three to five days for a letter to cross the country. But I'm not sure if they count the weekend, so it might reach them on . . . Tuesday? Wednesday? Even though I didn't add my phone number or email—I couldn't bear to admit I was using both—I've still been checking them constantly. They got Mom's number once, so it's not impossible they'd figure out mine, too, right? My letter also says the name of the motel. So every day I walk past the office, half expecting Alex to tell me there's a message waiting for me at the front desk.

Wednesday, Thursday, and Friday come and go without a word. And so does Saturday.

And the longer the wait, the weirder I feel. Because despite everything Mom said, I still miss it. I still miss everyone there. I want to spend afternoons with Meadowlark and the chickens again. I don't want to feel this confusion anymore, one piece of me in California, and another piece of me left behind on the other side of the country. I want every piece of me to belong in one place.

"Hey, you," Babs says, from the other end of the table we're carrying down the stairs. "Earth to Fern. Everything okay? You look like you're a zillion miles away."

It's Sunday morning, the day of the tag sale, and I still haven't heard a word from Dr. Ben or anyone else.

"Sorry. Just thinking."

We maneuver the table next to the rest of the furniture, which we've set up in the parking lot close to Birdie's.

Babs went all out. There are streamers and signs all along the street, directing traffic toward our tag sale. Anyone who buys something today gets a fifteen percent discount if they go for tea afterwards.

We haven't even officially "opened" yet, and already there are people milling around.

Babs puts her hands on her hips and stares at the sky. It's bright blue, with puffy clouds flitting here and there. And it's warm enough that all I need is a T-shirt. Like what an early-summer day might feel like back on the Ranch. "We got lucky with the weather. A brick of fog is supposed to come in tonight and drop the temperature about thirty degrees. It'll be foggy and dark." She wiggles her fingers at me. "And spooky."

I try my best to smile at her. Because if Eddie and I were still talking, she'd probably be here with us today, chattering on about how excited she was for this forecast. That maybe we could finally expose the truth behind the Spirit of the Sea. Our project is due in two weeks, but I haven't done anything for it since we fought. I'm sure Eddie has.

I wonder if she'll spend all of today trying to figure out the best way to catch whoever's pretending to be the ghost. I bet she's mapping and charting out every last detail, searching the base of the bluff for hidden paths. If anyone can figure it out, I bet Eddie can. Part of me is grateful we're not talking anymore, though, because it means I won't have to say good-bye. When and if that time comes.

Babs lifts my chin lightly with her knuckles. "Hey. Cheer up, Charlie. A long face will scare away the customers. How about you run in and get some tea for us to have out here while we sell? Ask Johnny for the thermal mugs."

I nod and, without a word, jog inside.

Maybe I should find a way to get into a fight with Babs, too. That way I won't have to say goodbye to her, either.

As the day—and our tag sale—goes on, I notice some of the things I restored aren't here. A couple of chairs, one of the tables I sanded and restained, a teapot with a broken handle I glued back together.

When I mention it to Babs, she says, "Huh. Must have sold quick."

I could have sworn I didn't notice them at all. But I guess it doesn't matter.

Most of the people who drop by seem to be more interested in chatting with Babs than in buying anything. She introduces me to a teacher at the local high school; the owner of Torres's Taqueria, a restaurant Mom and I haven't been to; a young family from San Francisco that just moved to the community; and even the mayor of Driftaway Beach.

It reminds me of what Eddie said about Babs, the first time we hung out. That Babs is more like the mayor of Driftaway Beach than the actual mayor. And she was right.

Tank drops by on his motorcycle, and he's the one person I get to introduce to Babs. I'm kind of proud of that, since she seems to know pretty much everyone else. She's delighted to meet him. She invites him to Birdie's at least three times, each time saying he'll get a steeper discount. It makes me smile to think of someone like Tank sitting at one of Birdie's lace-covered tables with a teapot in front of him.

Despite all the chitchat, we manage to sell almost everything. Even one of the old boxes of *National Geographic* magazines that Eddie said we should recycle, the broken kerosene lantern we found, the kayak paddle. Other than a couple of junky things that I probably should have put in the throwaway pile, we sell it all.

It's almost dark as Babs counts out the cash. She whistles. "Wow. Not too shabby. We made almost four hundred dollars today."

My half is $200, and I'm relieved, because it means Babs didn't overpay me when she fronted me the money the other day.

But instead of splitting it in half, she gives the whole stack to me.

"No," I say, trying to give half of it back. "You said we were going to split it. It was all your stuff."

"Yeah. And you did all the work." She stretches out her arms. "And I feel freer than I've felt in years. I didn't realize what a psychic burden it was to hold on to all that stuff. What a gift you've given me. I feel like I can do anything now. I feel light as a feather."

"What about the hundred I owe you?"

"Consider it a bonus."

Maybe she expects me to smile, to thank her for the extra money. And I know I should.

But instead, I start to cry.

"Fern? Fern, are you okay?" Babs asks me. She must think something's wrong with me, because this is the second time I've randomly burst into tears in front of her. I've cried more these past few months than I have in the past three years. "What's the matter?"

"I'm just . . ." I try to get a hold of myself. "I'm sad it's all over."

"Aw, sweets. Come here." Babs sweeps me into a hug that's warm against the cool evening air. "You know, if you want another organizing project, you should come spend some time in my garage. A nice way of putting it is that it could use your magic touch. An honest way is that it's a horror show."

I sniffle again. "Yeah. I remember. We picked up tools there a while ago. Your guest room could probably use some attention, too." She laughs at that. I pull away from her and wipe my face with the sleeve of my soft white coat. "I should get back. Mom's expecting me."

"Okay, honey. Give me a holler if you two want to come over for a celebratory dinner. We can get takeout. On me."

When I get back to our room a little after seven, the bathroom door is closed. I can hear the shower running, but Mom isn't singing. She hasn't been singing in the shower much this week. Not since we had that conversation about Reno. Things have been back to feeling a little awkward between us. That's probably for the best, too.

I open up her loaner computer from the library to check my email. My heart nearly stops when I see I have a new one, thinking maybe . . . But no. It's from Ron B. Tully. The subject line says "PS," and there's a little symbol that there's something attached to the email.

I open it up.

Hey, kid, listen. I don't usually follow up for free like this, but just giving you the address of that place and leaving it at that didn't sit right with me. I did a little more digging on this "Benjamin Wozniacki" and I can't say I feel good about this guy. Just wanted to pass this info along. RBT

I open the first attachment. The photo loads immediately. Staring back at me is Dr. Ben. Or no—Benjamin Wozniacki.

He looks younger in the picture. His hair is long, much longer than I've ever seen it. He's not smiling, either—it's only his head and shoulders against a gray background. At the bottom of the picture it says, "Albany Police Department." The second attachment is another, more recent picture, with the same gray background.

My heart almost stops. So Mom wasn't lying about that part. He *has* been arrested. At least twice, by the looks of it.

The next file is all text, and it takes me a minute to make sense of it. From what I can see, it looks like the document is claiming that Dr. Ben got in trouble in Orlando, Florida, that he got into some sort of fight, and they want to arrest him for it. I look at the dates. It's saying this fight happened last February.

I feel a buzzing inside of me. *Florida.* Mom said he went

there on vacation one time, instead of going to give lectures on sustainability.

As soon as the water goes off in the bathroom, I close out of the email, out of my account entirely, and shut the computer with a snap.

When Mom comes out a few minutes later, I'm sitting on my bed with my arms around my knees. She's in sweatpants, and her hair is up in a towel.

"There you are," she says. "How was the tag sale?"

"Good. Fine. We sold everything."

She comes over and motions at my bed. "Can I sit?"

I nod. She sits by my feet and reaches out to take one of my hands. I let her.

"Listen . . . can we talk? Really talk?"

"About what?"

"I've been feeling sick all week. Things were starting to feel so good between us, so open, and . . . I know it's been bad between us ever since I told you about Reno."

I nod. It has been off.

"But more than that, I know that it's my fault. I told Hugh—he's the owner of the company I told you about— I needed more time to think about the job. About Reno, period. I also checked to see if the Reyeses would be okay with us staying another month or two. They said yes. That would give us time to visit Reno, maybe more than once, so you can see it. And if you hate it, we won't move there. I promise."

I look up at her. "Really?"

"I don't want to do this to you anymore. I'm done making decisions without your input."

She's not the only one who's been feeling sick. I think about the email I just got. I think about my letter, and its backward journey across the country.

"Mom," I say, my voice shaking, "I have something to tell you, too."

Mom cocks her head, and I know she's about to say, *What, what is it?* when her phone rings. She grabs it from the nightstand, glances at her screen, and then ignores the call.

"Who was that?"

"Eddie's mom. I can call her back. What did you want to tell me?"

Even though Eddie and I stopped being friends, I know our moms haven't. They've gone out a few times to get meals, or take walks around town.

Mom's phone rings for a second time. "It's Fiona again. I should answer." She puts the phone to her ear. "Hello? Fi?"

I can't hear what Eddie's mom says. Mom's face is impossible to read.

"Yes," Mom says. "Yes, of course. I'll go take care of it right now, and then we'll be there. Uh-huh. Don't apologize. Okay, yes."

When she hangs up, she swallows, hard.

"We have to go to the Chattars' shop and lock it up for them."

"Why?"

Mom swallows again. "Eddie's in the hospital."

30

All Eddie's mom said over the phone was that Eddie got hurt. Badly.

"She didn't say anything else?" I ask Mom for the tenth time.

"No. I know as much as you. I'm sure we'll find out more soon."

After we lock up the shop, Mom and I head to the hospital. I feel numb.

When we get there, I don't like the hospital at all. The walls are white, the floors squeak, and everything smells like a mix of toxic cleaning products and sickness. It's so much worse than the doctor's office where I got my shots. Somehow, that already feels like a lifetime ago. I would let them give me a thousand more shots, a thousand more sharp stabs, if it meant Eddie would be okay.

We meet Eddie's parents on the third floor, in the waiting area. Eddie's mom is slumped over in a chair, and her dad has an apron on, like he was in the middle of cooking dinner when they rushed over here. They both stand when they see us.

"Thanks, Jamie." He takes the keys from her. "We didn't know who else to call. My parents are on vacation, so they can't get here until tomorrow."

"How is she?" Mom asks.

"We don't know," he says, his voice cracking. "She's got a broken leg and a pierced spleen, which is what she's in surgery for. But the doctors are more worried that she hit her head. They won't know how serious it is until she wakes up." A tear falls, and he brushes it away. "I don't know what she was doing. I don't know what she was thinking."

"What do you mean?" Mom asks. "What happened?"

"She was trying to climb the bluff," he tells us. "And she fell. I don't know why. I don't know why she would *ever* do something like that—"

"I do," I choke out.

All three adults look at me.

"She wanted—" I swallow. "She wanted to see if she could figure out the truth behind the Spirit of the Sea. She was probably trying to find a way up to the top, so she could hide and try to catch whoever was pretending to be the ghost. She wanted to prove it wasn't real. She thought getting evidence one way or another might mean you would stay here in Driftaway Beach. For good."

"Oh my God." Her dad presses his face into his hands.

"I'm sorry," I tell them. Because this is partially my fault. If I'd been with her, I wouldn't have let her climb. The bluff goes straight up. There are signs everywhere telling people not to climb. They show a little figure of a person falling, with pieces of rock falling with them. She wanted it so badly she couldn't see how dangerous it was. "I'm so sorry."

"It's not your fault, honey," Eddie's mom says. "It's ours."

"No. Don't go there," Mom says. "We'll sit with you. I can get food. Drinks. Go pick up a change of clothes. Anything you need."

"Okay. Maybe—maybe, yeah. Yeah, that would be nice."

We sit with them for a couple of hours. Eddie gets out of surgery, but they don't want to rush her waking, in case there are problems from her hitting her head. As we wait, I make all sorts of deals with myself. If Eddie's okay, I'll give all my money from the tag sale away. If Eddie's okay, I'll apologize for our fight and take the blame for everything. If Eddie's okay . . .

And on and on. At around ten p.m., I'm yawning so much I can't hide it anymore. Mom notices. "Let me take you home."

"No, I want to stay."

But even as I say it my eyes are drooping closed.

"You should both go home," Eddie's mom says.

"No. I'll drop Fern off and come back. I'll get food. You haven't eaten anything, have you?"

"No," she admits.

"Then it's decided," Mom says. Without a second thought, I give both of Eddie's parents a hug before I leave.

When Mom drops me off, I say, "You'll come get me if anything changes, right?"

Mom brushes the hair from my face. "Of course. And lock up behind me, okay?"

"I know."

But as soon as Mom's gone, my exhaustion vanishes. After twenty minutes alone, I realize it was a mistake to leave—to be alone. My head is buzzing with all sorts of questions, and the buzzing's only gotten louder with the empty space and silence and time to think.

After a little while, I pick up Alex's manuscript, hoping for a distraction. I'm more than halfway through since I started reading it, and it's so good that it helps an hour go by. But even his fast-paced story can't keep my mind away from Eddie . . . from everything Mom told me about Dr. Ben, about the Ranch . . . from the email from Ron B. Tully . . . from the letter I sent a week ago.

I call Mom, wanting to ask her to come back and get me. But it goes right to voicemail—maybe her phone's battery died. I call Babs, too, but she doesn't answer, either.

By eleven-thirty, I have to do *something*. I put on my coat and stick the remaining unread pages of Alex's rolled-up manuscript in my pocket. The first thing I do is go around behind the back of the motel, where there's a stretch of old pavement with clumps of grass and flowers growing through the cracks. I kneel and pluck a few of the orange flowers. California poppies, Alex told me.

And then I walk to the edge of the motel's parking lot. The waves are fierce tonight.

One by one, I toss the flowers into the ocean. As an offering to the Spirit of the Sea. Not for myself but for Eddie. She would roll her eyes at me, but I have to try. I have to at least try. Because if the Spirit can bring lost souls back home, then maybe she can make sure Eddie's okay. Maybe she can make sure she wakes up from surgery and is totally fine. She can help get Eddie back to her family.

But after I'm done, I still have that yawning emptiness inside of me. I don't want to sit and wait in our motel room. I can't be alone. So I decide to go somewhere else.

It takes me fifteen minutes to walk to Babs's house. It's spooky being out here by myself—every time a car passes, I jump a little. Mom would be so mad to know I'm out alone, this late. But then I'm there, at Babs's house.

First, I knock. Then I try the doorbell. But she doesn't answer. She's probably asleep. But I can't turn around and go back to the motel. The idea of Babs being in the other room is enough to comfort me. I'll curl up on her couch and fall asleep here.

I know she keeps a key under the fake rock in her garden, so I go to get it. The fog is bad tonight, which is why Eddie's hurt in the first place, but it clears for a moment, allowing a slice of moonlight to stream through.

"Fern?"

I immediately stand up, key in hand, and turn around. It's Babs. But she isn't coming from her house—she's coming from the sidewalk.

"Sorry, I— My mom tried to call. Eddie's hurt. I—"

I stare at Babs's clothes. She's wearing a black coat, but

underneath it . . . she's wearing a long white dress. A night-gown. The bottom is brown, like it's been muddied. Like she'd been walking on an unpaved path.

And in her hand is a reusable grocery tote bag. But what's inside is poking out, just a little. It's an old kerosene lantern.

It all begins to click into place.

That night when I was staying with her . . . It was this outfit I saw in her laundry room. This exact white night-gown, right down to the dirty hem. How she'd mentioned this morning she knew there was fog coming in soon. The broken lantern we found above Birdie's.

"It's . . . *you?*" I breathe.

She looks down at her outfit. "Ah. Yes." Then she grins at me. "I guess you've discovered the true identity of the Spirit of the Sea." Then she presses a finger to her lips, like it's a fun secret. Like I've stumbled onto a part of her identity that's small and silly. I think of the flowers I just threw into the ocean. The stupid, meaningless offering.

"But . . . people believe in this. Eddie's parents believe in this." *I* believed in this. "And now Eddie's in the hospital because she tried to climb the bluff. Because she wanted to prove the Spirit of the Sea wasn't real. And it's been you all along."

The smile disappears from Babs's face. "Wait, what? Eddie Chattar? She's in the hospital?"

I don't want to have to explain it to her. And I don't want to try to understand why Babs would do this. Why she would carry on a joke—a hoax—that hurt my friend so badly.

So I run. And despite Babs calling my name, calling out after me, I don't turn around.

When I get back to the motel's parking lot, there's a car idling, right outside the front office. It wasn't there when I left.

It's a white van. With New York plates.

I know that van.

Still breathing hard from my run, my hands shaking, I walk toward it.

As I do, the front door swings open, and the light from inside the van lets me see the man in the driver's seat.

I know that posture, those jeans, that casual cotton shirt.

It's Dr. Ben.

31

I almost can't believe my eyes.

The way the fog is making the edges of the van hazy, making *him* hazy, like he isn't real and is going to disappear at any moment. I've spent so much time imagining this moment. And now that it's here, it's like someone else is experiencing it. Or like I'm dreaming. Or a combination of both.

From this distance I can't see the expression on his face. I don't know if his eyes are steely and upset, or if they're warm and inviting. If they're happy to see me.

I take a step forward, and then another one. As I draw closer, his features become clearer. He looks exactly the same. His weather-worn skin, his salt-and-pepper hair, his piercing blue eyes. He's real. He's here. He *came*. "It's you. It's really you."

He laughs a bit, low in his throat. "Yes, Fern. It's really me."

"You got my letter?"

He pulls something out of his pocket and shows it to me.

My letter. The paper glows white in the foggy moonlight. "We left to come get you the day it arrived."

"We?" I ask.

That's when I hear the sliding van door open and close, and then the sound of feet on pavement. And before I have a chance to react, a pair of arms are thrown around me and I'm being hugged fiercely.

"Meadowlark!" I pull back, almost not believing it. Her blond hair is just as wispy and fine, and it's in a tangled nest, like she hasn't brushed it in days. Maybe it's my imagination, but unlike Dr. Ben, she does seem different. Taller, maybe? She's crying, and her pale skin is all blotchy. We both laugh a little as we hug once more, rocking back and forth.

"What are you doing here?"

"When I heard Dr. Ben was coming to get you, I said I had to come. I wouldn't take no for an answer. And he said I could. My mom thought it was a good idea, too. They said that when someone drifts, it takes family to remind them what's important."

"Are you mad?" I whisper. "I had no idea we were leaving. If I'd known, I wouldn't have left. I would have woken you."

She shakes her head. "I'm just glad you're okay. I'm glad we found you."

"I am, too," I say.

The words come out automatically.

But they feel strange in my mouth. Hollow. If Dr. Ben or Meadowlark notices, neither of them says anything. Meadowlark threads her ice-cold fingers through mine.

Dr. Ben smiles at me again. "What do you say, girls . . . time to go home?"

Home.

Despite all the bad things Mom said about him, Dr. Ben has never shown me anything but stability. He's been the father I've never had. Just like how Meadowlark has always felt more like my sister than my friend.

Being with them feels warm. Familiar.

Thing is, I *know* he's done bad things. But so has Mom. And so has Babs—obviously. And I have, too, haven't I? I think about my anger toward Mom, the way I've been so awful to her these past months. How I refused to make up with Eddie. How if I'd gone to eat lunch with her the other day, we could have started talking again, and I could have stopped her from trying to climb the bluff. The rush of guilt threatens to swallow me.

Maybe we're all a little bit bad.

Our car is still gone, and the lights are off in our room, curtains drawn, which means Mom hasn't gotten back from the hospital yet. I glance at the van. "We should wait for my mom."

"I already spoke with her. She's on board. She told me you could come with us or wait for her. She has to finish up a couple of things here, and then she'll follow in that rattletrap car of hers," he says, smiling. Smiling like he's not mad at all. Like he's forgiven us already.

"And she agreed?"

He nods. "It took some convincing, but she relented. She's far off the path, but nothing is unsolvable."

"I hired someone to find you," I say, wanting to prove *I* never got too far from the path. "I wanted to come home so badly."

Meadowlark hugs me again. "*We* wanted you home so badly. And you'll come with us, right? My mom put down a mattress on the floor of the van, with blankets and pillows. It's cozy."

Being able to ride home with Meadowlark is much better than how I imagined this would happen. I'll tell her everything. About everyone. But that nagging voice in the back of my mind returns.

"I think I should wait for my mom."

"If you wait," Dr. Ben warns, "Meadowlark and I will have to get back on the road without you. There's much to be done at the Ranch and we've been gone for more than four days as it is."

I feel a surge of panic at the idea of them leaving so quickly. They're here. They came because I asked them to. They're dependable, solid. They aren't asking me to move to Reno or pretending to be ghosts. They came for *me*.

And I should go with them.

"Okay. I'll come." I take my cell phone out of my pocket. "Let me just call my mom to tell her."

Meadowlark inhales sharply and steps away from me. "What are you doing with that?"

"I—"

I don't finish my sentence. Because I have no real excuse.

"Oh, Fern. You've been carrying that? Right in your pocket, by your internal organs?" Dr. Ben shakes his head like he's sad and disappointed all at once. Then he holds out his hand.

I don't think twice. I give it to him.

He presses a few buttons. Powering it off, I guess. "We can toss this on the way. Better to get rid of it entirely."

"Okay." I rub my hands on my pants. They've gotten sweaty all of a sudden. "So . . . did you talk to my mom in person, then? Was she still at the hospital?"

"Exactly," Dr. Ben says. "I spoke to her in the parking lot. Like I said, she's figuring out a few things before she follows us. We'll get on the road tonight, and then meet up with her sometime tomorrow morning. Sound good?"

Dr. Ben didn't blink when I asked about the hospital. He didn't pause or stutter. And he called our car a rattletrap, so he had to have seen it. So that means he *must* have talked to her, right? And maybe this is a deal I can make. Maybe if I leave Driftaway Beach right now, even when I kind of want to wait for Mom, Eddie will wake up and be totally fine.

And it's late. I'm done thinking. I'm done worrying. I'm done being confused about where I belong.

Because the answer is right here, staring me in the face. Making my choice for me.

"Okay," I say again. "Let me go get my things."

I don't take much. I find my work pants, which are down at the bottom of my drawer, my old sweater, and a few other things Mom and I brought from the Ranch.

After I gather my things, I scribble out a note to Mom and leave it on her pillow.

See you tomorrow. Love, Fern

At the last second, I also grab the money Babs gave me from the tag sale. It's hard to believe that was from earlier today. It already feels like a different year. A different life.

I count out half and leave it on the desk. I add to the note, telling Mom to give the money to Eddie before she leaves, for all the cleaning help she gave me. I shove the rest of the bills into the bottom of my bag. Just in case.

The van's engine is rumbling low when I get back out into the parking lot. I hear a door sliding open as I lock our motel room. It's the side door—and Meadowlark is hanging out of it.

"Come on!" she calls.

"Coming," I respond in a low voice. I don't want to wake any of the guests.

She was right—the back of the van is cozy. Even with built-in shelves, there's still enough room for a twin mattress, which we can easily share. There are blankets and pillows and a few bags of what look like jars of food. I crawl in back with her and am overwhelmed by the smell of lavender. The familiarity of it makes me ache.

"Ready?" Dr. Ben asks.

"Ready," Meadowlark and I both reply.

"Good. Meadowlark and I were able to get some sleep earlier today, so I have at least a couple of hours' driving in me."

"And then tomorrow Mom's going to join us?" I ask.

"Yes. Either tomorrow or the next day."

Meadowlark grabs my hand and kisses my knuckles. "I have a lot to tell you. So much has happened since you left."

I think about the last time I saw her. A tuft of white-blond hair beneath her blanket. Things were off between us. But now she's open and happy, and it feels the way it's always been. And Dr. Ben brought her to come get us. To get me.

So I unbutton my coat, sink onto the mattress, and smile back at her. "Like what?"

I hear the clicking noise of the doors locking, and just like that we're on our way.

32

When I wake up the next morning, the sun is streaming in through the front windows of the van and Dr. Ben is still driving. I see a slice of blue sky. I sit up and stretch. The van is hot in the back; too hot. My mouth is dry and tastes sour. I could use water, a toothbrush, and a bathroom break.

I glance to my left—Meadowlark is still asleep, flat on her back with an arm over her eyes. Her forehead is sweaty, and her cheeks are pink.

She told me about things that have happened on the Ranch for two hours last night. Who'd gotten promotions and special privileges; how one of the littles got in trouble for trying to smuggle a chick into the dorm; a new meal that had entered the weekly rotation.

She didn't mention how people reacted when they found out Mom and I were gone, and I was too scared to ask.

"Do you want to know about what it's been like for me?" I asked. "Out here?"

I expected her to drool over the details. To want to know about everyone, and everything. I wanted to tell her about Babs, about Birdie's, about the teapots and the petits fours. I wanted to tell her about the ocean. I wanted to ask her questions about the beaches and water in Florida, to see if she remembers anything, if it's totally different than it is in California. I wanted to know her last name.

Meadowlark hesitated. Then, from the front, Dr. Ben called back, "Fern. It's better to leave all that behind, don't you think?"

Meadowlark nodded in agreement. "He's right. I don't really want to hear about it."

"Okay. Of course. Sorry," I said louder, for Dr. Ben's benefit.

Once a little time had passed, I lowered my voice so Dr. Ben couldn't hear. "It could be a secret. Just between us. When you asked me to tell you about my rite back in January, I should have said yes, I should have—"

"Fern." Meadowlark stared at me. "No. Stop. I was wrong then, okay?"

"Oh. Right." I felt uneasy. But who knows. Maybe she'll change her mind once we get home.

I rub the sleep from my eyes and say, loud enough for my voice to carry to the front, "Dr. Ben? Can we stop soon? I have to go to the bathroom."

"Not yet," he replies.

"But I really have to go."

"Can you hold it for a bit longer?"

I'm not sure I can, but he seems set on his decision, so I don't ask again. I don't ask for water, either, because I know it'll make me have to pee even worse.

I lean against the storage shelves, which poke uncomfortably into my back. The van lurches and bumps. Meadowlark still doesn't wake up.

"Where are we meeting up with my mom?" I ask.

Dr. Ben glances over his shoulder at me. "Full of questions this morning, aren't we? We're running a little low on supplies, so we'll have to stop for some food soon, and then a rest stop, so I can sleep. Your mom should be coming around then."

I bite my lip to stop the rest of the questions I have from pouring out. "Okay."

I want to ask how he'll get in touch with her to let her know where we stop, or how he'll check in, since he doesn't have a phone, and since he threw mine away.

More than anything, I want Mom to be here now, too.

I wrap my arms around my knees.

I imagine Mr. Carlson looking at my empty seat later today, wondering why I'm not there. I imagine the bar next to my name on his clean-up chart staying exactly the same length for the rest of the year, since I won't be there to pick up any more litter.

I think about Babs, standing alone on the empty second floor of Birdie's.

And I think about Eddie. In the hospital. Hurt. That if—no, *when*—she wakes up, I'll be gone.

This is exactly what you wanted, I remind myself. *This. Here and now.*

To try to calm my thoughts, I close my eyes and think about the sea, the way it laps against the rocks. The way it goes in and out.

I must drift back to sleep at some point, because I wake to the sound of a car door slamming. I'm a little slumped over and my neck aches. I have to pee so bad it feels like my bladder might explode.

And the van is empty.

"Meadowlark?" I ask, sitting up. "Dr. Ben?"

The side door slides open. Meadowlark grins at me. "Wake up, sleepy! Time for breakfast."

I rub my neck as I hop out of the van. I still have on my clothes from last night—my jeans and my white fluffy jacket. I feel hitches in my sides where the seam of my pants dug in while I was sleeping.

"Hey, what's that?" she asks.

I look to see what she's pointing at. It's the last fifty pages or so of Alex's manuscript, poking out of my pocket. I'd forgotten I had that. I want to tell Meadowlark everything. About everyone I met, the books I've read, the things I've learned. And now she's finally asked me a question.

But I don't want to talk about it in front of Dr. Ben. "This? Oh . . . nothing. It's something for school."

"May I see?" Dr. Ben asks. He's doing some funny stretching moves by the driver's-side door. His legs are splayed, and he's rocking his arms back and forth.

"It's not that interesting." I motion at the diner. "Can we go in so I can use the bathroom?"

Dr. Ben stops stretching and stares at me. He holds out his hand. "Fern. I told you I want to see it."

Meadowlark looks back and forth between the two of us. She widens her eyes at me, as if to say, *What are you doing? Give it to him!*

Reluctantly, I pull the pages from the pocket of my coat and hand them over.

He flips through them briefly and then looks at me. "Is this a novel?"

"Yes. I mean . . . no. Not a real one. I mean, it is real, but it's not a book yet. My friend wrote it. And wanted to know what I thought about it."

"You made *friends*?" Meadowlark asks. "Out here?"

Suddenly, I feel all flustered. "He wasn't really my friend. Just someone I knew." I turn to Dr. Ben. "Can I—can I have them back? I'd like to know how it ends. It's about a different world," I add quickly. "It's not about anything real. Like, it's not set in mainstream society or anything."

Dr. Ben rolls the pages until they're a tube, and then points it at me. "I can tell from a single glance this isn't the kind of reading that will nourish your mind. I thought you knew better than this, Fern."

My cheeks burn, and my eyes are getting hot. "Sorry."

Dr. Ben tucks the pages into his back pocket. "Good. Let's get some breakfast now, shall we?"

After using the bathroom, I join Meadowlark and Dr. Ben at one of the booths. The diner doesn't feel like the kind of place Dr. Ben would approve of, but I keep that thought to myself. I pick up one of the plastic menus and start looking.

A waitress with a tired expression and a high ponytail comes over with a pen and a pad of paper. She eyes the three of us in a funny way. I guess it's because none of us look anything alike. Dr. Ben, with his salt-and-pepper brown hair and blue eyes, me with my green ones, freckles, and wavy brown hair, and Meadowlark with her pale, almost bluish white skin and stick-straight blond wisps.

"These your daughters?" she asks.

Dr. Ben nods tightly. "Yes. The three of us will all have the same thing. Plain oatmeal and chamomile tea. With lemon and honey, if you have it."

"I didn't have dinner last night," I tell him, putting the menu down. "Can I maybe get a couple of eggs, too?"

"How would you like them, hon?"

"No eggs," Dr. Ben says. "We'll have what I ordered. Thank you."

The way he says "Thank you" to her might as well have been "Go away."

It's pretty rude, honestly. I don't remember Dr. Ben being

rude. I have memories of him being powerful. Thoughtful. And wise.

Are my memories somehow . . . wrong? Or is he the one who's changed?

The waitress raises her eyebrows and slices the pen across her pad. "Fine. Three oatmeals and three chamomile teas, coming right up."

When she walks away, Dr. Ben leans forward. "Fern. I know the outside world is different from the way we live on the Ranch. But I'm going to need you to readjust back to normal. If you can't respect my leadership, we're going to have some problems. Do you understand?"

My eyes sting as I nod.

He makes a face like he's uncomfortable, and then shifts his body, pulling out Alex's pages from his back pocket. As he does, I *swear* I see the top of a cell phone poke out of his front pocket for a second before he shifts and it disappears. Not an old kind, like the one I have. Or *had,* I guess, since he threw mine away. The kind Eddie has. An iPhone.

I continue to stare as he flags the waitress once more. So Mom was telling me the truth about that, too. The one hundred percent truth.

She comes over. "Change your mind about those eggs?"

"No." He holds out Alex's draft. "Can you toss this in the recycling for us, please?"

"Sure," she says. And then she takes it away.

Which means I have no idea how Alex's story will end. And I never will.

Our tea comes. Meadowlark busies herself next to me, squeezing lemon and dunking her tea bag in and out of the mug of hot water.

I can't bring myself to drink mine.

Babs would have things to say about a tea bag being served in the cup and not in its own little pot. She says your first cup will be way too strong, and the second too weak.

Dr. Ben leans forward. "Fern. Drink your tea, please."

I take the mug in my hands and take a tiny little sip. The water's too hot; it immediately burns my tongue.

"Maybe . . . ," I start. But the words get stuck. "Maybe I should wait here. For my mom. And then I can drive with her."

Meadowlark stops stirring her tea and stares at me. "Why?"

Dr. Ben shakes his head. "I am going to say this for the last time, Fern. She has to get some things settled before she joins us."

"Maybe I should settle them with her. I'm not sure—" I swallow. "I don't think we should go any farther without my mom. I need to talk to her."

Meadowlark is staring at me like I've grown another head. She nudges me. "We drove for, like, *four days* to get you. Fern, seriously. What's wrong with you?"

I turn to her. "My real name is actually Frankie. Did you know that? My mom named me after a singer. A punk-rock singer. Frankie Bellows. She had lots of things to say. She screamed and yelled and sang all the words she wanted to."

I'm rambling now, I know. Meadowlark shrinks away from me with a horrified look on her face, like I've got a contagious disease.

"Did you really stop at the hospital?" I ask her. "Did you see my mom?"

She doesn't say anything. She won't look at me, either.

I can barely bring myself to look over at Dr. Ben, but when I do, he doesn't look angry. His expression is flat. But then he smiles, and there's warmth in his eyes.

"Of course we saw her, Fern. It's totally normal to be confused. That's what society does to you. All you need is a couple of weeks back with your family, detoxing in nature, and you'll feel better again. So right now, you're coming with us. Okay, Fern? That's the way it's going to be."

But I can't say yes.

I won't say yes.

I can take up space. I can make up my own mind. And my mind is screaming at me to not get back in that van.

Because I suddenly know, with absolute clarity, that Mom doesn't know I'm with Dr. Ben.

"No," I whisper. "I don't want to go."

"All right." Dr. Ben takes out a leather wallet, and from it a few dollars. He tosses them on the table. "That's it. I think it's time for us to go. We can talk more in the van. Breakfast can wait."

My heart is beating so fast I can barely breathe. "Can I at least— I have to go to the bathroom. Can I go before we leave?"

"You just went. So, no. You can't."

I slide out of the booth before he can stop me. "Sorry. This time it's number two. It's an emergency. I'll be right back."

Dr. Ben fixes me with a level look. It always felt like he had entire universes of knowledge and wisdom swirling behind his eyes. I used to think it was a gift only *he* had.

But now I realize there are universes behind my eyes, too. So I stare right back.

Finally, he nods. "Fine. Go. But be quick."

I head toward the bathroom. My blood is fizzing, pounding so hard in my veins I feel lightheaded.

I turn the corner into the tiled hallway leading to the kitchen and the bathroom. Our waitress is coming out of the kitchen, looking at her pad of paper. I stand there, stock-still. Then, before she can walk by me, I grab her hand.

She stops. I can tell I've surprised her. "Honey? Is something wrong?"

I fix my eyes on her worn-out name tag. Sheila. Then I open my mouth to say something, but nothing comes out, like someone's squeezing my throat.

"I . . . I . . ." I glance back over my shoulder, even though Dr. Ben isn't in view. The person who created the place I called home for six years. The person who I'd do anything to impress. The person I've been trying to get back to for months.

But I also think of Eddie in the hospital. Babs crying, telling me to wait, to let her explain. The special nook on the second floor beneath the fairy orb, all my unreturned library books scattered across the floor.

I want to visit the hospital after Eddie wakes up.

I want to study whales, and finish Alex's book.

I want to collect my goal of one thousand pounds of litter. I want to help Babs start that community garden, even if I have to do it from a different city.

I want to eat petits fours, to have sleepovers at Babs's house, and watch movies.

And more than anything, I want to tell Mom I understand. That doing what she did—leaving—was actually the hardest, strongest thing anyone could do, and I'm proud of her, and I'm proud she's my mom.

And I need to tell her that. I need to tell her that *now*.

So I take a deep breath.

When I speak, my words are clear.

"That man is not my father." The look on her face changes. I'm afraid my heart will leap out of my chest, it's beating so hard. "And . . . I need your help."

33

Everything that happens next happens slowly at first, and then all at once.

The waitress pulls me into the kitchen. There are cooks in black T-shirts, frying eggs and potatoes on sizzling griddles. Most ignore us, but one or two of them look over at me with curiosity.

I've started to shake.

"You wait right here, honey. I knew something wasn't right." She takes my cheeks in her hands. "I'm glad you spoke up. I have a daughter a little younger than you. As a mother, I promise I won't let anything happen to you. Okay?"

"Okay," I whisper. "Can I borrow your phone?"

"Yes." She digs into her apron and pulls out an iPhone, like the one Eddie has. Like the one Dr. Ben has. "Here, take it. . . . Serg," she calls out to one of the cooks, "please come wait with this young lady while I call the police. And make sure the man in booth seven doesn't leave with the other little girl."

The man jogs over. "You got it."

I dial Mom's new number, so relieved she made me memorize this one by heart, too. She picks up before the first ring finishes.

When I say, "Mom?" she starts hysterically crying. I tell her the name of the diner. And I can't stop apologizing.

She tells me not to be sorry, but to wait, wait right where I am. That she's getting in the car and that she'll be here as soon as she can.

The police come next.

It doesn't take more than a couple of minutes. Or maybe it just feels that way.

And this part is so horrible—the way Dr. Ben protests, the way he looks at me—I can't bear to think about it. I let my mind go big and blank and empty.

The police take Meadowlark and me to their station, to wait for Mom to come and get us.

Meadowlark won't talk to the police.

And she won't talk to me, either.

She doesn't say anything to Mom when she comes to pick us up, even though Mom hugs Meadowlark as fiercely as she hugs me, like she's also her daughter.

For the rest of that day and night, Meadowlark doesn't speak to me, not while Mom is arranging for her to come with us to Driftaway Beach, not on the long ride home, not even when she sees the ocean. I try. I try like Mom tried when we first left the Ranch, all those months ago. But when we get to the motel, Meadowlark marches into the bathroom, locks the door, and stays there.

When I go to knock, to try the handle, Mom puts her hand on my shoulder. "Give her some space, honey."

I barely sleep all night, but she doesn't come out of the bathroom again until her mom arrives the next day to pick her up. Dahlia flew on an airplane, which is how I know how bad this all must be. Airplanes, Dr. Ben has said, are worse for us than twenty years of internet exposure. Worse than drinking a cup of pesticide.

Dahlia raps on our door sharply. Even her knocking sounds angry.

Mom gets the door. When Dahlia comes inside, I have the strangest feeling. She looks exactly the same as I remember her, but it's like she's stepped out of a different universe entirely, into my new one.

"Where is my daughter?" she says.

"In the bathroom," Mom says. "Dahlia—"

"Meadowlark!" her mom calls. "I'm here. Let's go."

Finally, Meadowlark comes out of the bathroom. Her eyes are red and puffy, and her skin is blotchy, like she's been crying the whole time. She glances at me once and then looks away. My heart squeezes. She walks over to her mom, who puts a hand on her shoulder.

With her other one, Dahlia points at me.

"Something's wrong with you. Ben and my daughter drove across the country to get you, because you asked. You *asked*. And now look what's happened. You've torn apart your own family."

Meadowlark stands slightly behind her, staring at the

floor. I want her to look at me, even if she's sad or angry or upset. But she won't.

"Shame on you," she continues. "I hope you feel guilt over this for the rest of your life."

"Hey!" Mom snaps. She's standing just as tall and strong as Meadowlark's mom. "Don't speak to my daughter that way."

Dahlia only shakes her head. "Meadowlark, time to go."

"Meadow, please," I say. I don't want to part like this. I need her to understand. "I can explain everything, it isn't what you think, none of it is—"

Finally, she looks up at me. "How could you?"

And then, in a flurry of doors slamming, they're gone.

The whole day I wonder if I made a huge mistake. If there was any other way of getting myself away from them and back to Mom. Apparently, Dr. Ben is in a lot of trouble, both for taking me away without Mom's consent and for some other stuff he did, like that fight in Florida.

"Don't," Mom says, kissing my forehead, when I mention this. "You did exactly what you needed to do."

Later, I ask her if she can get Kestrel's—Alyssa's—number for me again. I call her and ask what I should do, what can I do, to not lose Meadowlark forever.

"You have to let people go at their own pace," she says. "You can't force anyone to accept or understand something they aren't ready to."

Suddenly, I can't wait to hear everything about Alyssa's

life. I want to know how hard the first few months were for her, how difficult the transition was. I want to know all her stories. Every last one. Mom says maybe we can stay with them in Truckee when we go to visit Reno.

After we get off the phone, I start writing Meadowlark a letter. Trying to explain. Trying to help her understand. I know the adults may not let her see it; but even if there's the tiniest chance it'll get to her, it's worth it. So I'll keep writing. Letter after letter.

If she does read them, maybe my letters will help, or maybe they won't. Alyssa was right. Meadowlark needs to see things for herself. No one can tell her. Mom tried with me. Even Eddie tried.

All I can hope for is that she'll see the threads poking out. And that she'll tug on them. That she'll eventually unravel the truth from all the lies Dr. Ben told us.

But sometimes, I guess people don't want to see. Or they can't. I know that better than anyone. I just hope one day she does.

In the week following Dr. Ben's arrest, some good things happen, too.

He can't come back and try to get us again, for one thing. We got something called a "restraining order," so even if he wasn't being held and charged by the police for other things, he legally can't get close to us without getting in trouble, which is a big relief.

But I bet he's mad enough about what I did that he won't try again. Not ever.

Another good thing—no, *great* thing—that happens is that Eddie is okay. She woke up the morning after I left. She has a concussion, a hurt spleen, and a broken leg, but otherwise, she's okay. She's going to make a full recovery.

The day Eddie is allowed to go home from the hospital, Mom and I spend over an hour at the nursery so I can pick out the exact right kind of flowers for her. I want to get something with roots, something that will last.

None of the flowers seem quite right, so I decide on a small potted prickly pear cactus.

When we get to their apartment, both of her parents hug us tightly. Mom lets me go in to see Eddie on my own.

She's propped up in bed, with Tuna curled up on her stomach. I didn't expect her to look so . . . bad. Her leg is elevated on a bunch of pillows, and even though almost a week has gone by since the accident, she's still got a black eye and a big scrape down the right side of her face. Her windowsill is covered in flowers, cards, and a few stuffed teddy bears.

"Hi," I say.

"Hey. Nice cactus."

"It's for you," I say, suddenly feeling stupid about my choice. "I'm . . . I'm really glad you're alive."

Eddie grins. "Me too."

We both start talking again at the same time. "I should never have gotten so mad at you the way I did—"

"Fern, I'm sorry I—"

We both stop. And something about the situation feels so ridiculous that we start to laugh. Tuna yowls at being jostled, and Eddie winces, clutching her stomach. "I shouldn't laugh. It hurts."

"Friends?" I ask.

Eddie nods decisively. "Friends."

For the next hour I sit at the foot of Eddie's bed and tell her everything. I tell her about Dr. Ben, Meadowlark, my journey in the van, the police. I tell her about figuring out the truth about Babs, that she was right all along. Eddie's not surprised by this, though; apparently, Babs already came to talk to her parents and apologize. I tell her I hope it means she can stay here in Driftaway Beach. That she can stay put after so much moving.

"I hope so, too," Eddie says.

I don't say that it's what I wish for myself, too. Because I do want to stay. I want to stay more than anything. Still, I feel like I owe it to Mom to at least visit Reno. To look.

On the way back from their apartment, Mom must realize this is where my mind is, because she brushes her fingers through my hair. "We can visit as often as you want. Maybe once I get my degree and save up some money, we can move back here. But I don't know how else to make it work."

I want to complain. I want to beg, to ask her to try and figure it out.

But a tiny voice tells me: Maybe she's right. Maybe this time, we *do* need a fresh start. Maybe it's time to sit back and listen to what Mom's telling me, for a change.

"Hey," Mom adds as she pulls into the motel parking lot. "Babs asked if we could come over for dinner tonight. She said she wants to explain some things to you in particular, so she asked if I could drop you off early. I asked her what she meant, but she didn't expand. Do you know what she's talking about?"

I think about Babs and her muddied white nightgown. Her pretending to be the Spirit of the Sea. Knowing Eddie could have died to prove something Babs knew all along is hard to understand. I didn't get it then, and I don't get it now.

But I also know what it feels like to want to explain something to someone. So if I ever expect Meadowlark to be open, to listen to why I did what I did, then I need to do it for Babs, too.

"I think so. And sure, I'll go."

My instructions from Babs are to bring a jacket and a good pair of walking shoes.

When I show up at her house, she's already waiting for me outside, sitting on her front steps.

"Hey, you," she says. "I suppose we've got a lot to talk about, huh?"

I nod. "Yeah."

She stands up and jerks her head lightly. "Come on. I want to show you something."

We walk for ten minutes without talking.

When we reach the bluff, Babs points to a patch of dense thickets surrounding its base. "We'll go that way."

"Which way? There isn't a path."

But then, like magic, Babs pulls aside one of the bushes, revealing a narrow—so narrow—path. So narrow it's almost invisible. You could have searched this area with a magnifying glass, but if you didn't know the exact branch to pull aside, you'd never find it. No wonder Eddie didn't.

I follow her up, up, up.

Once we reach the top, we're both drenched in sweat and completely out of breath.

The view of the sea stretching out below us is incredible. "Wow," I say.

Babs puts her hands on her wide hips and joins me in looking out from the edge. "I know. Wow is right."

"Won't people see us up here?"

Babs shakes her head. "Not over here." She points to the left. "You have to go to that side of the bluff for anyone down in Driftaway to be able to see you."

We're both quiet for a minute.

"So, it's been you this whole time?" I ask.

"Yes. Well, yes and no. It's been me ever since Birdie died. But I'm not the first woman in our community who's been the Spirit of the Sea. Other women, for many generations, have done it before me. It's . . . well, honestly, it's a bit of an honor. It was Birdie's thing first, really." She smiles sadly. "Oh, she loved the magic of it. She was shown the path by a woman who was getting too old to do the hike. And when Birdie died . . . I couldn't bear the idea of the tradition just . . .

stopping. Especially not with the way she died. So I started coming up. On every dark, foggy night I could. I did it so I could stand, look out, and hope that me being here might guide her spirit back home, back to me."

I swallow, thinking of Eddie, with her concussion and her broken leg. How it could have been so, so much worse. "But . . . you were tricking people."

"Tricking people was *never* my intention. I had no idea what Eddie was up to. When your mom told me more about the accident . . ." Her voice breaks. "I would never have kept it a secret. I would have told her the truth straightaway. I never meant for her to get hurt."

"But she did," I say.

"She did," Babs agrees. "I've spoken with her parents at length, and I will never stop being sorry. I'll carry it with me for a long time. I've thought a lot about it, and I think it's time to finally retire the Spirit of the Sea. Or at least my version of her. So no one else gets hurt."

I nod. Even if it's been a long tradition, Babs is right. No one else should get hurt. And if the first person who decided to become the Spirit of the Sea found her way up here, then maybe someone else will in the future.

Babs turns back to the view. "Birdie loved the ocean. Just loved it. And coming up here, at night, with the fog . . . It always felt so peaceful to me. But Birdie wasn't the only person I thought about. Before you got here, I thought about your mom, too."

"You did?" I ask.

"Yes. Constantly. I looked for her, too. For years after her dad's funeral." She laughs softly. "I even hired some local private investigator to find her, but no luck."

"Foglamp Investigators?"

She eyes me. "Yeah. How'd you know?"

"Just a lucky guess," I say.

"Yeah, well. I feel lucky I got to be the Spirit of the Sea. Maybe a small part of her *is* real, and she was the one who brought your mom back to me. Brought *you* to me. And that's more than enough."

We talk a little more about everything that happened. I tell her how confused I still feel. How I still believe in so much of what we did and how we lived on the Ranch, of growing our own food, taking care of the earth. That so much of it felt good, which is confusing, because obviously there was a lot of bad.

"Here's the thing, kiddo," Babs says. "Most experiences you'll have in life will be a mixed bag. The good and the bad tend to be swirled into every experience you have. Every person you meet. It's not so black and white as it feels it should be. It can be your choice to take the good with you and leave the rest behind." She smiles at me. "And look at all the good you've already taken with you."

I nod. Maybe she's right. We stand and look at the view together for a few more minutes in silence. Then a gust of wind whistles by, so strong I feel the chill on my skin.

"Can we go back down now?" I ask.

"Yeah." Babs takes one more look. "Yeah, we can."

Babs makes pizza for dinner.

I choose plain cheese and green peppers for mine, and Mom chooses mushrooms and onions. Babs dumps everything onto hers, plus some pepperoni—for good measure, she tells me.

But she doesn't eat a bite of it, even though it's probably the best thing I've ever had. The crust is moist and chewy at the same time, and the cheese falls off in long, stringy pieces.

Mom notices, too. She points at Babs's untouched slices. "Babs. Why aren't you eating?"

Babs clears her throat. "I wanted to give you a little more time, but I can't wait. I just can't. If I don't show you now, I'll explode."

Part of me expects her to drive us back to the bluff—to show Mom, too, maybe? But instead we go to Birdie's.

"So?" Mom says, getting out of the car. "What is it? Why are we here?"

"Follow me," Babs says mysteriously.

As she goes around the side, to the second-floor entrance, I try to make sense of it. Maybe she's already renovated it for the high-tea expansion and wants to show it to us?

But that's not what the surprise is.

When we get to the top of the stairs, Mom stops dead in her tracks. I do, too.

Because it's an apartment.

I mean, it was always an apartment—but now, it's *really* an apartment. The kitchen has a fridge and a stove. There's furniture now, too, lots of it. I notice some of the furniture I repaired while working here—the pieces missing from the tag sale. The fairy orb is still in the window, above my herb garden.

I run to the room where I kept the things to be thrown away—there's a bed in there. With blankets and pillows and everything. And there's one in the other room, too.

"What—what is this?" Mom finally asks.

"It's for you. I know rent is too high here. And I know you're considering that job in Reno. But I can't bear to get you and then lose you this quickly. So consider it a homecoming present. Rent-free, as long as you need it. That is . . . if you want to stay."

Part of me expects Mom to say no. To say no, because that's what she does—she doesn't accept help. And I can tell by the expression on her face she's struggling with it.

"It's too much," she starts, but Babs waves her words away.

"I didn't realize how lonely I'd gotten without Birdie. Not until the two of you showed up and some of that loneliness started to ebb away. Whether you like it or not, sugar, I consider you family—blood or not. I need some family in my life. So do this for me, and let me do this for you. Please."

In the back of my mind, a faint alarm goes off.

Dr. Ben also said family wasn't only about blood, and he used that idea to control us. And now here's Babs saying pretty much the same thing.

"Fern?" Mom looks at me. "What do you think?"

I take a deep breath and remind myself: it's my choice who and what to believe.

And I believe that while Babs might be saying the same thing as Dr. Ben, she isn't using the idea to control us. She's using it to love us.

"Yes," I say. "Definitely yes."

Mom starts laughing. "Okay. Then . . . yes," she says to Babs, then turns to me. "Yes. We can stay."

34

Four Months Later

Eddie puts her arm through mine as we make our way up the path. She's still a little unsteady because of her leg, but other than its stiffness, it's almost completely back to normal.

And so are we.

Her parents are up in front with Babs, and Mom's behind us.

"Are you excited about whale camp?" she asks. "It starts next week, right?"

I laugh and jokingly roll my eyes. "I think you mean 'marine conservation initiative.' And yes. I'm very excited. Especially to meet Haven Miller."

It's true—I'm so excited I haven't been able to sleep for the past three nights. I didn't win the scholarship Mr. Carlson nominated me for, but Babs helped so I was able to enroll for the entire summer. Ms. Diaz wrote me a recommendation for a partial scholarship, too. Not only because she and Babs have started dating, but because she thought I deserved it.

Haven Miller is one of the scientists who runs the initiative. He developed a solar-powered machine that skims garbage off the top of the ocean and raises awareness about the danger of microplastics that come off synthetic clothes when we wash them.

He's kind of amazing. And he's young, too.

Eddie bats her eyelashes at me. "Because he's so cute?"

I swat her. "No! Because he's a genius." But then I grin. "And yes. Also because he's kind of cute."

Eddie snickers loud enough that Mom calls out, "What's so funny, girls?"

"We're talking about Frankie's whale camp," Eddie says innocently.

I started using my real name soon after everything happened, and it still feels weird to hear it said out loud.

"What about it?" Mom asks. She was able to get the day off from the plant nursery for this. She's working there full-time now but is going to go part-time in the fall when she starts classes at the community college.

"Nothing," I say, shooting a warning look at Eddie. Because if Mom finds out I have a crush, I'll never hear the end of it.

It takes us longer to hike up than the last time I came here with Babs, because Eddie needs to stop a lot to rest her leg.

When we finally do reach the top, Babs unzips her

backpack and offers a thermos of tea and a bag of scones all around.

After we've rested and eaten, she takes out two small bags of dried flower petals. She wanted to do paper lanterns, but I said no, because even the biodegradable ones aren't good for the earth. So I told her what I thought we should do. We collected wildflowers after school one day and dried them by pressing them in between heavy books.

Babs hands one of the little bags to Eddie and her parents and keeps one for the three of us. Then she clears her throat.

"We are here today not to say goodbye to the Spirit of the Sea but to say thank you. Because even if she isn't *real* real, not in the way we think about what's real, I like to think the soul of her—the spirit of her—is." She glances at Mom, then at me. "Because she did bring family home to me."

She turns back to the sea. "But we're also here to say goodbye. Goodbye to Birdie, and to Skye. To send well wishes to Meadowlark. All of whom we love. Whom we miss."

We start with a moment of silence. There are some sniffles from Eddie's parents. They wrap their arms around each other and around Eddie, too.

They've decided to stay. For Eddie. And because, as Eddie's mom told me one afternoon, "It's finally time to stop moving."

They haven't decided if they'll keep on at the shop. Eddie doesn't know, either. Whatever they decide to do, I'm just glad it will be here, in Driftaway Beach.

I think about Meadowlark. Of course I do. I think about

her all the time, and I can't see how I'll ever stop. I write to her still, but she hasn't written back. Not yet.

But I also think about what Mom told me about those redwood trees, all those months ago, when we visited Muir Woods. How they're all connected by their roots, how they all literally hold each other up. With the six of us here together, I don't see how we're any different than those giant trees. And how lucky I feel for it.

After the minute is up, Babs says, "What do you say, folks? Are we ready?"

Everyone nods.

Babs steps forward. "For Birdie."

She casts a handful of flower petals out, but at that exact moment, the wind pushes them back, directly into her face.

We all can't help but laugh as she sputters to get the bits of dried flowers out of her mouth. It completely breaks the tension, the sadness.

"Let's try that again," Babs says with a grin, dusting some orange petals from her cheeks.

And then, like the wind understands the importance of the moment, it shifts toward the sea. Eddie's parents throw out handfuls of petals, and they drift and spin away from us on the breeze.

"We love you, Skye!" Eddie shouts into the wind.

In my hand the petals barely weigh anything, but they weigh so much.

I think again of Meadowlark. Of everyone we loved and left behind on the Ranch.

I hope they find their way home, like we found ours.

I let go.

Standing there, I can't help but feel my heart is full of petits fours. Of the color green, of gray whales and the spray of the sea, of sweet mango tea and all the books in the library.

I put my arm around Mom, and she puts hers around me.

Acknowledgments

First and foremost, I would like to express my deepest gratitude to my early readers. Thank you to Chris Denny-Brown, Katherine Lin, Aimee Lucido, Kaela Noel, and Lael O'Shaughnessy for reading this book in first draft form, when it was still a lump of clay. Your sharp suggestions and astute feedback were vital in molding it into its final—and much improved—shape.

Thank you to Pete Knapp, best agent in the universe, for your keen editorial eye and belief in this story. Thank you also to the incredible team at Park & Fine, including Stuti Telidevara, Kat Toolan, Danielle Barthel, Abby Koons, Andrea Mai, Jen Mecum, and Ben Kaslow-Zieve.

Thanks also to my amazing editor, Nancy Siscoe, who always has the best ideas. I feel beyond lucky I've been able to work with and learn from you over the past five years. Thank you to the rest of the brilliant team at Knopf and Random House Children's Books, including copyeditors Artie Bennett, Lisa Leventer, Jim Armstrong, and Alison Kolani;

managing editor Jake Eldred; production manager Tracy Heydweiller; marketers Caite Arocho and Katie Halata; and publicist Joey Ho.

Thank you to jacket art director Michelle Cunningham and interior designer Michelle Crowe for creating such a gorgeous book, and to Shelley Couvillion for the most beautiful cover in the world. It so perfectly captures the heart and atmosphere of the story.

I would also like to thank Rachel Richardson and David Roderick for creating and running Left Margin Lit, which is such a wonderful literary community space for East Bay writers. Getting out of my own house—and my own head—and being able to spend the afternoon working among other writers has been such a boon to my creative life.

I would be remiss not to mention the inspiration behind the setting of this story. Though Driftaway Beach, California, is a fictional town, it is heavily inspired by Rockaway Beach in Pacifica, California. I'm grateful in particular to Lovey's Tea Shoppe, for their delicious teas and petit fours, which I ate as "research" while drafting this book. Lovey's was the main inspiration for Birdie's, and their Pacifica location is well worth the drive should any readers find themselves in the Bay Area.

Thank you to all the amazing teachers, librarians, and booksellers who work so tirelessly to get books into the hands of young readers. Your passion and support are often what keeps me going after publication, so thank you, thank you!

Many people helped with specific and technical aspects

of this story. Thank you to both Virginia Rutter and Faridah Àbíké-Íyímídé for your expert knitting knowledge. To my nephew, Pierce O'Shaughnessy, for showing me how he navigated a computer when he was seven, to help inform Fern's memories of using a computer. (Pierce will be ten when this book comes out, if you're curious about how long it can take for a book to go from first draft to final product!) Thank you also to Nicole Ortega, who was extremely helpful in explaining what the process looks like for a homeschooler to transition into a Northern California public school.

On the home front, I owe a huge debt of gratitude to Nicole Constantine for taking care of my little ones while I wrote and edited this book. Thank you as well to those same little ones, Jack and Langdon, for being the cutest and best writing distractions ever. And as always, I'm so grateful for my husband, Chris, who has always been my number one cheerleader. I couldn't do any of this without you.

This story is, at its core, about a mother and a daughter finding their way back to each other. So thank you to my mother, Melissa O'Shaughnessy, for showing me what it is to be a mom, and to my daughter, Langdon, for making me one.